'Omar Sakr's writing does the wondrous, it manages to be harsh and beautiful all at the same time. I inhaled this novel. The story and the world and the language are exhilarating.'

Christos Tsiolkas

'Omar's intensely poetic narrative adds a new and powerful dimension to the Australian literary landscape.'

Alexis Wright

'Poetry in prose, this is a wondrous, beautiful novel.'

Sisonke Msimang

'Lyrical, bracingly honest, and shot through with dark humour, Omar Sakr's *Son of Sin* is a portrait of a bisexual Arab-Australian's coming of age in a country wracked with racism, homophobia, and Islamophobia; it is also a poet's novel that leavens the wrenching with the sacred. *Son of Sin* is a queer Arab coming-of-age novel that sings.'

Zeyn Joukhadar

'Omar Sakr's literary voice is a marvel. He writes stunningly of family, faith and dislocation, always with an urgent, compelling undertone.'

Hala Alyan

'*Son of Sin* is extraordinary. I loved this powerful, intoxicating narrative of the things that bind and break us. Omar Sakr wields language with a poet's hunger for truth.'

Hannah Kent

Omar Sakr is the author of two acclaimed poetry collections, *These Wild Houses* (Cordite Books) and *The Lost Arabs* (UQP). *The Lost Arabs* won the 2020 Prime Minister's Literary Award for Poetry and was shortlisted for the NSW Premier's Literary Award, the John Bray Poetry Award, the Judith Wright Calanthe Award, and the Colin Roderick Award. Omar is a widely published essayist and editor whose work has been translated into Arabic and Spanish. Born to Lebanese and Turkish Muslim migrants in Western Sydney, he lives there still. *Son of Sin* is his first novel.

IBN HARAM

OMAR SAKR

affirm press

affirm press

First published by Affirm Press in 2022
This edition published in 2023
Boon Wurrung Country
28 Thistlethwaite Street
South Melbourne VIC 3205
affirmpress.com.au

10 9 8 7 6 5 4 3 2 1

NATIONAL LIBRARY OF AUSTRALIA
A catalogue record for this book is available from the National Library of Australia

ISBN: 9781922992123 (paperback)

NSW GOVERNMENT
This work was developed with the assistance of Create NSW's Arts and Cultural Funding Program.

Cover design by Amy Daoud © Affirm Press
Typeset in Minion Pro by J&M Typesetting
Proudly printed and bound in Australia by McPherson's Printing Group

MIX
Paper | Supporting responsible forestry
FSC® C001695
FSC www.fsc.org

WHETHER YOU LOVE WHAT YOU LOVE

OR LIVE IN DIVIDED CEASELESS
REVOLT AGAINST IT

WHAT YOU LOVE IS YOUR FATE

Frank Bidart

Contents

Preface

My uncle Mehmet once told me how, when he was a boy, sleeping with his three siblings and parents in a one-room unit in Marrickville, he woke as a spirit—nudged out of his body by the foot of an angel—and that he took the hand of this angel, and was swept away across the land of the living and the dead. He was unafraid, a little Turk in a strange country; this was simply another translocation. He remembered an enormous shore, unending waters, how he did not sink into the sand; he recalled the black feet of the titanic angel, and how by the time he returned to his small body, curled up between his two younger brothers, his spirit feet had begun to blacken too. Mehmet Amca waggled his thick bushy eyebrows when he told me this, and said, See oğlum? My life should be a novel, isn't it? Call it Action, Romance, Mystery, Tragedy, Love, Everything. He died before the pandemic, alhumdulilah, before this story could be told, but I would like to hope that he is standing beside me now, his toes black and beautiful, his whole spirit shining like glorious night, and that he is about to lead me out.

Jamal Khaddaj Smith

I

The Night of Power

Soyam

He was beyond saving, and still he chose to pray. The choreography of faith was new to him; although witnessed a million times, as numerous as birds in the sky, this was the first time he'd tried to fly alone. Jamal raised his hands to his temple, as if laying on a crown. *God is greater.* Folded his arms, right hand over the left. *I seek refuge in Allah from the outcast devil.* He silently recited the Fatiha, knowing the Arabic sounds by rote, a music without meaning. He was praying in his aunty's bedroom, which everyone knew was off limits, and everyone used when they wanted privacy. The door opened and his baby cousin Amani poked her head in, goggling. Jamal put his eyes back to the ground, the red prayer mat under his feet, trying to focus. He wasn't meant to look up, but the door was still open, and he was starting to sweat. He had to get this right. It was Laylat al-Qadr, the Night of Power, on which the Archangel Jibril first revealed the Quran to the Prophet Muhammad with the word, 'Read!' On this night, the angels would descend to the earth, prayers would be heard, sins erased from their records. This one night in Ramadan was worth a thousand months, a lifetime, in terms of its significance to God, and Jamal was counting on that. Needed it, in fact.

It had been a month of firsts for him, beginning in Liverpool Local Court with his mother as she and a man in a wig stripped him of his last name. He was no longer a Khan. Hala was dressed in a grey suit, her hair tied back into a shining black bun, exposing the hard bronze planes of her face, her sharp nose; she looked like a powerful businesswoman as she told the judge that his absent father had never been part of his life, and didn't deserve to have even four letters tying him to his son. At fifteen, Jamal didn't have a legal choice in the matter, but if he had, he would have agreed. All his life, he had been kept apart from his Lebanese family by this other name and now, finally, he would be a Smith like them. He could not keep his eyes off his mother. Her performance was awesome to witness: an outraged woman of means taking full claim of her child. She didn't even have a job, but you would never know it, looking at her. Nor had she raised him for the first seven years of his life, but he was hers at last.

He bowed to the earth and the air and there, under his face, was a giggling Amani. His lips twitched. Upright again. *God is greater.* His aunty hadn't approved of the name change. It was haram in her eyes, and in Islam, to brand a boy in his mother's image. A father's name, his lineage, was meant to rule. Hala cheerfully didn't give a fuck. She didn't pray, didn't wear hijab, and told her sister to shove it up her arse. He's mine, and I'll be damned if I give that prick anything he wants, she said. The Department of Child Services had located his father, and so he met the man for the first time as a result. Jamal hadn't said anything, hadn't been able to even look him in the eye, he let Hala do the talking. As they left, his father grabbed him in a hug, and slipped a note into his hand with his phone number, telling him to call. He showed the note to his mother as soon as they got into the car, and it drove her into a fury; she called him at once to say he had no right to go behind her back like that, he had no right whatsoever, and she was going to prove it. Between that and what was brewing between him and Bilal, he had plenty to ask of the angels.

Jamal sank to his knees, brushing Amani aside, feeling benevolent and wise, having seen his aunties gracefully move curious babies out of the way like this many times, without breaking their prayer. As his head hit the mat, hands flat, elbows tucked in, an explosive fart popped out.

Amani! he shouted as she collapsed into more giggles, and he did too.

It was no use now. Sullied, he would have to do wudu again, washing his body and starting the prayer over. You're a menace, he said and chased her out of the room to her delighted shrieks, her chunky little legs wobbling fast as she could go, messy bob of curls bouncing. He went slow down the hallway to give her time to get away. Cracks split the white tiles throughout. It was bad luck to step on a dividing line, and this house was full of them. He skipped as many as he could, treading on the tips of his toes. In the lounge, two large brown couches lined the walls, and the box TV set blocked most of the light from the front windows. A large framed photo of the family hung above the couch: Mahmoud, big and bald, had his arm around Aunty Rania, who had her arms around baby Fatima. Ali, a tall teen, was smiling next to his dad and in front of them stood both Sara, with her frizzled mass of curls, and Jihad, all wearing flower-print Hawaiian shirts. Jamal had been there on the day, wearing a matching shirt, but he was not in the photo.

The lounge flowed into an adjacent dining area, with an alcove next to the kitchen. Aunty Rania was praying there, a white dove facing the old grandfather clock, and behind her, her mother sat on a chair, eyes closed, a dusky hill of a woman. After a minute, his aunty stood, taking off the hooded half of her prayer garment, becoming flesh again: she was short and round, with pale skin and severe lips. She stepped out of the bottom half and folded up her prayer mat. The clock, a creaky wooden antique with a broken plastic bird under the hours, loomed over her. Iftar was still an age away.

Wulah, inta soyam? she said. He was fasting as usual, but he and his cousins would be asked this question at least three times before dark fell. In the Smith family, you were weak until proven strong and strength was impossible; you might trip up and swear, might cave to hunger or to thirst, might come down sick (which they all claimed, at least once), might erupt into violence (which they all did, all the time). It was better not to try at all than to break midway, but they tried anyway, alert to possible faults, even eager to find them, to be the righteous one pointing fingers, shouting, Iftarat! Iftarat! You ate, you broke! To break your fast was to be the split spoiling the family ceramic. Rather than admit they were all so flawed, they competed to deflect attention from their own faults by jumping on each other's.

This was why he hadn't told anyone he was attempting to pray seriously. He didn't want to be judged if he failed or stopped. It meant too much to everyone. Jamal stuck his tongue out at his aunty, waggling the greyed-out slab as proof. A healthy pink would have condemned him, but the grey-white film showed his aunty he was telling the truth. Not a drop of moisture had passed his lips, not a crumb of food.

Good, she said, though her eyes were still narrow with suspicion. Behind her, Teyta finished her prayer and stood up with a heavy sigh. She was too old to prostrate herself, so for her, language sufficed. Amani had gone straight to her, bored with him now, and his grandmother beamed, her face lighting up bright as the sun, swooping to pick up the baby, crooning Arabic lullabies. Aunty Rania beckoned, and he followed her into the kitchen. Two large pots steamed on the stove and the oven filled the cramped space with heat, while Fatima, a smaller version of her mother, took up the remaining area, peeling a large stack of potatoes on the bench, hands stained with dirt. Seeing their preparations for the feast, Jamal's hunger doubled. In Ramadan, unlike any other time, the Smiths—the sons and daughters of Abu Ahmad—pooled their money, and there was always enough.

Rania wanted him to get extra groceries from the mall down the road, and she opened the fridge to show him the containers, the specific brands she wanted. He nodded in the right pauses, but he was distracted by the realisation that he was taller than her. Her eyes had to climb to his and, as though annoyed by the same thought, she flicked his nose hard.

Ow! Kholto!

Pay attention, you stupid boy! She stared at him hard.

I was, he said, pointing. Whose is that?

There was a long chocolate éclair on the top shelf of the fridge, just beneath the bulb that lit the cold interior, and the strips of whipped cream had a halo he could almost taste.

Rania's nostrils flared. You know what, just get the yoghurt, forget the rest, I don't trust you. She shut the fridge door. It was covered in old photos and rumpled print-out sheets that had instructions like, 'Say this surah 99 times and you will have a guaranteed place in heaven'. He stood in front of it often, aiming to trick his way into jannah, but he would always lose the count midway, stumbling over the numbers.

Forget what? he said, and she chuckled, thinking he was joking. She fished a tiny purse out of her bosom to give him a rolled-up twenty. He might see Jihad and Moses at the mall, at least. They stayed out until the last rays of light were leaving the sky, when blue verged on black, trying to time it so they arrived only at the exact minute they could eat. To sit in front of what you could not have, when you had thought of nothing else all day, was agonising. It used to be the case that he would roam the streets with them, playing cricket or footy, but that was before he got hooked on reading books, on the strange and powerful absence that came with making a world inside himself, and now he went outside less and less.

Get yourself a treat while you're out, love, Fatima said in a broad nasal Aussie accent. Her cheeks bunched up as she snort-laughed.

Skittie wuleh! Aunty Rania whirled on her and Fatima flinched, arms up, her long braid of brown hair twitching back like a snake.

It was a joke! Oof.

Oof? Aunty Rania looked like she'd tasted dirt. *Oof?* I'll show you oof, wuleh.

But she lowered her hand and turned away, the threat enough.

Aunty Rania said *girl* like it was the dirtiest word in the world, the *leh* rising high like a lash. When Rania's back was turned, Fatima was unbowed. She mouthed 'Psychooo', made cuckoo eyes, and stifled a laugh, her eyes glinting with mischief, and Jamal grinned as he backed away. The closer it got to nightfall, the more tense it became. Soon more of the family would arrive and the house would resound with their voices along with the melody of the Quran crackling out of Jido's handheld black radio.

Outside, the sun hazed the hedges, the uneven street, the Subarus and Commodores. He could see his jido, who other old men called Abu Ahmad, crouched at the top of the yard like a spade in the mud. He was a short thin man with silver hair, thick square glasses, and big ears. He should have been funny looking, but there was a keenness to him, an edged reserve that instead made him fearsome. Jamal didn't want to go. He wanted to sit and read, to leave this place with its hungers behind him. Besides, it was cool inside, with the broken tiles and the rattling brown box on the window valiantly conditioning the air.

Before he could go any further, Rania's screech yanked him to a halt. Wulah, ta lehon ya ibn haram!

Far out, what now? He glanced behind him.

His teyta sat in front of the clock, hunched over a large metal bowl full of mincemeat, onion and spices that she was rolling into kibbeh. She anchored him right away, every part of her solid as the earth, her wrinkled skin, the kerchief tying her hair back, the rhythm of her hands. Behind her, standing at the kitchen entrance, Rania stood with her hands on her hips, a younger and angrier version of the old woman.

Didn't I tell you to take the garbage out? Oh, you wicked boy.

He trudged back and grabbed the garbage bag, fuming. It wasn't fair, damn it. He should have gone with Jihad and the others earlier. When would he learn? As he walked past his grandmother, she smiled and her face cracked in a thousand places where life had left its lines. Yullah, habibi. Words soft as sand, warm as the sun, washed away the resentment before it could get a hold. He stepped into the heat, putting his shoes on and wishing again that he had real choices.

Jido turned at the sound of the screen door opening, the tip of his cigarette flaring amber, smoke rising around his head. There was a small metal tray and raqweh beside him, as well as an Arab coffee cup from which he sipped. The old and sick weren't required to fast any more than children, although that didn't stop Teyta from trying. Jido didn't speak much to his children or his grandchildren. The former because he didn't want to, the latter because he couldn't: none of them were fluent in Arabic. Rumours bloomed in the wake of his silence—he'd been a baker, a sniper in a distant war, a restaurateur, an orphan who fled from Lebanon and left behind his Arab last name. He remade himself and nobody knew if he liked the outcome.

The same choice was spread out before him, Jamal realised. His grandfather had done it and survived, but at what cost? He didn't know much about the man except that he could swing between silence and screaming in a second, that he loved to garden and watch Hollywood action movies, and that whenever he saw him, he was meant to kiss his hand, just past his hairy knuckles, bowing over it and bringing the kissed skin to his forehead. Jido was a king in a kingless country, and that made him frightening and unpredictable.

Jamal hurried past, the acrid scent of smoke spiking his nostrils, and neither spoke. There was still over an hour to go before iftar, and when you were this hungry, an hour meant anywhere between sixty minutes and a lifetime.

No food, no water, no cursing, no violence, no sex, no masturbation—not even smoke could pass your lips from sunrise to sunset during Ramadan. It was a hard reset, learning how to go willingly from feast to famine, to redefine feast as *anything*, as Leb bread smeared with zaatar and oil, as a splash of mai in a mouth. Harder still to go back to glutton afterwards. Think of the kids in Africa who don't have a choice, Aunty Rania would say to them. She never said, Think of the kids in Lebanon. Think of your cousins. The family left *over there.* It was always Africa, or India, because it was easier to imagine darker strangers suffering. She herself didn't fast. She had too many pains, and cooked for half the day what everyone would eat when the adhan rang out from the radio; no one could begrudge her that, and if they did, they could eat somewhere else. Jihad always argued the first day was the hardest, while Moses said the last day, but for Jamal it was the whole middle stretch, when the body had adjusted to lack, when what was strange and difficult became normal, routine. After the first week, he stopped wanting so much, and the absence of that sheer animal desire was oddly frightening.

Jamal never told anyone that he wouldn't mind being one of those kids in other countries if it meant he could touch himself. What's an olive to an orgasm? A pit to pleasure? The choice was obvious, the answer clear: he would die for this sensation. He was nine when he was introduced to it, in line outside the demountable classroom near the back field of Casula Public, pinned between a militant blue above and the mutant green of grass. Christian, a thin Anglo kid, was going down the line of boys, pretending to ignore the girls, even as he put on a show for them. He had three older brothers and he often spoke with their voice, their knowledge, to make himself seem older.

Jamal had retreated to the shady silver bench nearby, where he prayed for Mr Davis to hurry up. He was shy at the best of times, and Christian didn't speak to anyone without pitching it to be heard by the class. Jamal could hear him asking the boys, laughing as he went from one to the other—Have you ever—Have you tried yet—Do you?—until finally he stopped in front of the bench, grinning. Christian was not the smartest or the fastest in their year, not pretty or ugly, not gifted in any particular way, and maybe this was why he needed the most attention. His golden hair and freckly white skin were too bright to look at, and Jamal had to squint up at his weak chin.

Have you tried wanking yet?

What? Oh, yeah—yeah, totally.

His grey shorts were level with Jamal's eyes. The light behind him was blinding, a sea of blue and white. Jamal tried to focus on the bulb of pink kneecap, the pale expanse of skin. Twitched away to peek around the corner. Mr Davis was late again.

Christian's braces glinted. Oh yeah? What is it then?

Jamal flushed and squirmed in silence. Christian's laughter pealed out.

It's this! He grabbed his dick through his shorts, his eyes rolled up into his head as he started gyrating, and he moaned high-pitch moans.

Boys! Cut it out! Mr Davis's voice whipped Christian around, and he laughed carefree, crudeness discarded. No worries sir, it wasn't even me sir, I swear sir.

That night, Jamal had struggled to sleep. The blinds rustled with every puff of wind, letting in slivers of streetlight. He ached with a known and alien need. Listening for any change in the house, he pulled his underwear down, grabbed his softness, and closed his eyes. White light, lurid green. Christian in front of him, head tilted back, lips parted in false ecstasy. His metal mouth moaning. Jamal grew larger, jolted into hardness. He rubbed himself frantic, electricity shivering over and under his skin, and he was never the same.

It had been easier to fast when desire was yet a distant, unmet country. It didn't matter at first, he was young then—the angels on his shoulders would not record his sins until he was fourteen, and old enough to know better. He was old enough now and this was why he was thinking of prayer, and how to save himself. Already he dreaded to think of how busy he'd kept them, his angelic scribes. As he walked up the street, this thought preoccupied him: how could he protect himself from himself? He tried to soak up as much knowledge as he could, to follow the right rules, but there were no guarantees, and every day there was something new he had to do to be spared unimaginable torment, eternities of hellfire. It was haram to eat pork, to drink alcohol, to do drugs, to be with girls before marriage, to speak back to your mother, to disobey your elders, to listen to music, to piss while standing up, to leave shoes on their side or up, their dirty soles facing God. Each year it grew and grew, this tree of sin, crowned by the ultimate taboo: that no boy should love another boy, no girl should love another girl.

Every cousin and aunt and uncle added new fruit to it, voices low and serious, yet secretly gleeful. One night while squished between Sara and Jihad on the floor (they had bunk beds, but they all preferred to be together), Sara told Jamal that he couldn't sleep on his back—doing so opened you up, it meant any shaitan could get inside you, could take possession of your body. He immediately rolled onto his side, eyes wide open, and she breathed easier, stretching her bony arms and legs to fill the space he vacated. He never slept on his back again. His days were filled with stories of what the djinn, the free-willed spirits of the invisible world, could do to him if he wasn't careful.

Sara, fingers stuck in her fried hair, told them all the next morning that she'd seen a djinn. It was dressed in Ali's brown skin, his tall, muscled body, and walked by the room that she shared with the others, his features a grim parody of a clown, lips stretched from ear to ear. She had screamed, but no sound came out. Sara sat on an armchair, knees drawn up to her sharp chin, dark circles around her eyes, and as she spoke, Aunty Rania started praying, clicking furiously through her green prayer beads.

I was awake! Sara said. It was real. Seriously, Ali, was it you?

Ali shook his shaved head. Wallahi it wasn't, what the fuck.

Stop talking about them, Rania said. You invite their attention.

They each had experiences like that, and despite Rania's warning, they told them over and over again. Jamal's first began as a dream: he was in his teyta and jido's flat in Warwick Farm. Their lounge, with its flower-print couches, framed Quranic tapestries on the wall, and red Persian carpet, seemed carved out of another time. He was both present and not, could see everything and only the back of his head, as though he walked behind himself. He followed the figure into the hallway, to the first bedroom on the left, and as his double opened that door, he turned and smiled at Jamal. His eyes were molten black, and the look of malevolent joy on his face froze Jamal's blood.

He woke up. He was on the floor, enveloped by Jihad's and Sara's snores. He didn't see his doppelganger enter the room, he was simply there, his eyes windows of night, his hands around his throat. Jamal tried to scream and nothing came out, there was only a relentless wave of pain and fear. He told the others it stopped when he recited the Fatiha, and sometimes that was true. Other times, it went on, it seemed, until the djinn got bored. They had little proof of the divine without these episodes of devilry. In theory, one implied the existence of the other, but Jamal felt nothing except terror. No matter how hard he found fasting, Ramadan would always be his favourite time of the year for one simple reason: it was the only time the gates of hell were fastened shut and evil spirits denied entrance to the world. It was the only time he felt close to safe.

Iftar

Jamal's thirst for knowledge did not stop at sin: he knew every street in the area, every alley, every wooden and metal fence, and every tag on them. He knew where the fruit trees stretched their bounty above borders and the branches that had initials carved into them. He knew which yards held dogs, their barks, their bites, how high they could leap. When the boys were bored they used to run past Melissa's yard down near the park, yelling and banging on the wooden pales to rouse her two vicious pit bulls. The athletic animals would leap and scrabble upward, climbing a rope of snarls, always threatening to make it over. Once, Darren Hunter, a scrawny, scabby kid, matched each leap of the dun-coloured dogs, laughing and taunting them, until one jump brought him too close, canine jaws latched on with a growl, and blood arced into the air. He slumped to the ground with a squeal, his upper lip ripped clean off, a limp lick of flesh on the ground. It was stitched back on in the end, a darker band than it had once been, and they stopped teasing the dogs then. Darren's fucked-up black lip taught Jamal never to lose sight of fear's purpose.

He knew Mesake's house near the alley mouth as well as his aunty's, he knew the Hunters who lived opposite had the only Aussie flag in the hood, pressed up against their kitchen window, and that their dad Mick was a drug dealer. Mick looked like a chewed-up stick that had been dipped in a dozen paint cans. He ran a tattoo parlour out of their laundry and bikies were always coming and going.

Jamal turned up the alley, onto Kurrajong Road. He had barely managed a metre when a small red Corolla floored to a stop next to him, flinging gravel up in a wave. The driver's door swung open and Charmaine bounced out, tall and brown, flawless thighs showcased by ragged denim cut-offs, tits straining against her singlet. He had a second to gape at her before she slugged him straight in the mouth, and he staggered backwards, falling as much from surprise as force.

Give that to your fuck of a brother, she said, and spat. She jumped back in the car, speeding off. He stared, hand on his tender mouth. His hands were scraped raw from the fall, but he got up, and resumed walking. His legs jerked forward, out of rhythm, his pace picking up, as if the punch, the sudden violence, was repeating in his blood. He'd heard a rumour Moses hooked up with her, but hadn't believed it. All the boys wanted Charmaine and told stories of getting with her. The path blurred. He was almost running, so wrapped up in the injustice—he hadn't done anything wrong, it wasn't fair!—when he collided with Moses, Jihad, and Bilal on their way back from the mall.

Jemzy! Bilal's voice was warm and open.

Watch where you're going, bro! Jihad shoved Jamal back. He was a year older, and Jamal was already taller, which rankled.

Like his father Mahmoud before him, his cousin was balding early, his curls more sparse every year, and each bit of hair that fell took with it another inch of his patience, his easy smile.

Who hit you? Moses cut through the noise, and the other two stilled.

His dark hair was gelled back from his handsome face, his furrowed brow. Tall and fit and pale, he looked nothing like Jamal, who was shorter, slighter, darker. They had different fathers—one Lebanese, one Turkish, both absent. They shared that at least, along with their mother. Moses wasn't concerned for his brother's bruised jaw as much as he was for his own reputation; to fight someone in the area was to fight their whole family. No one wanted to fight Jihad because Ali was his brother, and no one wanted Ali's eyes on them, not even Mick. Knowing that made Jihad more reckless, the first to throw a punch. Moses, meanwhile, had few chances to prove himself. He was beloved, and his smile could charm even the devil.

Jamal stared at his brother spitefully. Your girlfriend happened, bro. He told them what she said and they laughed at him.

She's crazy! Phwoar! That's what you get with a glamour like that, boys, Filo girls don't muck around, ey. But that's what you want, wallahi. As they cracked up, she grew in their eyes and he diminished.

As if you got bashed by a girl, bro.

Jamal brushed past them, annoyed, ignoring their calls to come back, that iftar was soon. It took him a moment to realise that Bilal had followed him, splitting from the older two.

I told 'em it's too early to go in, he said, slinging an arm over

Jamal's shoulder. He was taller and wider than his cousins, a forward in the local footy team, whereas Moses played on the wing to best use his speed, and Jihad was the dummy half, small and determined. Bilal's hair was shaved around the sides, a ruffled black mullet growing out the back of his head like waves, and he stayed close, talking into Jamal's ear. Jamal tried to stay calm, but his heart had already begun to dance.

Before yesterday, he had thought himself alone, a unique devil, and if you asked, Bilal would be the last person he thought to name as belonging to this haram. He was like most boys in the area, loud and brash, his body an announcement, always ready to make a ruckus, to be the centre of attention, to make a fool of himself chasing girls. Nothing like Jamal, who could spend a day without saying a word, trying to avoid notice, to become a hush.

They'd been talking about Eid, the money they might get at the end of the month and the Adidas sneakers Jamal wanted, as they got off the bus at Prestons Public. The school spread out behind them, a huge gated enclosure, old demountable classrooms and long ghost gums at the fore. Jamal looked up at the broken pale stone of the moon, which was meant to confirm Laylat al-Qadr and Bilal rolled his eyes. Like you're gonna be the one who figures out which night it is! It could be any of the last ten days. He reached out and cupped Jamal's chin. You're too cute, bro.

Some dickhead honked their horn then, and Bilal's hand darted away so fast it might never have touched him. They crossed the road and went down the alley where they parted as usual, but in silence. Jamal went left to Aunty Rania's, and Bilal went right to his home around the way. He'd carried the warm flash of Bilal's hand on his skin, the charge of it, for the rest of that night and woke up determined to pray.

Okay, but what would you do if you died right now, like, *right now*, bro?

Jamal chewed his bottom lip. Bilal was acting as if nothing had happened yesterday, and maybe nothing had. Maybe it was all in his head. Saying 'Fall to the ground' would only earn him a punch for being a smartarse, so he didn't say anything.

Bilal continued, urgency in his voice, Say you had to face the Punishment of the Grave? He shook his head. I'd be fucked, he said, laughing. This was a common topic in the Smith family. Before Judgement Day even came, before the eternity of hellfire that might await, there was the grave, the waiting in which the body was still sentient. In his ancient history class, when Jamal realised that the Romans and Egyptians he was learning about had been waiting in their graves all that time, a hole opened up inside him into which part of his spirit fled and never returned. He tried not to think about it. The hole had a gravity all its own, and always threatened to take more of him away. Kholto Emne told them that the Punishment of the Grave was even worse than hell. It was the first test the newly dead had to pass: two angels, Munkar and Nakir, the Denied and the Denier, would descend and ask three questions:

1. Who is your Lord?
2. What is your religion?
3. Who is your prophet?

Emne's grey eyes gleamed in the telling, not from fear, but pleasure. These angels are nothing like the khara you will hear about from Christians, okay? Remember that the Archangel Jibril can fit the Earth on a single feather from his wing. Munkar's and Nakir's shoulders are miles long, in their eyes are the depths of space; one holds a hammer, the other a club spiked with nails, each instrument so large that all of mankind together couldn't shift them a single inch. They speak, and their tongues are flame. If you answer correctly that your Lord is Allah, your religion Islam, your prophet Muhammad sulAllahu alayhi wu salaam, then your grave will be graceful, peaceful and spacious, until the trumpets ring and the world ends. If you answer incorrectly, then the grave will be your first punishment, and you will feel every minute pass, every bite of the worms and insects, every bit of the dirt on your chest, in your mouth, under your eyes. And each day except for Friday, Munkar and Nakir will descend to beat you with their cosmic weapons, until or unless Allah orders them to stop.

Jamal's nights were sweat-drenched with visions of these beatings. Why would you be fucked? he said. He'd never heard Bilal admit he felt fear like this, too. As they crossed the road into the carpark at Casula Mall, everything was touched with the soft gold of the departing sun. Bilal shrugged, uncertainty flitting across his face.

Don't they know all your sins?

Jamal wasn't sure. There was nothing in the questions about sins. That was between you and Allah only, as far as he knew. What twisted and gnawed inside him was much more elemental: the angels would be speaking Arabic, the holy language of the Quran, and he only knew fragments, like yullah and habibi, like mai and haram, like immi and kholte. Hurry, darling, water, sin, mother, aunty. What could he say to them, the first divine servants of Allah, the immortal angels, that would spare him? Would they listen to English, or would he falter under their imperious stare, trying to wring an ocean from the precious few drops he had collected of his mother's tongue? Whenever his grandparents asked questions in Arabic, staring with dark and expectant faces, Jamal felt sure he'd failed before he even began to speak, and so he often didn't answer at all, waiting helplessly for an adult to offer a translation.

Maybe, Jamal said. But don't forget about your hassanat. They know your good deeds too. As they came close to the Liquorland side entrance, Bilal slowed.

Go first, he said. The dogs were on us before.

When all the boys in the area—Lebs, Samoans, Tongans, even a couple of Anglos—slouched into the mall together, security guards would descend on them like flies to shit. They were forced to split up. Sorry lads, no gangs allowed, Security said, even though the guards looked like them, a thick Maori man and a sallow, sweaty Leb. People get scared, Insecurity said. Over time, they learned even three of the boys counted as a gang, a threat, a breakable unit. Two should have been fine, though.

Were youse doing anything?

Nah, bro, what do you mean? Bilal's voice was angry. We're soyam.

Yeah? Jamal spun around to face him. Show me then.

Bilal stopped, surprised, as they came face to face. This close, Jamal could see the stubble along his jaw. Not like the fluff on his cheeks, closer to real manliness. Bilal opened his mouth, showed him his tongue. His teeth were a mix of jagged and even whites, his tongue was grey. He kept his mouth open for longer than needed, closed it slowly, blew a little kiss.

See?

Yeah, I can see that you need to brush your teeth. And then he ran into the mall, Bilal lunging after him, laughing. The tongue test was easily fooled. If they ever broke their fast, they would wipe their tongue on their shirts until it bleached, until it was so dry they wanted to retch. It was an old trick, one they all knew and applied to hide their shame. There was no proof you could trust, except the word—that was the measure of faith, and perhaps why they kept failing.

&

The moon's heft weighed on the sky as they walked home in the gathering dark. Bilal lumbered a few metres behind Jamal, because he was lazy or because he wanted to check out Jamal's arse. That thought sent tendrils of dread down his spine, and what was dread if not desire's other face, a question you didn't know how to answer?

Cars were piled up in Aunty Rania's yard and on the street. Her windows beamed a warm yellow, the babble of a hungry crowd washing onto the street. Moses, Sara, and Jihad were sitting at the table on the veranda with their cousins Saja and Doha, twins in matching blue tops. That meant Kholo Buktikh and his wife Wafat were here, too. They called him Uncle Watermelon because of his big oblong gut, or the way his sloppy red smile seemed to split his face in half, depending on their mood when asked.

Adhan, adhan already, bro! Jihad called out. Bilal practically ran inside, and they all laughed. There was still time. Jamal kicked off his shoes, looking through the front windows. Jido was at the head of the table, Teyta next to him. Kholo Khadeer shrunk the space, big as a truck, his chest a V8 engine, his beard a long oil spill. His wife Emne darted between the kitchen and the table, her flowing mauve hijab making her seem like a butterfly or stage magician. Next to Khadeer, his older brother Buktikh looked small and harmless, his clean-shaven oval face grotesquely babyish. Ali took up the last spot, a slim brown blade of a man with dark bags under his eyes. A second fold-out table had been set up and a bunch of cousins Jamal couldn't remember the names of were seated there, one nestled in a black niqab. This was only a small part of the family—Kholo Ahmad and his children lived in Melbourne, and Kholto Nazeero lived in Bankstown, with her uppity Turkish husband who thought he was above them all.

Jamal had to tread around a half-dozen children in the lounge, their paper plates full, mouths covered in sauce. The kitchen was a hive of activity. He'd barely lifted the plastic bag with the tub of yoghurt before Fatima snatched it out of his hands. He slunk back to the couch, where his aunty Wafat was keeping an eye on the kids, rocking a baby in its hezezeh. Her face was heavily made up within her floral hijab, blush on her cheeks, red on her lips, eyes sparkling.

Wulah, b'dok aroose? Inta wu Saja?

He sighed. She would not stop asking him if he wanted to marry her daughter, Saja. It started out cute, because the two of them were close and loved spending time together, but Wafat had stopped laughing as they got older, her question laced with intent. He did not want to marry his cousin, not at fifteen, not ever, but he couldn't say that. Wafat and her husband were cousins, and she seemed insistent on making a tradition of it. The adhan went out, the long call to prayer; there was an elongated pause, then loud clatter as collectively the Smith family broke. Now, it's now, now! Some shouted, as if the others didn't know. Wafat left to get her own food, but not before giving him a last lingering look.

Fatima clumped over to him, body dipping to the right with rhythmic thuds, her brown chain lock of hair bouncing to the beat. Her shorter leg hit the ground harder and louder when she was tired.

I put this for you, she said, nodding at the plate. It was filled with his favourite meal: fatteh jage and bulgur, a yoghurt-based chicken dish with brown wholegrains. There were hot chips and chicken nuggets on the coffee table, salad and fried kibbeh, and icy cans of Coke and Fanta. Baby Amani was busy lifting one red can to her mouth. She had the same grey eyes as her mother, Emne.

How come? he said, taking the plate gratefully.

Ash'had! she said. And you're welcome, gronk.

He raised his right forefinger and recited, Ash-hadu an la-ilaha illAllahu wa ashadu anna Muhammadan rasulAllah. There was no God but God and Muhammad was his messenger. He started eating and had to bite back a moan as creamy deliciousness, melted butter and paprika exploded in his mouth.

Okay, fine, Fatima said, tossing her hair back. I was the one who told Mum to tell you to get extra. We don't even need it. She hated peeling potatoes and was annoyed he didn't have to, just because he was a boy. She'd also hoped he would read between the lines and come back with sweets.

Read between the lines? he scoffed. You said it straight out!

And you still didn't get it, ya majnun.

Nuur. Even your mum got it, and nearly gave you an atleh.

Jamal ate until he felt pain, which was well before he finished the plate. He could never get used to this part, where a whole day spent fantasising about how much he would eat ended so unsatisfactorily. It wasn't that he was hungry still; it was hunger's ghost roving in his blood, powered by all those dreams. While the kids ate, the adults had their first coffees and smokes of the day. Above their table, smoke swirled in thick eddies. Jamal would never smoke, he couldn't even look at a lighter without feeling nauseous. Saja came in from the veranda, small and swathed in cloth, the blue of her jilbab flowing past her waist. She managed somehow to be in perfect control of its every swish, to not be swallowed in it, so you knew beneath it she was slim. She perched on the arm of the couch next to him, folding her dainty hands on her knees.

My mum go after you again? Saja had a button nose, unlike the rest of them, and so everyone reckoned her a great beauty, Jamal among them.

First thing, he said, and she laughed a bright, tinkling laugh.

Me too. She screwed up her face and parroted her mother's heavy migrant accent, 'B'dek areese, inti wu Jamal?' A million times at least. She's got issues, cuz.

Tell me about it. He leaned closer, whispered, Who's the ninja? indicating the niqabi.

Oh my god, cuz, don't. Saja laughed and slapped his arm. That's Emad's wife, Najwan, he met her at Lidcombe Maccas after he went on Hajj last year.

There was no chance of being overheard, but Jamal still looked around. Saw Emad in his dark grey thobe, his long brown beard and skullcap, head to toe an immodest declaration of his faith and modesty. He had a cheeky smile and an easy soft manner.

Behind him, Kholo Khadeer came stomping out of the kitchen, the house shaking with each of his steps, roaring, Who ate my éclair? I've been looking forward to it all day! He looked so furious and so sad, this large éclair-less man, his beard a hungry bush. Silence encroached on the noise around them, a sudden embarrassment. The parts of his cheeks that weren't covered with hair went pink.

I dropped it off this morning and I told you—he pointed at Rania, who was tiny next to him—I told you to make sure no one touched it.

Jamal shook with the need to laugh, while Fatima hid her double chin in the couch, and Saja carefully looked away, biting her lips.

Aunty Rania tried to mollify him, but he shook her off, his big belly wobbling.

It's not about the éclair, ya. It's the principle!

That was too much, and Jamal snorted so hard he pushed Saja off the edge of the couch. Her yell covered his laughter. No one noticed, anyway. The moment of quiet had only been a moment. There was a constant flow of people in and around the house. Kids taken inside to be washed, or pulled apart from screaming fights, or put to bed; plates refilled, discarded; more food being brought in from the kitchen or packed away. His grandparents shifted to the lounge, Jido in his blue striped pyjamas, Teyta in her white linen pantaloons and loose green top. Jido fixed his eyes on the TV, although Jamal wasn't sure why. It wasn't like he could speak

English. On the news, muted and grainy footage of Western jets bombing a distant city.

Wein ummok? Teyta said to Jamal. *Where's your mother?*

Like he knew. She never fasted, and rarely came to these dinners except to pick up Moses and Jamal. His eyes drifted over to Aunty Rania and back again as he tried to find the Arabic to reply. Between them, an untravelled sky. His grandmother never stopped trying to reach him, though they shared only a handful of words. She often singled him out for the chore of massaging her feet, and he'd sit on the couch with her heavy legs on his lap, trying to press into her hard skin, her iron muscles, to show he knew what she was trying to say. Unlike the others, he ran towards her, not away, when she yelled, Tah lehon! *Come here.* Through her, Jamal knew love did not have to be spoken.

Without looking from the TV, Jido barked, Lek, skittie wuleh! The *leh* a lash. Teyta rocked back, false teeth clicking as her jaw snapped shut. Jamal wished he hadn't seen it, the pain and fury that flared and floundered in her eyes, how she opened and closed her mouth like a fish yanked out of its nature, then looked away, her hands twitching; how he knew that she, like him, was drowning and unable to escape. Jamal shoved another bite into his mouth, and then another. He knew better, and he didn't care. He ate until his stomach expanded, until the food was crammed right to the back of his throat, until he felt sick.

The living room emptied within the hour. Jido and Teyta went home, and the men decamped to the end of the driveway, where they stood in a grim circle, smoking and talking. The women stayed in the lounge, some cleaning up, some eating, all talking and laughing. Jamal sat near them, as usual. He didn't want to join the men. They were out there pretending to be serious, the patriarchs, the providers, but he knew they'd been sent out of the house because they were useless, because they got in the way of the actual work, and because the women wanted to talk without being interrupted. He heard it all, the budgeting, the bargaining, the parenting tips, as well as the weirdness and rawness they saved for each other. At one point Najwan lifted her baby son right up to the eye-slit in her niqab and declared, Oh my god, I love him so fucking much! She shoved her face in his belly and he giggled. Like, it's not normal, wallah. I would suck his little doodle if he wanted, she said, and the women screamed with laughter. I don't care! I don't care what anyone says! I'd eat his snot. Anything, anything he wants. And they cackled, the younger ones, while Rania led the disapproving clucks of the older women, and the words sin and shame bubbled over them.

Jamal kept his face turned away, curled up around his book. As long as he was reading, he was invisible; he could see the men, hear the women, and be part of both worlds. Why would he ever give this up? Bilal poked his head in, around the screen door. Yullah, we're going to the mall, he said, and Jamal put his book down without a word to follow him out. Fatima hissed, Make sure you get me some Ferrero Rocher. And a Buffalo Bill!

They passed through the circle of their cousins and uncles like the wind, unremarked upon, unseen, not-yet men.

Where's Jihad and Moses?

Already gone, Bilal said.

The streets were dark and quiet and they glided along, as if the soft night was inviting, no, pushing them forward. The mall proper was closed, but Coles stayed open late. They crossed the road near the baseball field, going through the sloping grass towards the library, and the back of the mall. Bilal confessed to the great éclair heist, and they laughed themselves silly about it.

Did you see his eyes? Faaar out. If looks could kill, forget it, we'd be gone!

Haram but, Jamal said. I'll get some now so he doesn't have a heart attack. That set them both off again, their laughter bringing them closer together. Jamal brushed up against him, breathless, and Bilal's foot slipped, sending them both to the ground. They fumbled around, rolling, hands grasping for purchase, flashes of warmth. Jamal half on Bilal, half off. His eyes flicked from the green of the field to the lights blaring over it, settling on the dark glass of the library windows. Bilal followed his eyes.

Eidre b' this library, Bilal swore. What's it got that I don't?

Internet, Jamal said, knowing that *books* was an unacceptable response. Besides, he loved going online, where being a nerd was basically the default, and aside from his school friends on Myspace and Bebo, there were endless forums and chatrooms full of people who would talk to him.

Oh, so it's like that, Bilal said. Can you watch porn there or something?

No, but you can read it. Jamal smirked. And it looks like you're studying.

Bilal whistled. All this time we thought you were just a nerd, you were being a horny cunt? He put his hands on Jamal's shoulders, on his neck, sliding them up to Jamal's face. Fingers on his jaw. Touching his lips. I've got a lot to learn.

Jamal shifted without thought, aligning his hips with Bilal's.

Tell me what you read, Bilal said. Voice heavy. Trees whispering above.

I—

Jamal couldn't bring himself to say the words. He'd never told anyone what he wanted, never said aloud what lived inside him, and even now, an urgency for touch wrestled with a fear of being known. Watching was different to reading and both were as different to doing as life was to death. He remembered when Anthony, the slim Viet boy with a cloud of black hair who lived down the road, had found one of his dad's porn videos in the garage and Jihad promptly arranged a viewing. Anthony arrived with Aiden and the Hunter brothers, Rick and Darren, in tow; he was always hanging with the Anglo kids. Aiden's family owned the only mansion in the area, an old estate on top of the hill with a blue slate rooftop. He looked well fed, his teeth were white and even, and he was the only boy in the area who rivalled Moses; naturally, they were best mates. Next to him, Mick's sons looked like dirty starving ghosts.

Aw fuck, it's Chinkie porn, Darren said as the video started, his black lip twisting. They saw a naked Asian woman crouch over the chest of an old fat man and take a long curling shit. The boys hooted because it was gross, but they didn't care because she was still naked and, later, Jamal couldn't tell what had him feeling so tight and hard, full of an inexpressible energy: her pert tits, her gaping, or the close-ups of the fat man's cock. They watched intently, carefully spaced out around the lounge, kitchen, dining table and hallway, wherever they could contort themselves into seeing the screen, all of them jerking off and yelling, Don't look bro, don't look bro, don't be gay!

Jamal had been closest to the TV, so close to the glare of the light it was almost unbearable, in full view of them all, unable to look away from the screen, unable to touch himself. He sat still, the focus of all that desire.

Staring at Bilal now, and seeing a reflection of that want, unlocked something in him, but the words he had read would not come.

I'll show you, he said.

He moved down, feeling Bilal's muscles flex beneath him, lifting his shirt, kissing the heat and hair. Bismillah, he thought. It was muscle memory, this half-prayer. Entering a house? Bismillah. Reaching for a pot on the high shelf? Bismillah. A reflexive reaching for safety. In the Name of God … His fingers trembled on the cold belt buckle.

Jamal undid Bilal, pulling the leather belt tight, flicking the metal pin, letting go. Each inhale roared in his ears and panic fluttered at the back of his throat.

I knew, Bilal whispered. I knew you wanted it.

He did, more than anything, and still he hesitated. He could hear Rania hissing in his ears, Ta lehon ya ibn haram! *Come here you sinful boy!* How many times had he heard it? A hundred times, a thousand, more: as a shout promising violence: laced in an affectionate chuckle: a rasp: a whisper almost to herself, an echo as he was lassoed to her from wherever he'd been, a soft song of ibn haram, ibn haram. O you son of sin. His other name, his true lineage. He'd never thought of the words in English, tuned rather to the tone, the sound that could predict future pain, but they unveiled themselves to him as he pulled Bilal's zipper down. He hurt more than he knew how to express, he was hard in his pants, and he could not move.

Jamal resisted the faint pressure on his shoulders. He could feel Bilal's breath on his ear, and the tenderness in his voice, real Romeo shit, might have worked better if Jamal hadn't heard him try it on Lizzie, Tania, Charmaine and every other girl they'd come across. He thrilled to the idea that he was wanted enough to replace them, before his anxiety returned in a wave of static.

It's just us, Bilal said, and Jamal buckled.

Just us, he thought. No demons left in the world, no spirit to whisper wrongdoing, just this desire. From us. Jamal drew down the denim until he saw the insistent shape of a hard, thick cock pressed against black briefs. His tongue was dry again. He licked his lips and looked up. Bilal had never looked more serious: his usual dopey half-smile, the glint in his eyes replaced with intense focus.

Jamal leaned in and pressed his face softly against the clad warmth of a cock. He'd thought and dreamed about this often—not this boy, but the kneeling, the wanting, the taking, the tasting—and nothing compared to the reality. Bilal's thick muscled thighs. His hairy funk. The sourness of his sweaty underwear. Jamal soaked it in saliva, lapping at the thick twitching dick, like he was still afraid to have nothing between him and his desire, needing even this thin layer of protection. And then he couldn't take it anymore, he released what was his, opening wide to suck on the brazen bald head. It was warm and hard and perfect in his mouth. He couldn't believe how it seemed to fill everything inside him.

He was a faggot, oh God he was a fag, and he fucking loved it.

Jamal and Bilal ran up the hill as fast as they could, sweets forgotten. Jamal was faster, but Bilal was fitter, and as one pushed ahead, the other would soon overtake. They never tried to match each other; their difference, the fluid distance, was as necessary to them as getting away from what they had done. Jamal's heart thudded in his throat, his jaw ached, his mouth tingled with a tang that burned a line into his stomach. He could die, he could die right now and he would do so happy—he had never been more alive. They crested the hill and crossed the overpass bridge, terrified and ecstatic, broken and whole. Jamal made it to the roundabout first. The road ahead led to Prestons, the turn down and around to Bilal's house. He slowed to a walk, heaving. His face was wet and dark patches stained his shirt. He didn't check to see if Bilal had followed him or gone his own way. He could guess.

There were only two cars in the yard when he got back to Rania's and one of them belonged to his mum. He took his shoes off on the veranda, his mind spinning. Through the screen door, he saw Hala on the couch, laughing. She'd brought hulew; three aluminium trays of Arabic desserts were laid out on the coffee table. When he opened the door, she turned to face it as he had once, and he was seven years old again.

He'd stood on these cracked white tiles as Hala, wearing Chanel sunglasses, jeans and a white singlet, stalked into the house like she owned it.

Hi Kholto, he said to her, because every adult was an aunty or an uncle, and the woman he had thought of as immi—his mother—grimaced.

No, Rania had said from her seat. *I'm* Kholto. That's your mum, give her a hug.

And he faced two women, made strange by a sentence. They could not have been more different. One was tall, thin and brown, alluring and poised; the other was pale, soft, matronly, her auburn hair tied back in a bun, eyes pinched with worry. Love. Sticks and stones, he thought. He would never be afraid of sticks or stones again. He jerked a step towards glamour, the newcomer, and then another, for no reason except that he was expected to, until finally he was within her arms, resting his head on her hard collarbone. He sensed her deep discomfort. Whether at his reluctant hug, obvious ignorance as to her existence, or some other pain, he didn't know. It would be years before he thought to ask the question she might have feared, and years more before he could voice it: *where were you?*

He had stepped away then, unable to look at his not-mothers. Aunty Rania announced that Hala was there to take him home, but he heard what she meant: she's here to take you away from your home. In that moment, he understood why his cousins had been sent outside to play. He understood them, Sara and Ali, Jihad and Fatima, *as* cousins, and he realised it was only Moses—who he didn't see much, because he lived with Teyta and Jido—who had ever called him brother back. He heard at once all the buried instances of near revelation from every bout of bickering: he doesn't know, he doesn't get it, shh you can't tell, you're not allowed, that's not your—, she's *our*—! He'd thought of them all as one, and why not? Family was who you lived with, who you woke next to, who you bathed, ate and fought with, and that afternoon, they were butchered into adjacent pieces of language.

Oh, there he is, Hala said brightly, reeling him back to the present. Look, I got your favourite. Her voice was unexpectedly girlish, high—she was in a rare good mood, and he was conscious of not wanting to ruin it, but still he wavered there on the threshold. He took one look at the Znoud, fat rolls of deep-fried pastry with a gooey cream centre, the thick lengths drenched in honey, and rushed inside, his gut a pit of wild snakes—he made it to the toilet in time to expel it all, every bit of white, every dash of sin.

Bet on God

Princess! I'm home, yes, I am, who's a good girl? Hala's dog yipped and barked, a fluffy white bolt dashing to and fro on the backyard veranda. Hala laughed and tickled her pet, and Jamal watched, smiling, because it was rare to see his mother express joy of any kind, except with her beloved animal. She unlocked the heavy black security door, calling out as she did so that they had arrived.

Wayne was sprawled on the floor of the lounge, back against the black couch, glittering half-images flowing over his hairy legs, his green-tinged stubble. He was a grubby-looking little Irishman, his features squashed in like a plush toy. He couldn't be any uglier, Hala had said to Rania earlier, stirring the tar-like coffee in her cup. Honest. He looks like a leprechaun, but he's got the best heart. She wrapped the words in a warmth he had never heard her use with another person. Jamal remembered the night she found the end of her rainbow at a slot machine in Crown Casino. She'd gone out, her black hair ironed straight, the gifts of men bright around her slick dark dress, lovely as any field of stars, leaving her sons to their own devices. Bored after a while, Moses had grabbed one of her lighters, flicking it on and off, over and over.

Is this how you did it, bro? You wanna know what it's like, you mad cunt? And he leapt on top of him, holding Jamal down, the metal tip close, threatening.

Don't, Mo, come on, don't—please!

Moses grunted. Don't be such a bitch, it's nothing, look. He pressed the tip into Jamal's wrist, who screamed and thrashed, surprising them both; the metal was so hot it seared a red circle into his skin. Moses jumped up, panicked, running to the fridge and coming back with a bag of frozen peas. I'm sorry wallah I'm sorry, he said, and there was real fear in his voice. I didn't mean it. Jamal's wrist throbbed with pain, and his brother was extra attentive and kind to him, letting him choose what channel to watch, showing him that he cared, he really cared, and this was why Jamal would never forget that night, why he was still awake when Hala stumbled home with Wayne, the two of them giggling and shushing each other.

She joined him now on the floor. Wayne's lips were pursed around an unlit cigarette while he chopped up thick knots of green in a wooden bowl. The snip of the scissors, the clack of metal against the grain, were as familiar and regular as breathing. Hala took the cigarette, unwrapping it to mix the tobacco in.

Where's the other one? Wayne said, still cutting.

Running around, Hala said. He'll turn up.

Probably at Maccas, Jamal said. He wedged himself deep into the back of the other couch, as if doing so would prevent him from being told to go to his room.

Didn't youse just eat? Wayne's eyebrows shot up. Bloody hell.

They had, but the older boys didn't want kibbeh or fatteh jage as much as they wanted Big Macs, and to chat up girls in the carpark. Jamal didn't say that, he'd already blundered by speaking—bringing attention to himself usually resulted in getting kicked out. If he was quiet, there was a good chance they would forget about him, and he could lie here with them, under a blanket of smoke, watching shows like *Seinfeld* and *Becker* and *Frasier*, laughing when they laughed, watching the air turn silver, watching himself disappear.

Who cares? Hala said, miffed that his focus wasn't on her. Honest.

She grabbed the red Tally-Ho packet, pulled out paper and a filter, lining it with the chopped mixture. She licked the edges and expertly rolled a joint. Sparks flared from Wayne's lighter once, twice—he shook it—then they were smoking, and Jamal was forgotten. Forgotten, but not alone, which was enough. All the knots binding him began to loosen. Jamal touched his face, feeling the fluff on his cheeks. It was nothing like Wayne's green-black scruff. Jamal had asked why his face was like that when they first met, and Wayne had sighed with regret. His father warned him to wash his face in the morning if he wanted to avoid it, but he hadn't listened. Jamal woke early the next day to dunk his face with ice-cold water as Wayne lathered white foam and took a razor to his skin. That became their routine, and Jamal wouldn't trade it for anything. It had nothing to do with the water, or the ritual, nor after a while the fear of becoming a grizzled green. He'd simply never been invited to stand beside a man before, and at his first opportunity, he took it.

The footy was on, men in tight shorts tackling each other all over the field. White lights, lurid green. Dragons against the Knights.

What's the bet? Jamal heard the words coming out of his mouth as if from a great distance. He had slipped somewhere deep into his body.

Knights by 13 plus, Wayne said.

Either the Dragons were in for a belting or the odds had been too tempting to pass up a punt. Jamal almost wished he'd been here earlier. He knew the number to the betting agency by heart and often called on Wayne's behalf when he was busy rolling a blunt or jumping in front of the TV. His first bet had given him the bug.

They'd been in the car as usual while Wayne slipped into the dim interior of the TAB at Lurnea shops; Moses looking out his window, twelve, a young Adonis. There was no question that he took after their mum, or that he was her favourite, and Jamal felt keenly their differences in age, looks and love. Hala had signed Moses to a child model agency, and it seemed to Jamal that his brother often sat now in the same pose as his framed headshot, as though having seen himself once as beautiful, he was always trying to be so again, to recreate the recognition it had given. At nine, Jamal didn't have to worry about that. There were no photos of his large head, his sharp disparate teeth. Restless next to his perfect brother, Jamal unclipped his seatbelt and got out.

What are you doing? Moses said. He told us to wait.

Jamal didn't answer, but he heard the other door open and close behind him. There was no way Moses was going to be outdone by his little brother. It was dank inside the TAB, and a dozen screens angled down from the ceiling, lit up in an array of colours above a couple of high tables. It smelled like the inside of Moses's footy bag after a match: old sweat, unwashed feet. Wayne was by the wall, tapping a pen against an unfilled ticket. He looked up as sunlight shadowed them in.

Come here, he said irritably. Might as well make yourselves useful.

He was trying to predict the weekend's scores, and like any gambler, he split his faith between calculation and pure chance. Jamal and Moses gave him random numbers, eager to be included in men's business, and as a reward, got to have their own tickets. Wayne gave them twenty each, and the games, which they liked already, soon became much more than that. They'd lie in front of the TV at the end of every week, paper prophecies clutched under their chins. One Friday night, in the closing minutes of a Broncos game, Jamal looked down and realised he had accidentally picked the number eight for both teams.

It was eight all. Two minutes to go.

Hey, Jamal said, I've got the score. Eight and eight.

Wayne snorted. No, you don't, give it here. He snatched the ticket out of Jamal's hand. Fuck me, he shouted, you little good thing! You beauty! D'you know what this means? What the odds are? This is an easy twenty fucken grand. He charged at the screen, his face alight, fist clenched over the ticket. Hala was on her feet, too, letting out little yips of excitement. One minute left. Every pass, every tackle, he leapt a little off his feet, he couldn't help it, he was shouting, they were all shouting, this febrile lightning ripping through them, making the hair on their bodies stand on end; they'd never been more of a family than at that moment, lit up with possibility, right until the dying instant when Darren Lockyer kicked a field goal and robbed them of a fortune, or at least a desirable future. Sixty seconds was not long to dream, but the four of them had dreamt so powerfully the future had been in the room—a new car, clothes that didn't have holes, a holiday, their own home—tangible as smoke cloying in lungs. And then it wasn't. As the whistle blew, they collapsed on the floor like marionette dolls with their strings cut. Wayne tore up the ticket in a fit and left the room, cursing.

Jamal thought about this often, the moment of possibility when even his small ugly body briefly became beauty.

Don't you have homework to do? Hala glared at him, but somehow the glare did not pierce his skin as it usually did, it slid right off.

He shrugged. No, he said. It was easy, so easy to lie. He had always wondered how Moses and his cousins lied to their elders with such ease and confidence, knowing the beating they'd cop if caught. Now he knew: it was easy to lie when you were no longer alive. Earlier that night, he had knelt and died. He had sucked a dick into his mouth, putting another boy into raptures, and he wanted to do it again. This life, this world, was already over, and nobody but he knew that he had crossed an uncrossable line. They were all ghosts, still operating by the old rules, while he had become a new being.

Yeah, well, go to your room anyway, she said.

He hopped up, feeling oddly elastic and elated.

Wait on, Wayne said. How come you're not out with him? All you do is read. You're too old to be such a cat. He gushed out smoke. I'll tell you what—

Jamal kept grinning, his cheeks tight painful hubs. Those words meant a bet. The prediction: he couldn't sleep outside for a night by himself. The stakes: a cool hundred. Any other night Wayne might have been right, but there were no devils, no spirits to fear. This would be easy money. He was definitely getting those Adidas sneakers and he would look sick as on Eid. He couldn't wait to see Bilal's face when he rocked up to Lakemba mosque in them.

Before going outside, he needed to shower. The narrow bathroom was tiled a deep green with swirls of black throughout. Three glass panels stretched from one wall to the other, with opposing black nozzles, creating one double shower. He and Moses used to shower together, facing each other like two sides of an unfortunate coin, until Jamal turned ten and shy. Over the years, as this shyness intensified, Moses only became more confident, delighting in teasing his brother. A burgeoning football star, he developed into a fitness freak, taking every chance to show off his body, his abs, the V of his navel pointing down.

Look at these guns, bro. You wish you looked like this, Jemz. You fucken wish.

Jamal stepped up to the basin, trying not to be disappointed in the image, the hair that covered his chest and arms, his belly. He brushed his teeth free of the horrid aftertaste of vomit, gargled Listerine. The mirror had a light-green glass frame that curved and bubbled like breath. Whenever he undressed here, he felt as though he was stepping into a strange sea, a witch's dream. Goose pimples rose on his skin. He stepped into the shower, let the hot water fall and cleanse him. He liked it boiling hot, needing steam to rise and cloud the glass, to hide where he began and ended. His dick was hard and he stroked it with conditioner until he came. Bilal hadn't touched him earlier. Hadn't said anything except, Watch your teeth, and then, We better go.

By the time Jamal dragged his blankets and pillows out to the front yard, he was clean and happy and tired, but no longer so certain of his prospects. The cut grass of the lawn poked through the blanket, and he struggled to get comfortable. His breath plumed. His eyes darted around at every dog bark and passing car. He could hear the TV inside the house, and Wayne laughing. It was all a game to him, but games could be won and Jamal was determined this once not to lose. It was the Night of Power, and angels were everywhere. He had meant to pray for freedom, to be rid of whatever it was that ran under his skin like an angry current. Instead, he had fallen further into it and the fall felt like flying.

He stood up, arranging his blanket beneath him to face towards what he hoped, somewhere, was the Kaaba. He knew where Kholto Rania's house was from here, and the direction she faced from there. In front of him, the lounge-room window, Wayne, his mother, a continent, the oceans. He raised his hands and began praying. He bowed. *How perfect is my Lord, the Magnificent.* He dropped to his knees, pressed his head against the ground, crunching the grass under it. *God is greater, God is greater, God is greater.* Standing, he saw a blue Subaru WRX with a flared spoiler approach. It came to a stop at the kerb. He bowed again, prayers untroubled. Prostrated himself. He looked to his right, then left, saying peace be upon you to absent brothers, as the car door opened and Moses got out. Jamal lay down again as Moses slapped hands with the other boys and their goodbyes collided with the music pumping out. The Rexy sped off.

What are you doing, ya goose? Moses said, stepping over the low brick boundary that circled the yard. He was eighteen and his good looks had only grown since they were boys. Girls fought for his attention, and Jamal had a bruise on his chin to prove it.

Sleeping here. Wayne bet me I couldn't, Jamal said. He didn't get up, and Moses stood there, blotting out a portion of sky.

I don't get it, his brother said. He never did. Moses didn't care about Wayne's games. He knew who his dad was, a handsome man with dark curls named Abraham, and they had even met him once before he went to prison. Besides that, Moses was not one to dwell on anything, he moved through the world like a shark, going forward and never back. When the bets began, Jamal had never met his father, didn't even know his name. There wasn't a challenge he could let pass, no matter his fear, or perhaps because of it. Now, it had become a tradition, one of the few things that bound him to the man his mother loved.

Where were you? Jamal said.

Moses shrugged. Out, he said, and walked over to the back gate.

They had been drifting apart, and Jamal didn't know how to stop it. He was certain, though, that some of the blame lay in these bets, and the changes they had provoked. It was Wayne who had sneeringly claimed that Jamal couldn't read a whole book. He was given *King Arthur and His Knights of the Round Table*, a volume with thick pages and small ink drawings. He loved the feel of it, even as he struggled to piece the letters into words, and the words into pictures. He stopped following Moses around like a lost puppy as the pictures came to life in his mind. The orphan boy who became a king, chivalrous knights, the witches and wizards and dark woods all fit perfectly in a world rife with spirits. He understood it and understanding felt like stability, though he still worried at the past, turning over the men in his life, from his uncles Mahmoud and Khadeer, to Abraham and Wayne, like pieces in a broken puzzle.

Now Wayne thought he was too much of a nerd, that he'd overcorrected. Jamal rolled onto his side. He was fatherless, or he had too many fathers, and neither felt right. The one time he'd asked his mum about it, she said that he was an accident and his dad was a cunt. He didn't ask again. He told himself he didn't need anything, not a father or a mother, not even a half-brother. He told himself he didn't need his bed, that he wasn't scared, and no spiders would crawl into his mouth out here. He told himself things in the hope that telling was enough, that words made their own truth.

Inhuman shrieks and dark applause split the quiet. He scrambled up, heart bursting, but it was only a splotch of bats descending on the palm trees next door to feast on fruit. He was just starting to relax when the first explosion sent him reeling. Dimly, he was aware of Wayne laughing and lighting another bunger. But that was a worry for the body, its muscles and aching eardrums. Jamal was no longer within: he was on the air. Outside of his flesh, time failed, and he followed the flash to the fire.

&

Five-year-old Jamal sat on the couch, in the paling light of dawn, fiddling with a lighter. Nearby, close enough to touch, Fatima played with two rolls of toilet paper in Mahmoud's furry green armchair. She was two years old, a chubby little girl with bouncy brown curls who reigned as the youngest in the household. He had been the adored one before her, but she loved him with such thoughtless abundance, he did not feel lesser. Their parents slept, as did Ali, Sara, and Jihad; the house was hushed.

The two of them had developed a conspiracy of sorts in these unguarded hours where they would play together, but separately, with her nestled in Mahmoud's seat while Jamal sat in their mother's next to it, only a side table with the phone and tissue box between them. Fatima had draped the armchair in ecstatic white whorls, within which she was ensconced like a cherub among clouds. Jamal kept dragging the lighter's ignition wheel, sometimes fast and sometimes slow, loving the rough scratch of it against his thumb, absorbed totally in the feeling, the brief flare of flame, the flicker of heat and colour. Between breaths, a thin orange serpent crackled into being, racing across the pleated white paths, setting the clouds on fire, charring the green chair black. Fatima giggled, playing with the roll in her hands, unconcerned, while all the air in Jamal's chest went up in smoke.

In an instant the chair was ablaze, and he staggered away from the slap of heat and fear. He didn't know what to do. Mai, he thought, mai. He needed water, but it was miles away, stuck inside the kitchen. He sprinted over to the sink, springing off the tips of his toes in an effort to keep quiet. Beyond water, all he could think was that he didn't want to wake anyone. He'd be in more trouble for that than ever before and trouble already lived in his shadow. He was lucky the ahwa cups were in the bottom cupboard, within reach, and that he knew where they were because he was always asked to fetch them when guests were over. He grabbed one of the tiny coffee cups printed with blue vines, filled it with a mouthful of water, and gingerly carried it back to the burning chair and baby. He upturned the cup's contents in a tiny liquid arc and the fire laughed.

He ran back to the kitchen, filling it again, his ineffectual vessel, knowing it could never be enough. This time he splashed Fatima with a dash of the water and she seemed to notice him, and the heat, and began to cry at last. He played out this absurd, desperate ballet twice more. The fire continued unabated, crackling, *growing*, and he stood in front of it, overwhelmed. It had been seconds, it had been years. Screams were trapped inside Jamal's throat, but overriding everything was the fear of waking Mahmoud, the man who ruled the house, and who he knew never to call father.

He took one step back, then two, screams coiling irrepressibly in his muscles, until at last, he ran. He entered his room in perfect, dreadful silence. Jihad and Sara were asleep on the mattress they shared on the floor. Jamal slipped in beside them, nauseous and dizzy. Everything was still and quiet. He couldn't hear if Fatima was crying still, his heart's painful din blotting out sound. Or maybe that was the roar and sizzle of fire. He squeezed his eyes shut. He heard Ali yelling, and nearly pissed his pants. Ali had found her, thank God, his room was closest to the lounge. Everyone was in an uproar, Mahmoud most of all. His chair was unsalvageable, a smoking black and green wreck, as was the adjacent couch. Fatima, to everyone's astonishment, was untouched, not a hair on her head singed, as though that entire time all the hosts of heaven had stood guard over her.

Jamal did not confess. He stayed on his side, knees brought up to his chest, his eyes shut, thinking with all his might, I'm asleep I'm asleep I'm asleep. They knew it was him, he had known they would. Wherever a wrongness occurred in this house, it started with him, the strangest of them, and so it was that Mahmoud, a bull with a goatee, dragged Jamal's limp body over to the only unburned couch left, swearing all the while. Jamal curled into as small a ball as he could make, nose deep in the couch. Mahmoud grabbed the vacuum cleaner from the linen closet, and with everyone gathered behind him to watch in fearful silence, he whipped Jamal's body with the heavy end of the power cord, its cold metal fangs biting into his legs and thighs, his arms and belly, over and over, releasing at last all the screams in his chest.

This was his earliest memory: he left his sister to die: a conspiracy of flame: the tenor of terror hounding his steps: a man he loved beat his body until it bled: he prayed for someone else to save them.

&

Jamal flitted up to the trees, hung upside down with the bats. They knew he was there, and there was neither welcome nor rejection in their song. He was simply present. He knew this feeling. He had been a spirit before, and he would be again. He was always being called scattered, forgetful or lazy, and like anyone else he could be those things. Mostly, though, he was no longer there, his body emptied. He wondered if, in those moments, the angels stopped recording, but knew it was not so. Whatever limitations applied to man did not apply to them. They occupied all times. This knowledge dropped into him like a stone in a lake, and he rippled with it. The night gained a voice, and with this voice, it spoke:

It was one, ya subbi. Not a host. One angel stood guard over Fatima that day.

Jamal trembled. From his new vantage point, he watched Wayne creep out with another lit bunger, this time accompanied by Moses, both of them showing their teeth. He watched his body leap into the air as the next blast ripped out, his muscles and bones and blood working in tandem to provide a semblance of life. He saw the many fractures that spread through the whole, rivers of colour, he reached out and—

Aunty Rania had guests over that day, two men who looked like old bricks, and their wives in finest garb. They were sitting on the veranda drinking ahweh, smoking argileh, and shouting happily over each other. Rania was inside, brewing more coffee, and Jamal was leaning against a wall, waiting for orders like a good little soldier, when a brown sedan sped up onto the kerb and nearly crashed into the fence.

A short man in a rumpled suit came running out, yelling, Wein Rania? Wein Rania? Ya Allah, ya Allah, Mahmoud ma'at! Mahmoud ma'at!

Jamal heard the urgency, the pain in the man's voice, but couldn't grasp the meaning. He knew only that the man was asking for his Aunty Rania, and so he sped into the house, as the guests on the veranda slowly got to their feet. Jamal raced to his aunt's side at the stove, where the pot-bellied raqweh was filled to the brim with coffee, the long handle sticking out. The rich smell of ahweh poured over his head and Rania looked down at him with a smile.

Shu?

Mahmoud ma'at, he said.

Shu?

Jamal swallowed. He was trying to say it right but he didn't know Arabic well, nobody had taught him, and he had only his poor mimicry to rely on.

There's a man outside, Jamal said. Mahmoud ma'at.

The raqweh crashed to the ground, hot coffee spilling over the tiles in a boiling black cloud, and Aunty Rania, her face punched in with shock, bolted outside to hear the man say Mahmoud had died. It wasn't fair and it wasn't right that a child parroted those words, that Jamal was the one who hurt her with the news, and would be remembered always as the messenger. It wasn't fair that he saw Ali and Jihad, Sara and Fatima, come together in grief and weep. Wasn't fair that he wept, too, but alone.

&

Jamal looked down at the brick house with its black security bars on the windows, the husk on the grass the men were tormenting. They were bleeding, couldn't they see? Memory flickered out behind them like the most extraordinary wings, huge and brilliant white shapes full of images. One, a kangaroo, leapt off the canvas. It shook itself, glanced up at him and said, Fuck off we're full, then soared into the dark where it became something else. Jamal remembered meeting the animal at a coastal resort Wayne took them to after a big win at the casino. It was their first and last holiday.

They had a cabin with two rooms, a TV that didn't work, and just enough trees and bush around to suggest wilderness. Jamal crept onto the balcony in the morning, needing air, and the wild became more than a suggestion. He saw the kangaroo come towards him over the misty earth, huge and brown, a long muscular monster, all grace. The balcony jutted above the ground and still the animal loomed over it.

Jamal shrank back, focused with horror and awe on its thick claws that dug with ease into the wood of the rail. Wayne stepped up beside him, closing the sliding door behind him softly.

Don't make any sudden moves, he said. This thing can kill you in a second.

Jamal didn't need convincing. The roo radiated power, its black eyes pinned on his own. Then Wayne laughed loud as thunder, seizing his shoulders and shaking him, startling the rodent spirit of Australia in the process. It vanished in a second.

It was probably just hungry, Wayne said. God, you're too easy.

He took great satisfaction in Jamal's fear, the same way that Moses and Jihad did. As if his weakness made them strong. In Wayne's case, that wasn't quite right—he often boasted that his own father used to do this and much worse to him. Maybe Jamal's failure to overcome his tests reassured Wayne that no boy could pass them, that they were designed to fail, that it wasn't his fault.

They lasted three days at the resort. By the second day, Hala was bored and angry. Whatever she had imagined for a holiday, this was not it. There was nothing to do—who was she meant to talk to, the fucking trees? Lie on the beach all day? For what? And the food here? Yuck. She would rather die. Did he think she was really a Smith or something? She was a Khaddaj! She hadn't crossed an ocean for this shit. Get her high or get her the fuck out of here. She didn't know why she was shouting, except that the place was too quiet, she could hear herself think, and to think was to remember. To be around her in that state was like walking through a cloud of wasps: every step invited pain. To be her in that state was much the same.

They all went to sleep early that night. Jamal lay on the bottom bunk, listening to his brother snore. In the darkest hour, the djinn made itself known. The outline of a giant face, sketched in lightning, burned blue above him, like it was trying to press through from the other side and couldn't fit. He could feel its fury. The force of it pressed on his chest, turning the blood in his body to lead. He screamed into the void, he prayed, he lost language itself, the space between words becoming larger and larger, the hole within darker and wider. By morning he was wrung out, red-eyed, shaking, his throat a long ache.

Moses told him it was just a dream, and to stop being so gay.

These words ran all over his wings as he launched his bunger. *Stop being so gay, stop being so gay.* Jamal blinked: those weren't wings, they were enormous feathers, a minuscule part of the whole. At the dark tip was another night, another house: Jamal playing chess with Moses, the house quiet as a secret. Moses went to the toilet, and Jamal lay looking over his queen, his king, their retinue and pawns, strategising victory. He heard the toilet flush, and the sound of someone climbing the stairs, first with soft treads, then a shocking flurry. Jamal reared up as a figure with a large black teardrop for a head sped into his room, roaring, a wall of sound and rage. He barely made out the words, Give into me! He shrieked until his high voice broke, stumbling back and up onto the bed, blubbering. Wayne took off the balaclava, his leathery face folding in on itself as he and Moses laughed until they too were crying.

Give me all your money, he'd said, but Jamal heard *Give into me.*

&

The bats closed over him, sharing the heat of their hearts, urging him to let go of fear. There was so much of it. He did not return to his body, or let go of anything. He left the street instead, its fibro and weatherboard houses, footpaths lined with trees, trees lined with spider webs. He was going home, he was going back. It was time for suhoor, a dark snack. He had not woken for it in years, not since he stopped calling this house home, stopped calling Rania his mother, and her children his siblings. He flashed past Lurnea High, past Paterson Avenue, bordered by the park that rustled with the wind, each tree a tower of blood and memory singing to their kin. Flashed up the alleyway, setting off Melissa's barking dogs, and now the sun was shining, and Jihad and Sara were with him, each of them holding one of Fatima's hands and swinging her into the air. He watched his younger self shout, Bet ya I can beat you home! and start running. He watched Jihad take off after him: Sara curse them: Fatima wander onto the road: the eyes of the driver widen: the bonnet bend and bounce: the body rise and rise, and fall.

Fatima survived her three broken ribs, her torn skin healed and her shattered leg was bolted back together only a touch shorter. She was blessed, no one could doubt it, to have survived not one but two disasters, of fire and metal, before she reached five years of age. And she was cursed, no one could doubt it, to have needed to survive so much at all. The distinction did not matter, Aunty Rania said. Either way, it was clear she had to bet on God. She put on the hijab after that, the first of her sisters to do so.

Jamal blinked and he was above her driveway. His aunty, his mother. The house was unlit, sleeping. Nothing was as it used to be, and he was to blame. Why else would he be haunted by these jagged edges? And yet angels did not record deeds before the age of fourteen, so perhaps he was not seeing his sins, perhaps this was no divine manifestation but his own wretched tally of wrongs. The moon vanished behind a bank of cloud, and the ruffled dark shivered with disappointment, as if there had been a lesson there for him to learn and he had failed it.

Ay, move over.

Jamal blinked again, brought back to his body by his brother's voice. Stars glared above. Grass poked into his back. His neck cricked as he unfolded from the foetal position. Moses got down beside him. Jamal made room on his doona, and his brother scooted in close, his aftershave a cloying stamp.

What are you doing? he said, wiping his face with his shirt.

Listen, Moses said.

Jamal heard his mother's voice on the air, a rising tide. Wayne's voice was muted by comparison. He would go again, maybe for the last time.

I died today, bro, Jamal said. His voice was scratchy, his throat sore.

Don't be such a drama queen, Moses said. Charmaine felt so guilty she gave me a blowie. Chin up, you took one for the team.

I took one all right, Jamal said, grinning.

I saw you praying by the way, Moses said. Definitely in the wrong direction, and on a dirty blanket, so it won't count but on ya for trying, Jemz.

Jamal smacked his lips. God's everywhere, though. Everywhen. Knows it all. Biggest know-it-all, but I still get shit for reading, bookworm this, nerd that—

His brother shifted up onto an elbow and grabbed his face, turning him sharply to look into his eyes. Are you stoned? How many times have I told you not to stay in there with them?

Jamal snorted, jerking away. Whatever, don't be such a drama queen. How'd you smooth things over with Charmaine anyway?

Moses sighed theatrically. I'm a sexy cunt, that's how. You can't teach this.

You're the worst. Like actually, on the list of the worst people in history, you're at the top. It goes you, then Hitler.

Don't hate the play—

Oh my god, kill me. I was having a great time by myself, you know.

Nuuurrr. You pissed your pants, don't lie. Then Moses dived on top of him, and Jamal was laughing and writhing, and they pretended not to hear the door slam, and the car start up as Wayne left them for the last time, leaving two fifty-dollar notes behind.

Everyday Jihad

Ali Ali Ali! Jihad's screams electrocuted the living room.

Jamal, Kholo Khadeer, Aunty Rania, Fatima and Ali were on their feet instantly, staring out as Jihad appeared, sprinting towards the house. Ali moved first, summoned by his name, rushing out to meet the police crash-tackling his little brother to the ground. The difference between them was immediately apparent. It was almost cruel that he was so tall and Jihad so short, like distorted copies of the man who made them.

What did he do, get off him, hey, hey! Fucken calm down! Ali shouted, leaping over the veranda railing. Cops poured down the driveway, taking to him like water to sand. They crashed against him as a wave and fell apart in pieces. There was a reason no one wanted Ali's eyes on them, there was a devil there, an absence of fear tied with a willingness to hurt. He went to work with quick heavy blows, standing tall for all the world like he was used to being one man against everyone else. Jihad thrashed beneath the cops holding him, going berserk. Hands wrenched his head back, then a jet of wet fire squirted into his eyes and he screamed a high girlish scream.

Ali, eyes weeping and furious from multiple hits of pepper spray, shouted, Shut up you little bitch! and Jihad strangled his cries into strained moans, rubbing his face into the ground, hoping the dirt would douse the burning.

Kholo Khadeer charged into the fray. Where Ali was lean, Khadeer was a mountain of fat and brute strength. Tall and wide, he had made a name for himself as a bouncer in the Cross, and more besides. One night, Ali told them in an awe-filled voice that he'd seen Kholo come over after his shift, the whole left side of his Statesman riddled with bullet holes as though he were still in Beirut—but now he worked as a truckie, hauling cargo. He hit like a truck too, and the cops scattered again. Ten cops became twenty, cars piling up in the street with blue and red spirals, neighbours popping out all over to stare as three grains of sand drowned.

Inside the house, Jamal's shirt clung to his body as sweat poured out, but he couldn't feel anything, he was on the ends of the batons rising and falling, he was crunching Kholo Khadeer's nose into a red flower, he was inside Ali's heart as his ribs cracked and his collarbone snapped, he was falling out of Jihad's eyes in long wet trails as his cousin was overwhelmed by what he had dragged into his mother's yard. He was everywhere and nowhere as his arm slammed the front door shut, the motion reflexive, unthought through, as if closing the door could close the world. He flung his arms out, trying to hold back Aunty Rania and Fatima, both yelling and pushing against him, but he couldn't hear anything beneath the great honking bellows of Kholo Khadeer and the swell of sirens. There was a split second where Jamal almost seemed to gather from the danger a power over the woman who had raised him, to say with his body, *I'm doing this for you*, but it flickered and was gone. He couldn't say whether he let his arm fall, or if he was shunted aside. She opened the door and ran out onto the veranda casting curses at the cops, telling them to leave her boys alone.

Again, Jamal closed the door. He snapped, Stay here! to Fatima, who was still only a girl. She elbowed him in the side, saying, Move, to get a better look out the window. They stood there and watched as all three men were arrested, shoved into the back of paddy wagons. It was only then that Jamal felt able to venture out and get Aunty Rania, who sobbed and swore in Arabic, casting curses on everyone present, on their fathers and mothers, sisters and brothers, on their houses. He crushed her to his chest saying, I didn't know what to do, Kholto. I didn't know what to do. I was trying to protect you.

He knew what she was thinking because he was thinking it too: he should have been out there. He should be in that box, too, beaten and bloodied. The last time he froze, he'd ended up in the paddy wagon, nine years old. He could feel the steel, smell the chlorine. Rania shrugged him off. Wheezing. Face swollen red, mascara smeared. He crept back inside. She talked to the cops for a while, then followed them to the station to write a statement. No doubt calling his cousin Habib on the way, who was a lawyer and a legend in the family. He'd done his HSC six times, repeating it until he got the marks he needed for law school, and now he drove a Porsche. It was the Porsche everyone talked about.

You should be like him, Emne often said. Jamal would rather eat his old shoes than do the HSC more than once, but he never said that. He was in Year 10, and the countdown was on for him to demonstrate whether he was going to be anything more than a flop like the rest of them. Everyone expected greatness from him, because he read books, and the simple fact that he enjoyed doing so told them that he must be capable of something incredible. A brain like that, they said, you're lucky. Don't forget us when you're rich! They were all drop-outs doing odd jobs, or on Centrelink, and increasingly, they looked at him like a future lifeline. The thought cut into his mind every night, that he liked boys as much as girls, that they would cast him out one day, and then what would happen to them? To him? He'd lost a home once, or at least his understanding of home, and it had felt like dying. A great disruption, a tearing, freedom and pain all at once.

He stared at the empty yard. The real joke of it was that the books he was reading were fantasies. He was no more a genius than any of them, no more capable of getting them out of their circumstances. Behind him, he could hear Fatima on the phone, recounting to her friends what had just happened, starting out tremulous, scared, but by the third call sounding almost bored, like the story was a blade and each telling dulled the edge. It was a tactic he was familiar with, but he was starting to think these edges would never dull, that running over them repeatedly only deepened the cuts they made, leaving you with tattered and bloody feet.

Habib got Jihad out a few hours later, but Ali and Khadeer weren't released. They had priors, and had assaulted police officers, but Habib was going to sue the police for excessive force. They were all sitting in Kholto Rania's living room, Moses and Bilal too, Kholto Emne and her kids. Habib was in his element: he wore an expensive grey Armani suit, his hair gelled and shining, and he seemed to be rehearsing his court case, talking about how racist and fucked the cops were, how much worse it had got since 9/11. Even he—here his eyes widened, he gestured to his suit (he didn't need to point to his Porsche, it was a gleaming alien thing in the driveway, more out of place than the police the screams the blood had ever been)—even *he* had been stopped by cops on a dozen occasions, always because they were looking for a suspect of 'Middle Eastern' appearance. Sometimes his smooth polish dropped away and his words thickened, as now when he said, Seriously, all this, twenty cops, for what? All because Ji was driving on a suspended learner's licence? He's just a kid for fuck's sake.

It was the kind of line Jamal expected his cousin to bristle at, but Jihad, sitting next to Habib, in the same worn black trackies and hoodie he'd been in earlier, didn't seem bothered. He was hunched over, a bandage over his bruised and swollen right eye, and there was something different in his carriage, something that wasn't there before, that made the word 'kid' ridiculous without him needing to say a word. That word had been robbed from him. He was sixteen and the stubble on his face was thick, and his eyes, so often crinkled with mischief, were hard stones.

It's been like that forever, he said. First time I was in a paddy wagon I was ten, me and Jemz, mahak?

Jamal nodded, smelling the chlorine again. Reckon your mums are proud of yas, you little grubs? the white cop had said, as he dragged them out of the Whitlam Centre. They'd been sneaking into the pools that summer. It was easy to do: just go in through the back entrance for the squash courts and gym, take your shirt off in the restroom, wet your hair at the sink, and walk past reception like you'd been there for hours. People were always coming and going. The hard part was the smell of hot chips and burgers, the fridges full of Coke. When they got hungry, they stole what they needed. With all eyes on Jihad and Moses, Darren and Aiden rifled through people's bags for money. No one suspected two white boys could have less than everything, so they usually got away with it. It was the best week ever, and like most of their best weeks, it ended when someone yelled, Cops!

Moses, Darren, and Aiden got away, legging it across the fields towards Hoxton Park Road, but Jamal had frozen. Jihad told the cops they didn't do nothing, that it was the other boys who done it, they didn't even know them. Coppers didn't buy it, though. Said they had to take them home to talk to their parents. That's all, just talk. But they put them in the cage anyway, and there was a big green golly on the floor left by the last animal in there.

Fucking pigs, Jihad said. Ali had shown him the bugs in his car once, told him to act as if the walls were always listening, because they were. Half the people in the area are doing fucked shit, but are they being tailed around the streets? Nah, just us.

We can't even go to a Dogs' game without an army of cops following us, Moses added. They were warming up now, the fires of injury burning bright, every slight rising to darken the air. Jamal remembered the thrilling power of being with the boys at a Bulldogs game. The crackling atmosphere, Ace the blind old Anglo leading them in team chants. Boys and men with their doumbakkas, banging the drums, a thunderous music, the chanting and rhythmic clapping, the way the mass of them could at any moment part into dancing circles, the boys with their arms out like wings, swinging their hips, dusky skin and dark hair gleaming under streetlights. The way they could roar with one voice, the loudest and proudest fans in the NRL, because the Dogs had Hazem El Masri, El Magic, their prince. And what did it earn them, this pride for the national game? Harassed on the trains, harassed at the game, and in the news. Habib was right that it was getting worse, Jamal thought, but it had never been good.

&

Jihad put his lips to the bent Coke bottle, held a flame to the cut hose sticking out of it, and sucked as the water bubbled and smoke filled the plastic.

They were at Bilal's house, partly because he had a sweet set-up in his garage, with a ratty fake leather couch and TV they played video games on, but also simply to have a reason to move. Most of what they did came from an inability to sit still, to stay put, and it was this more than anything that made the boys so curious and fascinated by Jamal's transformation into a reader over the past two years. How can you just *sit there*? they'd ask, eyes bugging out. Jamal hadn't spoken to Bilal, they couldn't even look at each other, but since Jihad had included him earlier, offering him a way into what was happening, he had come along.

Jihad raised his head, releasing smoke in a rush. I'm in love, boys, he said.

Two hours in jail and you fell in love? Jamal said. Fuck that was quick.

They all cracked up, even Jihad, his spluttering laugh sending them all further into hysterics. He had that gift, the ability to take people with him into whatever he was feeling.

No, you gronk. With Lana, he said.

He'd been with her last night, and it had been perfect. You know perfect? Fucking perfect. He could not have been flying higher if he tried. He was in love and that love pulsed in his chest, it was in his lungs, and all he had to do to feel it was think of Lana, which he did all the time, like a child touching a flame to prove it was hot. This girl was not like the others; okay yeah they kissed, okay she let him finger her, but there was something in her baby blues that called to him and when he wasn't talking to her, he was still thinking about her, about what he'd say, and how she'd answer. He drove all the way to Cronulla for her: what was that, if not love? His L's were suspended, but he didn't give a fuck. He'd stayed with her all night, talking and touching and kissing.

Thought I was that fucken hectic, coming home today, he said. I was two streets from here, all right, two streets and then, whoop-whoop, I heard those sirens and khiri tukhti. My stomach went like that, bro. Slammed the brakes and fucking legged it.

You know me? Cathy Freeman wouldn't have caught me, I was that fast, and cheering, thinking I was sweet—then I look and see them still coming, kus ummon and my heart, bro. I'm going to jail, I'm going to die, but I can't stop. I jumped over a fence like I was Van Damme, nearly broke my ankle, and all I'm thinking is I just gotta get home, if I get home it's all good and just as I make it, fucking bang! I'm telling ya, this munyak thought he was Goldberg, bro, the way he tackled me.

As he got to this part, Jihad was on his feet, comically mocking his own fear, how hard he went down, and they were all laughing so hard, too hard maybe, crying, but it was fucking funny, no one could deny that.

Is that how you got the cut, cuz? Bilal pointed to the bandage, the stitches over Jihad's eye.

Nah, he said. That was the cop chick—did you see her, the redhead?—she and this other cop were walking me to the paddy wagon, all right. Jihad had the biggest smile on his face.

No way, don't tell me—

I go to her, give us your number! He threw his head back and roared with laughter, the world rang with it. Next thing you know I go headfirst into the paddy wagon door, kus umma.

When they got their breath back, Jamal said, But weren't you just telling us you were in love?

Jihad frowned at him. I am, he said. Bro, I reckon it was Laylat al-Qadr last night, all right, and eidi-al-Quran, wallah, I asked God to make Lana my wife. I was just being a smeek with that cop. Ask Lana yourself, I called her and told her about it (he held up his Nokia 7610 here), she laughed too. That's how I know she's the one.

Jamal shook his head in disbelief. Watching Jihad gesticulate excitedly, pumped with adrenaline, almost feverish in his declarations of love, as if he could distract them all from his wounds, Jamal thought again of being in the paddy wagon when they were kids. How fun it had seemed at the time. He'd stood up to the small grate at the top left corner and stuck his fingers through, wiggling them at the cars in the lane behind them.

They can see us, Ji! They can see us! he said, flashing his fucked-up teeth in a grin. A little kid playing a game. Jihad had hissed at him to get down, to be quiet, his face flushed with shame. Jamal sat down again, wondering idly why there were no seatbelts.

How come you're never scared? he'd asked as they got closer to home.

Whaddya mean? Jihad said. You could build a house with the bricks I'm shitting. And then laughed. Tried to hold on to the bench as the wagon swayed. They both knew there would be a beating waiting for them.

What do you think it'll be? Jamal said. Shahayta?

Jihad thought about it. The spoon maybe, he said. His mum loved that damn wooden spoon, long as her arm. But it could always be worse. He pursed his lips. Remember when you got the hairbrush?

Jamal shuddered. His aunty had a heavy ornate hairbrush shaped like a handheld mirror. Metal bristles with blue caps filled out the oval head. He had sleepwalked into his aunt's room and pissed all over the bottom of her bed, thinking it was the toilet. She bashed his face with the brush, and his arms, which he'd raised to shield himself, and his legs when he curled up into a ball, the hard mirror falling again and again, showing only pain. He had raised red welts all over his body, and later, he'd wandered the street crying loud as he could, hoping someone, anyone, would come out and ask him what was wrong. Nobody did. They had their own problems.

Fuck that, Jamal said. Then, You should have run.

Fingers of light speared the cage through the grate. Made the green golly shine.

And left you by yourself? Jihad shook his head. No way, you're my brother.

Looking at the nasty cut, the stitches an angry railroad of shadow arcing above his eye, Jamal wished he'd been there today, wished Jihad hadn't been alone so that he had an excuse not to run. Why was it, he thought, that they were always willing to do more for each other than for themselves?

To Feast, To Fury

Jamal stared at the racks of sneakers, his pocket itching. It was late-night Thursday shopping and Westfield's was packed, pop music blaring over swirls of teenagers, some still in school uniform, while others had already been home and back, done up and glossy. He had $150 in his wallet and he felt powerful with it, powerful but afraid, because the two went together—the former, being unnatural, could be lost or taken away. It was frequent, this loss and this taking, in Liverpool. People got rolled all the time, especially in Bigge Park on the way to the station, after school.

If you don't hurry up I'm gonna rob you myself, Fa'ailo said.

Jamal rolled his eyes. In the sliver of mirror between shoe racks, he watched Ilo gather his hair in his hands, pulling the long dark wave back and retying it. Ilo was the kind of big that always had other boys asking, Why don't you play footy, bro? You'd be unstoppable! He never answered, would brush them off with a laugh. His laugh was light and high, a fey music that had drawn them together. On Orientation Day, sitting side by side, the white woman doing roll call had mangled both their names and they'd shared a groan, then a laugh. Seeing his eyes light up, the dark freckles dusted across his cheeks moving together like a flock of birds, Jamal mirrored him, felt the same light enter his blood, the joy of recognition. They had been friends ever since.

Jamal knew which shoes he wanted, but he was stalling and the reason walked out of Footlocker's back room. Bilal spotted him straight away, and angled towards him, his stride so wide-legged it was comical, like his dick was so big he couldn't walk straight (it wasn't, although it was big enough, and the thought of it, thick and cut, the knob pushing into his throat, was enough to make his mouth water). He'd recently been to the barber, the sides of his hair razored bare, his stubble now the finest rain, a sweeping sharp curve across his face.

Hey cuz, you getting your Eid clothes? Bilal said, as their hands slapped together. Jamal nodded. It was the second-last day of Ramadan, and he, like most others, was putting together his outfit. On Saturday, they would go to Lakemba mosque at dawn to pray with thousands of Arabs and Africans, Malaysians and Indonesians, a cross-section of the world, the young all decked out in their gleaming best, ready to chat each other up. Bilal gave Ilo a startled look, eyes widening. Who's this? You should play footy, bro.

Uh-huh, Ilo said, his voice flat and hard. Then to Jamal, I'm going for a smoke. And he walked off, his back straight, expression grim.

What's his problem?

I dunno, Jamal said. He hates hearing that. He won't even play PE.

What a fat shit, Bilal said. It was a fucken compliment! Yaraat I was that big.

Jamal was sure that Bilal meant it that way, and he was equally sure Ilo couldn't take it as it was meant. Brand names and block colours blurred in front of him. He doubted there was any point in saying there was no way to assert how your words would be received, that they could change on the air, like when his mum called him a mistake once, and the word was there now always, under his tongue, whenever he saw her. He doubted, and doubt ate his voice.

Look, Bilal said, whispering now. I can't give you a discount, cuz, I just started here. And—he looked around, shuffled closer—I'm sorry, okay? About everything. It's all good, yeah?

Jamal nodded, unsure exactly what he meant, if he was sorry for what happened or the strained silence that followed, and relief cascaded down Bilal's face. He wanted things to go back to what they were, Jamal realised, and the door that had so briefly opened inside him sealed again. He bought his shoes, a blue he thought matched Bilal's eyes, and left quickly after that. Ilo was waiting for him in his usual spot, in the Westfield's carpark, near the entrance to the cinema. He looked worried and guilty all at once.

Sorry, he said in a rush. I'm sorry, I dunno what—

It's fine, Jamal said. He didn't care.

Ilo paused. But did you? You okay?

Jamal wanted so much to tell him about Bilal, but he couldn't. They still had a year left at Liverpool Boys, where faggot and gay got shouted every day, and anything remotely feminine was met with scorn and violence. When Jamal had started carrying books everywhere, he got his fair share of shit, but it lessened as he grew taller and his beard came in, making him at least look the part of a man, which carried weight among the still-beardless boys.

Ilo talked over the silence, tapping ash from the end of his cigarette. You know my dad wanted me to be a footy player? Even before I got big. Every weekend, I'd be out there on the field, fucking hating every minute of it. I'd try to avoid it but sometimes I'd get the ball and just stand there while they jumped me—like, seriously, who wants to get hit for fun? Then he'd bash me when we got home anyway for 'embarrassing' him.

The impulse to make a joke hit Jamal, a need to return or undo what he'd just been given, this quiet hurt part of his friend, because he didn't know where or how to put it alongside his own pain, the stories that bubbled up in response. He pictured Ilo's dad, a man larger than them both, a solid mass of muscle with a protruding gut over his floral 'ie, hitting little Ilo with his oaken arms, and fury coursed through him. The force of it was shocking, a heat pulsing through the dense fog of his mind until there was no fog, only the clarity of rage.

That's fucked, Jamal said. Fuck those guys, fuck him and fuck footy too.

Amen, Ilo said, and giggled. He rested his arm on Jamal's shoulder, and they leaned a little closer together, bound by a thin ribbon of smoke.

&

Jamal caught the bus home with Moses. His brother's face was drawn with exhaustion. He'd started working at Bakers Delight, which meant he had to get up at 4am, to bake with the dawn. The black half-moons under his eyes did nothing to diminish his beauty, the classically handsome angles of his face; if anything—Jamal thought with disgust—the emergence of flaws highlighted the strength of his features. He smelled delicious too. Do you have to sit here, Mo? he said, stomach rumbling. I'll eat you at this rate.

Moses laughed. Imagine working with it all day. He sounded pleased, a thrum of pride beneath his tiredness. You know the amount of hassanat I'm gonna get?

The more difficult the fast, they'd been told, the higher the reward for accomplishing it. Between his new job and Sara's at the Tip Top factory, they had access to all the bread they'd ever need, and extra money too. Aunty Rania told them what a good sign this was, because Jido had been a baker in Tripoli, before the civil war launched in earnest and the country collapsed. When he arrived in Sydney as one of the first wave of migrants fleeing Lebanon, he landed a job at Tip Top. They wanted him to make Lebanese bread for them, which none of the national chains had then, but he refused, and later opened his own bakery. It was the beginning of his great fortune, the means by which he brought his wife and children over. Obviously, he'd lost it all (how, she never said), but there was no doubt that the good and grand began with loaves in an oven.

The ride from Liverpool to Lurnea took twenty bone-rattling minutes, but it felt longer, in part because the sun was losing its purchase in the sky, and the spools of lavender and pink, orange and red, visibly changed with each passing moment; to see time was to sink into it, in the act of noticing. Jamal staggered off the bus at the end of it, nauseous with motion sickness, and followed his brother down the street to their home. He could see their neighbour Shane taking the bins out; a plump man with a circlet of grey hair around a large bald spot and a jolly air, he waved at them, and Jamal waved back. He and his wife Sally had a perfect white Christian life: a sumptuous, cement-rendered townhouse with a cobblestone driveway that looped around a centrepiece fountain, and two grown children, Susan and Max.

Susan used to take Jamal and Moses along to her local church youth group, which they agreed to because they were bored and she was a beautiful eighteen-year-old blonde girl. The other kids were all Anglo offcuts, like Gary, whose face resembled Arnott's pizza shapes, and who thought painting his nails black made him, if not a rebel, then at least worth noticing for something other than his mass of purpling pimples.

Remember Susan, bro?

Moses smirked. You never forget your first, Jemz.

You're a fucken bullshit artist.

He's bluffing, Jamal thought, but there was a surety in his voice, and a swagger in his walk, as they went around the back. He tried to remember if there had been any signs of this supposed first. Susan had been engaged to her British friend Jack, a weedy guy with long brown hair, who led the youth group with her and was *just like, super down with Jesus*, because he thought they looked alike, and the image of himself suffering but glorious, haloed in painted glass windows, was about the only thing that made him feel something.

Even you guys believe in Jesus, Jack had said the first time they went, with a painfully encouraging smile. He was roaming the room handing out snacks while he talked, and stopped in front of their table, his Adam's apple bobbing as he swallowed.

Yeah, Jamal said reluctantly. Isa was one of our prophets.

That's right, that's right, Jack said, nodding emphatically. He held out a bowl of Cheetos. Tell us more about Jesus in Iz-larm—you know, we can learn from you too. He looked tremendously pleased with himself for that allowance.

But he was wrong. Jamal couldn't think of anything else. What little he knew at that time came from gossip and the occasional scripture class at Casula Public, where a bored hijabi taught a group of five that Islam meant surrender to Allah, and that the Prophet was perfect. Satisfied with these truths, she made them recite the Fatiha for the rest of the period—until Jamal found out that scripture was optional, and non-participating kids got to stay in the library. Jamal had looked to Moses for help, but he was staring at Susan with a vacant expression. As the silence dragged on, Jamal started to panic and blurted out, Jesus was not the son of God!

Gary sniggered, and some of the other kids laughed. Jack smiled and launched into a speech about how tolerant they should all be, as if what Jamal said was as silly as 'pigs can fly' instead of a literal imposition on his narrative, a declaration that it was false. Jack withdrew the bowl of Cheetos as he spoke, adding that it was time for an activity break. In the hall, the pews had been pushed to the sides, and they used the space to play indoor soccer. That's what had kept Jamal and Moses going back—games and free food were worth a boring lecture any day—or so he'd thought. For Moses, it had clearly been more than that.

She gave me a handie behind the church, Jemz. Full made her Jesus jiggle.

What?

Her necklace, you know the one with Jesus on the cross, fell out while she was jerking me. Said she loved my big Arab dick. He paused, his expression changing. Watch out for the religious ones, bro, they're the worst.

Fucking hell. So that's why she stopped taking us?

Moses shook his head as they went up the steps. Nah, that was after she got married.

The screen door, with its thick iron bars and black security mesh, was ajar and he swung it wide open as he stepped into the kitchen. They never used the front door. That was for deliveries and police. Moses walked up to the fridge, opened it, and grabbed a can of Coke. The hiss of it opening, the gurgle as he swallowed, the long ahhhh of relief were all so familiar, so normal, that it took a minute for Jamal to realise why his dry mouth was open.

Bro, he said, and shock plastered itself on Moses's face.

Oh fuck! Astugfirullah I wasn't even thinking, I just—he held the can in front of him like it had turned into a snake, and such was the pain in his eyes that Jamal almost expected it to slither out of his hand.

No, no, no. That can't count, come on. One sip. One sip. He was muttering to himself as he poured the can down the sink, let it fall with a clatter among the stack of dirty dishes, crowned by a raqweh which had covered everything with grainy darkness. Things had gone to shit since Wayne left. Hala smoked more and did everything else less. She'd gone back to working nights, and they saw little of her, to their mutual relief.

Yullah, are youse ready? Hala followed her scratchy voice into the kitchen. She looked exhausted, but her eyes were fever-bright.

Her hair was tied back in a loose ponytail, and she wore torn blue jeans and a white singlet that had 'Hot Stuff' written in bubblegum pink across her bulging chest. Jamal couldn't help thinking of the week she got the implants, one of Wayne's last gifts to her, how she'd been tottering around the kitchen, almost unbalanced by her new ballast, when one of them suddenly caved in and she cried out, trying to hold herself together. She had to go back into surgery to get it redone after that. He tried not to look there at all, but when he did, he was sure at any moment her tits might pop.

Moses iftarat, Jamal said.

You fucken dog! he said, aggrieved. It was an accident, Mum. Just a sip now.

She shrugged. What about you, she said to Jamal. Are you still soyam? When he nodded, she told them to get in the car, and they did just that, racing to Aunty Rania's house. On the way, Moses kept arguing his case.

It's not fair, he said. There's only ten minutes left, I don't care, I don't care, I'm still fasting. Hala told him it didn't matter, not in Islam, and not to her. She wasn't invested in what they did, the only Muslim customs she adhered to were abstaining from pork and alcohol. The latter she was so adamant about, she never even let Wayne have any in the house. Rules were rules, she said, and there was no use pretending if you'd broken them. Maybe this was why she didn't wear hijab or pray—she considered herself irredeemably broken.

When they got to Rania's, there was only a smudged fingerprint of light left on the horizon. Hala led the way inside, Jamal and Moses following.

Jihad looked up from the couch. Are youse fasting?

Jamal and Moses both said yes at the same time, and Hala whipped around, furious. No, you're not wulah, cut it out! she said, finger stabbing at Moses.

I am! he screamed, his voice breaking.

Jamal was stunned to see tears in his brother's eyes. Moses had struggled for this moment all day, and he couldn't accept losing it, the favour he thought he'd gained. He backed away from the door, lips trembling, then with a final look of pure hatred he shouted, Fuck you! He flipped her the bird and bolted, screen door crashing behind him, and disappeared up the driveway and into the dark street with all the speed he had. After a minute of horrified silence, Hala pointed at Ali, who was frozen like everyone else, and with perfect calm said, Go get him.

Ali looked like a man condemned, but he nodded and went out. He was the only one who could do it. He was taller, faster, older, and Moses would obey him for the same reason that Ali obeyed his aunty: it was expected, and expectation, enforced over time, became instinct.

The waiting was awful. There were too many people for it to have been quiet, with Fatima and Rania in the kitchen, and Teyta and Jido in the lounge with Jihad, but whenever he thought about it later, Jamal would not be able to recall a single sound. His eyes were fixed on his mother, her growing anger felt as a prickling all over his skin. As her eyes narrowed, Jamal followed them to see two shapes coming out of the gloom, Ali leading Moses gently with his arm around his shoulders. He came inside first, softly saying, Come on, cuz. Bite the bullet. Moses hesitated on the threshold, sniffling and cringing. Jamal had always thought of him as *old*, not just older—he had fixated on his height and muscle and the three years that separated them—but looking at him now, he saw only a boy.

Moses opened his mouth to say sorry, but Hala spoke over him. Fuck me? she said, repeating his words back, and her voice was so quiet and dangerous Jamal shrank back into the couch. *Fuck me?* She lunged towards her son with a scream, smacking him in the head at full extension, then slamming him into the door. He fell beneath her flurry. She was so crazed, her hands bashed repeatedly into the screen door as she swung, and chaos erupted—Ali trying to stop her and failing, Moses scrambling over the couches, his face red and bleeding where her rings had cut into his face, Teyta squawking in Arabic, heaving her bulk off the couch, the adhan blaring out of the radio releasing them—and all the while Hala followed Moses across the living room yelling, Fuck me? Fuck me? as she belted and scratched and clawed at him for all she was worth. She may well have killed him if not for the fact that her own mother was hit in the face by a careless backhand, and fell to the floor with a cry that muted everyone.

Hala came to a complete stop. Strands of hair had fallen loose in dark lines across her face, and she looked lost. Oh ya immi, she said, dropping to the ground to help the old woman up. As Teyta rose, Hala stayed on her knees, dazed and panting, as if unable to bear her own weight, or unwilling to look her mother in the eye.

I'm so sorry, immi, forgive me please, she said, and kissed her mother's hand repeatedly, pressing it to her forehead. Aunty Rania swooped in from the background, ushering Moses into the kitchen and out the back. From there, she called Kholo Khadeer, and it was agreed that Moses would stay with him for a while, until things calmed down, but Jamal didn't know that yet. He was staring at his mother, who had made herself abject in a way he had never seen before, sobbing into her mother's hand, while behind them, the dinner table was laid out with a feast slowly turning cold.

Jamal stayed at Aunty Rania's that night. Hala went to work—she was now driving for a fancy taxi company that catered to the rich—and while he could have gone back to their house, he didn't. He was old enough to be alone and young enough to admit he didn't want to be. He lay on one of the two three-seater couches, in the warm glow of the TV, and Sara lay on the other, both of them outfitted with blankets and pillows. She'd got home late from her shift, missing all the excitement, and was only now eating while everyone was asleep.

Far out, was all she said when he told her. Bet the Brady Bunch loved that. That's what they called the Anglo family who lived across the street and one house over, because they kept ringing the cops about 'domestic disturbances', which ranged from the Smiths having a barbecue to a birthday party, or more than two visitors. Jamal supposed he should be thankful they didn't understand that the only unusual volume in an Arab household was silence, because after a while the cops had stopped taking the calls seriously and they hadn't shown up tonight. Jamal knew silence was unusual because he inhabited it, because he loved it; the silken texture of absence made him feel at one with the world, as if the quiet was coming out of him. Once, after reading for an hour, he'd stood up to go to the toilet, and in standing, startled Kholo Khadeer, who clamped his meaty hands on Jamal's shoulders and roared, Wulah, I forgot you were there!

Don't you have blood in you? Move, ya! He shook Jamal hard, as though he were a dud Coke can he could fizz up and explode.

Can you still call 'em that when you have a crush on Steve? Jamal said.

Ohmygod shut up, Sara said, looking around nervously, and laughing.

She wasn't fasting (she had her period, she announced gleefully), which was probably for the best as she was too thin already, her chin and nose pointed arrows, her frizzy curls burned into dead straight lines around her bony head. She loved it when Jamal stayed over, it gave her an excuse to sleep in the lounge room, to be close to the front door and sneak out to meet boys. He was sworn to secrecy, of course. Ali would be furious if he knew, but he didn't, because he was out most nights too. Having someone else's secret made Jamal feel strangely full, as if he didn't have room for it, too hollowed out already from containing his own growing desire. Sometimes, like this night, she didn't go anywhere, and she read books opposite him, novels like *Flowers in the Attic*, which they'd seen the movie of on TV and was about a rich white woman who kept her children locked in an attic and how the older two, brother and sister, had sex while stuck in there. The boy said it was rape, and the girl said it wasn't, like they had stolen each other's lines, trying to package them with different meaning. It made sense, and it didn't. Maybe that was why the movie didn't show the scene at all, or maybe it was only in words such confusion could be addressed safely.

Sara would pass him the books when she was done and he'd read them, both of them turned on their sides as they read, backs to each other, trying hard not to breathe, not to move, a thickness on the air. Not caring at all about the story so much as the permission it provided to imagine sex, however taboo, without guilt, because it was not their minds conjuring it. Sara was four years older than him, and he sensed in her a desperation he knew the taste of, but stranger too, more removed.

She was expected to marry soon, she said with dread. Rania had married Mahmoud at fourteen, already pregnant with Ali, while Hala married Abraham at fifteen. Abraham beat her often, and she'd begged her parents to let her leave him but they refused, until she jumped out of their second-storey window while six months pregnant with Moses. Her ankle snapped and so did her marriage, thank God, but Moses was unharmed, her charmed one, and it was only part of the reason she adored her first son above the second. Sara told him this was why she was in no hurry to marry, and risked everything to break the rules and sneak out to see boys, to flirt, date, kiss without a chaperone, without the burden of binding and sundering families. He didn't respond. She had given him the hidden knowledge of women as if it was his already, and he was trying his best to take it in without showing her how much it changed his world.

At dawn, thousands of men put their arses into the air, pressed their foreheads into the road. Cameras flashed in their hundreds, a glittering swarm. Most of the men had their own prayer rugs, but some didn't, including Jamal, who was still bleary-eyed and cold. He'd spent his money on his shoes and didn't have a jacket. Ali and Jihad were on either side of him, solemn and serious. Jamal copied the motions without thought. When salah was led, the imam's voice was everyone's voice, his prayer everyone's prayer; Jamal only had to follow and it felt as close to bliss as anything, to not have to worry about what he could remember. It didn't last long. He had another man's feet next to his head, and he kept thinking about the grinning white politician behind the Mufti, his obvious pride, like a man with a prize-winning dog. It made the whole thing a show. He prayed, as usual, for God to fill the hole in his heart, and then the masses broke into a milling cluster of hugs and handshakes. Eid had arrived, a grand permission to have and be happy, and for a second, Jamal almost got swept up in it, until he saw Moses in the crowd, his face a bruised shout. Kholo Khadeer was next to him, impressively large as always, his hand on his shoulder.

Jamal greeted his uncle, kissed his cheeks—they were almost the same height—and by way of hello, gently crashed into his brother, who was busy scanning the crowd for his mates.

Where's Mum? Moses said.

Jamal shrugged. Haven't seen her. I stayed at Kholto's. Then he said, Are you going to Jido's? instead of what he really wanted to ask, which was: Are you coming home?

Moses said, Eventually, and then called out to someone, and took off without another glance. Jamal looked around and realised he was alone among men. He retraced his steps back to Ali's car, and waited there for his cousin to return.

&

Last Eid, the line of Smiths had snaked out of Teyta and Jido's flat. The old man's armchair was by the front door and it was there that

Jamal's uncles and aunties paused, one by one, to kiss their father's hand, pressing it to their forehead, before rising to kiss him three times on the cheeks. They would then replicate the ritual with Teyta; on this day, she was as much a queen as Jido was a king. Jamal had done the same for his mother for years, feeling strange and resentful, but it wasn't until then that he understood they were subject to the same power, all links in one chain, passing love up. When that love was supposed to come back down, he didn't know. Today, there was no line, only his aunty Rania and Fatima. He could smell the warra eynab on the air. Thin rolled-up vine leaves stuffed with rice and placed on top of lamb and bones, it took three days to cook, and they only got to experience its succulence once a year.

He looked out the window, eyeing the concrete ledge. They were on the second level of the flats. As Rania kissed her father's hand, he wondered whether he could step out onto that ledge, then jump, and if the fall would feel like forever or nothing, if the pain would be an instant knockout or a numb shock followed by a belated reckoning. He wondered whether his mother had felt the wing of an angel curling around her life-heavy belly when she leapt. He wanted to hate her, to think of her with the same clarifying fury that came to him in service of Ilo—for taking his brother away from him, for how afraid he was of her—but he couldn't. He didn't understand her nearly enough to be able to hate her. How could she come back here every year, how could she stand it? Then he was kissing his grandfather's skin, a spike of tobacco diving into the back of his throat, and his jido weathered this assault of rough pecks and whispered greetings, his eyes on his TV, still in his pyjamas.

The three of them filled up the flat, but somehow it still seemed empty. He wondered if his uncles and aunties had coordinated to avoid the ugly scar of yesterday's violence, or if it was coincidence. His grandmother was sitting on the bench in the kitchen, directly opposite her husband, as far from him as she could possibly be in the small space. She accepted their kisses with delight, and into Jamal's hand she slipped a fifty dollar note. It was only children who were meant to get money, but she would never stop giving.

His grandmother told him to eat, eat, and he looked at the huge silver bowl of steaming food he loved, enough for a village, even though the village wasn't there, and he couldn't bring himself to have even a bite. He said that he wasn't hungry, and she looked at him like he had confessed to the greatest sin.

Laysh? she said.

Mabaraf. I don't know.

The screen door rattled then, and his mother walked in. Tears pricked his eyes and he looked down hurriedly, blinking them away. Teyta put a plate of warra eynab in front of him, Yullah, she said.

Ana b' hubek ekteerd, he said, a phrase he had carefully memorised for her—*I love you big*—and she chuckled, putting her warm hands on his face and kissing him over and over, a stream of Arabic coming out of her mouth faster than he could follow, but he could see the light in her eyes and breathe in her smells, the soft citrus of mandarins, an unnameable spice, and he guessed then that this was why Hala kept coming back, that the place and the man meant nothing in the face of what she would do for this woman, her mother, and with that came the first hint of how vast her anger at her own children must be, how deep the hurt.

After

This is what our grandfathers fought for, and we're not going to let these fucken Lebanese take it away from us! The crowd roared. Thousands of white people, beers in hand, Australian flags everywhere, waves and waves of pink and sunburnt skin surrounding a gaggle of mics and booms. You're not welcome, get out! A noose of white men chased dark-haired, olive-skinned people through the streets and across the sands. Cops escorted the habibs out, ducking from thrown bottles, Anglos draped in Australiana pushing and shoving against them, the camera wobbling, screeched curses swooping like magpies to pluck blood from ears, Get the fuck out! Get the fuck out! They were dancing and cheering and furious, there were kids smiling and women laughing, then a man pushed his face into the camera, screaming, Go fucking home! Dozens like him inside a train bashing two brown boys. Cops swinging batons, pepper spraying everyone, trying to push back the frothing white mob. Fuck! Off! Lebs! Fuck! Off! Lebs! One big policeman laid into the lads, wide as a barrel, throwing his weight behind the baton, herding them back—Jamal, Moses, and Jihad cheered him on from

Aunty Rania's living room. Get 'em! Fucking get 'em! What a legend, they crowed.

You flew here, we grew here! the young Anglos chanted back, as if the way Jihad's parents had arrived carried over to him, and he would always be stuck in the process of arrival. Like they seemed to be, still on their white colonial ships, terrorising a beach two hundred years on.

Aunty Rania tutted. Why are they doing this? What's wrong with them?

Coz we keep getting their girls, Moses said, grinning, then had to duck as she hurled her shahayta at him. Oof! he laughed, but his expression changed as she got up with the other shoe in hand, shaking it menacingly. She was almost smiling—the throw had been more for show, like she hadn't yet decided if she would allow his cheek.

Oof? I'll show you oof, wulah. She dived at him, and he dived out of the way, taking off out the front door, still laughing. He was always escaping. Even when he swore at their mum last year, he fled successfully. He had walked back knowing what was waiting, and so it was on his terms that he got bashed. He still hadn't returned to living with Jamal and their mum, as if testing how long he could stay away, how much he could live on his terms. If he was hoping Hala would relent first, would tell him to come back, he would die waiting.

Aunty Rania settled for giving Jihad an atleh instead, smacking him twice around the head as he squawked with outrage—Wot! I didn't even do anything!—and ran for the door too. She let out a pleased huff, dropped her open-toed shoe back to the ground, slipped her foot into it, and gathered the other. The news footage continued, talking about the Bangladeshi students who were hospitalised by a mob who couldn't distinguish nationalities beyond what they felt was foreign: a darkness. The riots were revenge for a lifeguard being bashed, and now there was talk of revenge against the riots.

Well? Aunty Rania said. She was waiting to see if he would run after Moses and Jihad. He didn't want to: his heart was beating like a dozen batons. He felt sick to his stomach, but couldn't look away from the screen. Besides, he figured they'd probably be running to Bilal's place and geeing themselves up for a fight. He and Bilal didn't speak much anymore, or at all really, not since Ramadan last year.

They bashed a lifeguard, Kholto, he said.

So? she said, and went back to her seat. People get bashed all the time without all this. She gestured at the screen.

Jamal shrugged. He didn't have an answer for her beyond racism and the rage of men, which was hard to talk about with his aunty, who still remembered Lebanon, and who knew what her relatives there were going through. She was grateful to be able to say she was Australian, to have some kind of life, and if that meant getting dirty looks on the street, or harassed by the cops, then so be it. It was the smallest price to pay for what they had. Jamal didn't think there should be a price at all, and the only thing that felt small about it was him. He'd heard the Aussie lifeguards had been staring at the Lebanese boys all day, making comments, making sure they knew they were being watched, pinned by a Southern Cross gaze. That one Leb had finally snapped, What are you looking at? And that's all it took. One look sent and returned. Or maybe it had been the other way around.

Either way, Jamal was no stranger to what a look could do. He'd been sitting on this couch late one night when he was struck by the same blend of query and threat: what the fuck are you looking at? And he'd blinked, horrified to find that he was staring directly into Ali's dark eyes and must have been for some time, his spirit off somewhere else entirely. There was an expression of distaste and upset on Ali's face, which was narrow and long with a stain of stubble across his jaw; he surged across the space between them and slapped Jamal, whose head rocked back.

Fucking watch yourself, Ali said. You're lucky you're my cousin, anyone else I'd have stabbed in the neck.

He could shift like that in an instant, from static to violent. Fury was a constant, always within reach, and it charged everything with the quality of a fight—even, and perhaps especially, the intimacy of a stare. Ali shared this with Hala, and maybe it had to do with whether they were rising to or falling from a high, or something else entirely. Maybe the day Hala ordered him to drag Moses back, Ali looked so haunted because he was dead sober and seeing himself for the first time. Jamal wished he could fold his cousin's and his mother's wildness into his faith, into Islam, into surrender, but they, along with God, kept drifting away from him. It was Ali who taught him that to stare was to challenge, and a challenge had to be answered with such force that it was never repeated. That's what they were seeing on the news. He knew that, but any knowledge contained in memory was akin to smoke, and however hard he tried to hold on to it, it escaped him.

&

Jean Grey would annihilate Storm, you're being ridiculous!

The breezeway was empty, except for their table. It was too early to be arguing, but Emir was fired up, pale cheeks turning pink, and Ilo was laughing. Ilo loved Storm; she was beautiful, black and undeniably powerful. More than that, she could control the elements, harness the world. Emir loved Jean Grey because she could read minds, and because she was unassailable as the Phoenix. She could burn everything the fuck down, just like he wanted.

Unlike Ilo and Jamal, Emir was short and round, a Bosnian boy who was easier to pick on and the boys knew it. He hated it here with such obvious vehemence it was somehow reassuring, the way he performed it, with his spiked-up hair, pentagram necklace, studded straps and hissed *hail Satans*. It was directed so visibly outward, at everyone not at their table, that it seemed he was also saying the opposite to them, just as obviously and constantly, and so the three of them bonded beneath his spite. If Jamal had joined the chatter, he would have argued for Rogue, who wanted to touch without harm but couldn't. Like Ilo, he didn't care about who would win in a fight, he wanted only to declare who he loved most.

He didn't join in, though. He was reading *The Chamber of Secrets* again. He'd read the Harry Potter series a dozen times, he knew every spell cast by a character, and what each was meant to do. He had even practised casting them. The books were his shield against the darkness of the world, or the darkness within, and he returned to them when he felt most at risk of falling prey to either. He liked this one especially because the Dursleys put bars on Harry's window, much like the bars on Jamal's window, and a lock outside his door so he could be kept inside, much like the one on Jamal's door. Jamal didn't have a cat flap, but Moses would bring him a sandwich once their mum calmed down or fell asleep. Hala didn't cook much. Wayne had been the one who cooked, the one who asked if they'd done their homework, who remembered to give them money for lunch at school. Moses had taken up that responsibility, reminding Hala to leave some coins for Jamal on the table, but it had been a year and he still hadn't come back. He liked living with their uncle; there was calm, there was order, there was food every night.

Jamal looked up when the two fell silent, to see his friend Adam walking towards him with an uneasy smile on his pale doughy face, nervously smoothing the blue-red tie he'd started wearing when he became school captain, head of the prefects. Principal Erskine flowed beside him in a pressed suit, tall and gaunt, his head a long spotted egg. Jamal stared at the old man's leathery skin, trying to come up with an excuse for whatever he was about to be accused of, or asked to do.

Jamal, is it? Would you come with us, please, Principal Egghead asked, but it wasn't a question, and he was already flowing back towards the front office. Adam lagged back a step, Sorry slopping out the side of his mouth. The front office had a thick blue carpet and fresh paint on the walls—it had recently been burned black for the third time—with thick columns and potted plants spread throughout. He'd been to the vice principal's office a number of times, but never the headmaster's, and he was disappointed to find it was pretty much the same desk, chair, and fatherly frown. The principal sat behind his desk, and Adam hovered by the side of it, as if unsure whether to join the old man or to sit with Jamal.

Adam here had a great idea, Principal Egghead said. I'll let him tell you about it.

Adam squared his shoulders and gave his pitch: the riots on the weekend had been disgusting and horrible, and they needed to show a united front now more than ever to advocate against racism and bullying. Jamal noticed the flashcards gripped in Adam's hands, the speech he'd written in his familiar blocky handwriting. He was painfully earnest and resolutely fair in a school that despised anyone who tried or cared. They had become friends when they went to the protest against the Iraq War together, getting the train into the city, marching with tens of thousands, faced by rows of police on horses, rows of water cannons. It was because of him that Jamal even went. Moses and Jihad would only have laughed at them, Err, look at these fucken heroes! Hero was the dirtiest word, a lie, and it was thrown at anyone embarrassing enough to care, to think they could change the way things were. It was just like Adam to see the riots on the news and think he had to try to fix it, to think that his actions mattered.

Basically I've already written it, Adam said. And I think if you read it with me, that would send the right message. His eyes were bright blue, and in them, if you looked hard enough, you could almost see the words *Prime Minister* written in gold. His future was a bright shining ribbon, Jamal's a dark beckoning hole. There was no suggestion that Jamal should write his own words, voice his own opinion. His body, his willing participation, said enough. He agreed to do it, because he could see how tightly wound Adam was, the big vein in his temple pronounced against his fair skin, and because he was a coward who didn't know how to say no. An hour later Principal Egghead stood on the steps of the assembly line and delivered his announcement to a thousand boys in blue rows, Jamal and Adam to the side, waiting to be introduced. Fear gurgled in Jamal's belly. He regretted saying yes. He scanned the audience, and saw the questioning looks on Ilo's and Emi's faces. He couldn't do this, who the fuck was he to say anything?

Adam's hands were white-knuckled on his cue cards, but otherwise he seemed fine. He spoke calmly and resolutely into the microphone, his voice a soothing drone. Jamal's mind wandered to the last time he had to speak in front of the boys. In Modern History, they were given an assignment to write a diary account from the perspective of a Jewish prisoner in Auschwitz, and they were encouraged to be as creative as possible. Jamal's account had been one of a boy who watched his family being raped and killed, shot in the back of the head and dumped in a mass grave, whose shaved head was pissed on by the guards, and who suffered every degradation he could think of—it made him sick to write, brought him no closer to any Jew, and he was awarded top marks. He had to read it in front of the class, and they were all audibly grossed out. Later, when they covered the 'Arab–Israeli conflict' in class, there was no suggestion they empathise with Palestinians, or take on their perspective, and Jamal didn't know whether to be glad of that or not, if empathy meant only imagining their torture.

Adam coughed. Jamal realised he was meant to be reading 'his' part of the speech, but there were a thousand pairs of eyes in his throat, it wasn't possible. That's when Jamal saw it, the sight that unlocked his jaw, a gleaming where there shouldn't have been anything—a long silver pube jutting out of the principal's zipper, turning ginger at the root. There he was, noble in his expensive suit, adorned with age and all the seriousness of his position, his skin, and he was no more than a ridiculous pube. Jamal let the laugh break out in his heart as he stumbled over his friend's words about how racism was unacceptable and bullying was bad and they all needed to come together. Half of the sentences were blacked out by the principal's pen, and Jamal had to skip over the little islands of ink drowning *Aboriginal* and *colony*. When he was done, the boys clapped because it was over and they could go now, but to Jamal, the applause sounded like an approval he'd never had before and the force of it washed over him.

&

Despite the dark, Hala was home. She didn't work every night; sometimes, he wasn't sure she worked at all. He'd been at the library after school to study (and post shit on fan forums and read erotica and play Neopets and, and, and), which usually meant the house would be empty by the time he got there. She was asleep in the lounge room—she rarely slept in her bed anymore—her hair a snarl, the blanket on the floor, her snores sawing at the walls. There was a twenty on the table for him to get dinner, a small red sign she hadn't forgotten he existed. She looked worn to the bone.

The other night, she had shaken him in the middle of the night, her voice hoarse and urgent: Jamal, Jamal, get up, come on, couldn't you hear me screaming?

He snapped awake. What?

There was a man sitting on my chest, she said. I was screaming. She put a hand to her head. There were deep purple gouges under her eyes. Oh, fuck. Come on. She motioned to him and he followed her out into the hallway, and then the lounge. She sat on her favourite leopard-print cushion and began chopping up.

He was fat and had long hair, she said. It was a Kaboos. The horror seemed to ease a little as she fit an explanation to the trauma. It's my fault for sleeping on my back. You should never do that, 'cause if they come at you like that, they can crush you, keep you from breathing, and that's what was happening, I was suffocating. Oh God.

He sat with her until she lit her second joint, and relaxed into the smoke.

It's okay, she said. I'm okay. You can go.

Her face softened in sleep. He picked the blanket up and put it over her. It hadn't always been like this; there had been days when she smiled and laughed as much as she yelled, when there seemed in her an inexhaustible power, even though she was on her own then, and they moved from one rental to another every couple of months. Wayne had changed all that. He had been handed a sun, and left them with this guttering candle, this melted woman. Not because he beat her, he never had, but because she had loved him and he had loved her, and it hadn't been enough.

Jamal went to his room. There was nothing to do. He couldn't focus on his books. His friends would still be on their computers, on MSN and Myspace. He had no phone and his brother was elsewhere. He thought about the feeling of Bilal's cock in his mouth, and he was instantly hard. He took his pants off, changing the memory into a fantasy in which he was on his knees. In the fantasy, he did away with the awkwardness of his body, the complaint of his arms holding up his head, the ache in his jaw, the unpleasant push from above forcing him further onto the warm muscle until he gagged and spit spluttered over his lips and chin and onto Bilal's balls. He kept the trail of hair down from the belly button, he kept the moan, the twitches of approval, the shivers, he kept the way he became a vessel for lightning, the way he brought a boy's world to a stop, laying him out with only his lips. Jamal's erection was painful, a short spear that stuck out from his body and would not dissipate. He got up, his heart pounding. Fantasy wasn't enough anymore.

He stuck his head into the hallway; he could still hear snores. He dashed as quietly as he could into the bathroom, his dick bouncing stiffly in the air, his shirt still on. It had to be here, the only room with a lock on the inside. He took his shirt off, naked now except for his socks. He grabbed the bottle of conditioner, poured some onto his hand. It was cold on the tiles and he was starting to wilt. He had a plan and the plan was surfacing. His eyes settled on his mother's skincare products, the cylindrical L'Oréal moisturiser with its curved cap, as his wet fingertip pushed at his anus. It felt weird, an unbelievably strong ring of muscle, and then he was inside. He paused, gasping a bit at the pain, but he was hard again so he kept going and began to finger himself. Soft and tight. As it became easier, pleasure radiated into his gut. He grabbed the L'Oréal bottle and slathered conditioner on it. It was hard to grip it after that; bent over the sink, arm reaching backwards, he couldn't quite force it in. He put it on the tiles and squatted above it, feeling the conditioned top as a cool force, the push and push and push until—agony.

One of his knees almost gave way as he dropped an inch down, and the thick bottle tore into him. All the air was driven from his chest. Eyes watering, he rose, intending to get off it and put an end to this, but when he reached the tip, feeling once more in control, he did it again. The pain was searing, and somehow, that was right, that was what he wanted, because he was behind it, because it had a purpose. Still, he had to stop after a minute; it hurt too much. He lay down on the deep green, welcoming its chill. Afloat again on this strange sea, he spread his legs, and began to fuck himself in earnest. Ow, he whispered, oh fuck, God, and bliss was flooding his system when he heard a sound—there at the window was the pale moon of Moses's face, mouth open in horror. When their eyes connected, he said, What the hell?

Panic crushed Jamal's heart with an icy fist. He scrambled to his side, his wet hands half-sliding on the tiles, and the bottle in his arse slipped half out, but dangled, his interior muscles hanging on grimly and painfully, so he was forced to slow down, squeezing his eyes shut to not see the disgust in his brother's eyes, to not cry. He took it out incrementally, the white-pink bottle smeared with shit and blood. It was the most excruciating minute of his life. He was dripping sweat and freezing at the same time, and oh God, he'd been *seen*, really seen, in the midst of his want, and the shame of that was overwhelming. How long, how long had he been there, watching? He looked over his shoulder, but there was no one at the window, only the blank night. He'd thought his life was over when he tasted Bilal, but he was wrong, so wrong—that was when his life began, and here, here was where it ended, naked and known, with blood dripping down his legs.

Directions

His mother was still snoring, the back door was still locked, and the chance existed that he had hallucinated his brother, but he knew better than to hope. He did not sleep, thinking over every instance of being called gay by Jihad and Moses, how his aunty Emne had overheard them once and told them to shut up, it wasn't funny to joke about something so disgusting, tfeh. Rania had agreed, saying if any of them ever turned out that way, she'd hang them herself. He pored over every instance, every expression of language and movement, trying to calculate how much of a joke was a joke, and how much a real rope. By morning, Jamal had renewed his plan to leave home, had even packed a garbage bag full of clothes and books. He couldn't live like this, inside the terror of being kicked out. He had to leave. The result might be the same, but at least if he left first he would be the one doing the hurting. He was going to bury the night deep inside himself, and focus on the HSC. He decided his best shot was university, not because he was smart but because the only thing he knew how to be was a student, and because it would give him a reason to be away from his family.

He needn't have worried. Moses didn't return for another couple of months, well into Jamal's final year of high school, and when he did, he came bearing flowers, he kissed his mother's feet. The Prophet Muhammad sulallahi alayhi wu salaam said the way to paradise lies at your mother's feet, which in Hala's case were brown, her toenails painted pink and glittering with diamantes, fake diamonds that outlined a heart. Her perfect toes reminded Jamal of her freelance beautician phase, when she'd done a course in make-up and nail art, and took him out of school for a day to use as her canvas. She drove him into the city, got him a hot chocolate, and then spent hours painting his face at the Napoleon Academy. She coated his skin in thick white layers, and inked black flames (or was it bat wings?) around his eyes, before putting a curly black wig on his head and taking a photo of him with his tongue stuck out. Her smile that day was so wide and so bright he wanted to live in it.

Moses didn't act any differently when he moved back in, which was relieving at first, before it swiftly became a problem. He still made jokes about how gay or weird he thought Jamal was, only now they were weighted with what he knew. In the drive-thru at Casula Maccas one night, he said from the front seat, How are you reading a book right now? I don't know how we're even brothers, I swear. Just admit you're gay already. He laughed and Jamal groaned, but Hala turned towards him with a frown, her gaze focused and clear.

What? she said, passing him the bag of Big Macs. Why are you saying that?

Nah, I'm just joking, Moses said uneasily. It's not like it matters.

Don't be ridiculous, she said. Then looked at Jamal through the rear-view mirror, pursing her lips. You're not gay? It was a statement more than a question, but he felt the catch at the end, the need to respond.

N-no, he said, feeling sick. It wasn't a lie, not really, he liked girls too, after all.

Good, coz I'd break your fucking legs if you were, she said, and put her foot down on the accelerator.

&

Warwick Farm had its own Harbour Bridge, and the boys cheered for it as they trudged past. It was a small replica in front of a car dealership, but it was impressive enough for Rabih to declare he didn't need to see the real thing. Why go all the way to Circular Quay, a full hour on a train, when you could see it here and get KFC too? Adam rolled his eyes, muttering about savages, and Emir sneered back, I know you are but what am I? The sun blistered the blue, and Jamal stayed close to Ilo, connected by one earphone, listening to Destiny's Child. It was Wednesday, sports day, and they were walking along the highway to distant tennis courts near Cabramatta Creek, led by the Dragon, her habitual cigarette dangling out of her mouth. Old Barb was little more than bones and white hair, but she had more energy than all of them combined and walked a furious pace. Jamal had cared enough once to actually play, but they were close now to the end of everything, the end of school, these five days in which, despite everything, they weren't alone. The prospect of being at home every day loomed larger and it drove him to study harder and longer; he wrote and rewrote flashcards until his fingers cramped and his eyes ached. For the first time, he felt information sinking in, felt himself gathering the reins of his life, aiming in a direction, and even though the animal he rode was unknown to him and the way shrouded in fog, he had a measure of hope that he might make it out okay. Emir and Ilo had no such plans, like most of the other boys, they were going to get a job and help their families, so Jamal saw them less as a result. Wanting to make the most of these hours, he wandered after Emi into the broad slice of bush that surrounded the creek near the courts. Ilo stayed behind, content to sing softly at the shaded tables, keeping the old bird company and scabbing a smoke off her.

It never failed to surprise Jamal how completely the outside world vanished even a metre into a canopied sky. The trees were enormous, the ground uneven and soft, treacherous in its gorgeous weft of leaf and mud, hiding loose rocks and thick roots. They had learned to tread carefully, but still fell often, muddying their pants and hands. The creek patterned the dappled dark with its wet music, accompanied by insect chirps and the call of birds. Emir was ahead, whacking a stick in lazy arcs at the ground, following what passed for a track.

Watch it, Jamal said, as he came within range of the stick.

Emir whirled, pentagram necklace bouncing. En garde!

Nah, Jamal said, and Emi deflated with a sigh. I'm fucking bored, he said and threw the stick into the bush. They walked further in together, talk turning to Ilo's upcoming birthday, their plan to get him the DVD boxset of *Inuyasha*. The tree line deepened around them, the slope up to the courts becoming steeper, and as they turned, it felt as if they were being cupped by the joined hands of the earth. The distant shouts of boys reached them. Their time here was almost up.

Ugh, Emir said, kicking at the dirt. Can't wait for this year to be over.

Why wait? Jamal said. It's not like you have to finish.

He got an angry look back. The 'rents would kill me, that's why.

Maybe that was true, or maybe, like Jamal, Emir felt the end approaching and wanted to hold on for as long as possible. They stopped as the path opened into a huge green grove crammed with the layered chittering of flying foxes in their hundreds. According to the warning signs they'd ignored, this was a reserve, a restricted area because they were a protected species. They looked and sounded like bats to him, and Jamal wasn't sure what the difference was between them, if any.

Fruity fucks, Emir said, following his eyes up to the colony.

I know you are but what am I? Jamal said, and Emir elbowed him in the side. They stood there for a moment, looking at the small dark creatures, the thunder of their living, their joyous consumption.

Must be nice, Jamal said.

What?

To be a protected species, he said. If only we were.

Emir grinned a sweet crooked grin. Yeah, then we could stay here forever.

&

Water pelted down and steam misted the glass panels of the shower. Jamal had turned both showerheads on as high and hot as they could go. His skin reddened as he paced between the two scalding jets. The exams were behind him and he should feel free, he knew he'd done well, but he struggled to feel anything. He closed his eyes around the flames of the last month. Ilo's backyard: multiple tables of food, a hundred of his rellos, his Maccas crew, Emir and Jamal, a circle of heat in the centre of the yard, the heat rising out of the fire and out of them, laughter a long song in the night. People drifted off, the night became heavier, and the fire dimmed, until it was just the three of them. They were having sleepovers almost once a week at this point, Jamal taking every opportunity to not be home.

The fire was a hot joyful leaping. Ilo sat closest to it, face curtained by dark waves, his short curly beard hairs prominent around his mouth and chin only, black and gleaming. Jamal thought again that he might be the most beautiful man in the world. Emir, on the other hand, was a knot in time and space that seemed to draw air in so tight it became uncomfortable.

Do you remember when we became friends? Jamal said, and Emi smiled, brushing self-consciously at his new moustache. He'd transferred in Year 9, a chubby boy who carried a hostility and sadness that had no end.

God, yes, he said woozily. He'd had a beer or two—Bosnian Muslims apparently didn't have any issue with alcohol, which fascinated Jamal. The idea that there could be more than one way to be Muslim, that it wasn't all or nothing.

Modern history, Emir burped.

In the margins of his exercise book, Emi had drawn a stick-figure man atop a cliff pushing a rock onto another unsuspecting stick-figure man below, when Jamal reached over and drew above his would-be murderer, another man with another rock, and grinning at each other, they created a cascading series of this moment, always the same—a ledge, a figure behind a boulder, a never-ending Damocles loop. It grew from there, sorrow to sorrow, grim dark laugh to grim dark laugh, fantasies of ruin and revenge. They were inseparable after, in love with their books and comics and games. In Science class, leaning over a Bunsen burner, Emir would whisper swearwords in Bosnian and Jamal would whisper back in Arabic, teaching each other insults, and later they even learned to write notes to each other using ancient Viking runes they read about in the library, to be even more alone with what they had to say.

We were sick, Jamal said.

Full depresso, with an extra shot of what the fuck, Emi agreed. But how could we not be, surrounded by those cunts.

They staggered back up to the house—Ilo to his room, Emi and Jamal to the lounge. The dark wood floors creaked. The hard green couch had been folded out, with pillows and blankets in a neat pile. Squished into the corner was an old piano and above, along the walls, large silver keys glinted. Inside them, ghosts. Emi fell onto the couch in a sprawl, and Jamal fell into a restless black. Until a sharp tug, as of a fish on a hook, brought him to the verge of waking. Then again, another and another, followed by the sudden sense of a frustration not his own. He shifted, and the hand on his soft dick jerked away. His eyelids fluttered, but did not open. Did not want to open. Awareness seeped in: he had been sleeping. He was in Ilo's house. He lurched off the couch, stumbling down the hallway to the bathroom. The not-yet light of dawn blued the dark. His jeans gaped open. Throat thick with the previous hours, Jamal stood on the cold tiles of Ilo's bathroom, staring down stupidly, dizzy with déjà vu. He had been here before, swaying fuzzy, wondering how his zipper kept opening at night, berating himself again that these jeans were old and he needed a new pair, that he had to stop being so forgetful. He went back to bed after pissing. He lay down next to the boy he had loved, the boy he did not know any longer, and they both pretended to sleep.

Jamal had gone home early the next morning, throwing up a couple houses down from Ilo's. He told himself he had eaten too much. The next few days, he couldn't sleep. His mind kept returning to the feeling of being hooked, being dragged to the point of pain, the lurch into wakefulness. Overwhelming shame he could deal with, but the inexplicable guilt and, worst of all, strange hope—even then—that this might mean that he wouldn't be so alone anymore, was crushing. Earlier today, unable to bear it any longer, he'd logged on to MSN, firing off a message to Emir before he could talk himself out of it.

Are you gay?

What? Why would you say that?

Your hand. I was awake.

He waited.

Finally, Emir replied: *lol oh yeah sorry, I thought you were my boyfriend.*

Bullshit, Jamal thought. I know you! He shook with how much he knew him. His eyes were wet with how much he knew him, and when they weren't anymore, he ached with the loss. The inadequacy of it, the flippant tone, drove a brand into Jamal's chest. It hurt more than the moment itself, which still, even in the future, stayed wrapped in a haze of grief and dream. He had for so long aligned himself with Rogue, wanting to touch without harm following, he'd never imagined what it would be like on the other end of it—to be touched against his will and feel something so private it was innate, part of his spirit, taken away. Please don't tell anyone, Emir said, and Jamal had that same fear laced throughout his body.

He couldn't make the water any hotter, the steam any thicker, and still he felt cold. He did not remember leaving the bathroom or falling asleep. He slept until almost noon, as did Hala and Moses, all of them for different reasons. It was chance that led to Hala waking first, stumbling out to relieve herself. Later, much later, he would imagine her sitting on the toilet, staring at the faint words that had been ghostwritten into the glass, in giant letters across the room, and he would laugh so hard he cried.

By the time Jamal and Moses got up, she'd had her morning coffee and was waiting for them in the lounge with her thick leather Chanel belt, the buckle's golden C a dull gleam. She made them kneel on the carpet.

Who was it? she said, her voice calm. Tell me now.

Who was what? Moses said. He looked at Jamal, and Jamal shrugged. He had no idea either. Hala's eyes narrowed.

You think I'm an idiot, do you? she said, and the belt snapped through the air to dig into his thigh. 'Fuck You', is it? Who is *you*, ya akhu sharmuta, is it me? She was shouting, the belt lashing down repeatedly, leaving long purple tongues on Moses's legs; he screamed with each hit.

Was it you? she said, turning to Jamal.

He said no, and the belt came down.

Was it you?

No.

And the belt came down.

Was it you?

No.

And the belt came down.

They were rolling on the floor, trying to get away from it, away from her, jerking their legs back, closing in around the pink-purple crisscross when the pain was too much so the belt fell on their arms, their shoulders and backs. It was Moses who came to his senses first, who realised she wasn't going to stop, and surged to his feet. That was all he did, stand up, but it was enough.

Hala's chest heaved, and she had to tilt her head up to look at him, but she was unfazed. Well, fuck me, maybe I did it, hey? she said, and laughed. I'm the loony one! Yeah, right! Moses didn't say anything, his face wet with tears, and Jamal stayed on the floor, staring at his mother's feet, her diamond hearts, knowing deep in his bones that if heaven existed, it needed better directions.

II

Mercy, Mersin

Returns

My son, my lion, my king! As the plane descended into Turkey, Jamal recalled his father's words, his strong hold—the ecstatic growl of recognition and ownership in his ear, the feel of warm hands on his neck and cheek, head close, the chewy smell of tobacco, the rough pebble of his stubble, the light parting sting of his lemon cologne. His name was Cevdat, but he went by David, a legal change he'd made to escape paying his debts. They had met in the Italian Forum in Leichhardt, a multi-tiered plaza of restaurants that roasted the dark with lamps, laughter and the smell of pizza. Cevdat was a touch shorter than his son, pot-bellied in a brown suit, his thick head of silver hair netted with black. He had a big easy smile and his skin shone a brassy gold; Jamal's first thought was that he looked like an Indian car salesman.

Listen, Cevdat said to him, pulling him closer. Your mother promised me that she had her tubes tied, son. She lied. Don't get me wrong, I'm happy you're here, but you need to know. She left you on my doorstep and ran away, what was I to do? I had a family already. It's a good thing Rania took you in, trust me. It was as though he was still there, on Aunty Rania and Mahmoud's doorstep with a baby neither asked for, the words spilling out of him in a torrent.

Jamal breathed in through his nose. He didn't know what to say to that. His father's family sat at a table behind them, eating and talking; he'd known them for only a week and they had already betrayed him. His uncle Mehmet was a tank of a man, packed with muscle and fat, his hair dyed jet black, his eyes a deep Mediterranean blue, and he was looking over at Jamal, flushed with guilt. A week ago, a short woman with russet hair and huge owl-like eyes had stopped at the cafe Jamal was working in and stared at him for a solid minute. She ordered a bottle of water and he rang it up at the register, shying away from her unblinking stare until she said softly, You're a beautiful boy, and left.

No one had ever called him beautiful. He was the awkward, graceless one. He'd shot up a foot and grown an unflattering goatee, like any teenager, just to prove he could. He wore Ali's cast-offs and old Adidas shoes; no one looked twice at him. The weird lady returned two hours later with Mehmet, who immediately embraced him, his blue eyes watering, sobbing into his neck, saying, Oğlum, oğlum, over and over again. My son, my son. I'm your umja, but you're my son, he told him. Never forget it. Jamal stood in the circle of the crying man's arms, unsettled that his resemblance to his father was strong enough to stop a woman in her tracks and send her racing off to find her ex-husband. He heard his mother again, saying, *Your dad's a cunt*, with vicious certainty. Jamal learned he had half-sisters, a half-brother, a new extended family, an entire additional language and history to sit outside of, looking in. He agreed to meet them if they promised not to tell his father, and they said, Of course, of course, lying through their teeth.

This was destiny, Cevdat said to him. How many times did I pray to God for my son? Ask your uncle, ask anyone. Every day.

He was earnest and sincere and charming, and Jamal didn't trust him. They had met once before, when the government caught up with him for the child support he owed, and he had been as sweet and charming then, too. Days later, Jamal read the papers his father's lawyer had sent to Hala, disputing paternity, asking for a DNA test. He laid out the story that she had left a baby on his doorstep, assaulting his then-wife in the process and doing considerable damage to his property before fleeing. He painted her as a manic fury given flesh, and Jamal, reading the cold words, had felt such an overwhelming tangle of sorrow and shame that he could only be glad when Hala took the whole stack and threw it into the bin.

Do you see now? Hala said to him that day, her dark eyes hot even as her voice remained even and cool. Once a cunt always a cunt. She took him to the local court that month and stripped him of his father's name.

I told them I didn't want to see you, Jamal said, and Cevdat sighed.

Don't be mad at them, son, be mad at me. I know I have a lot to make up for, believe me. Don't you want to know your dad?

Jamal clenched his jaw. Oh, now you're my dad? I saw what your lawyer sent.

Cevdat laughed, surprise and relief flashing across his face. What, that? That's just lawyer shit, son. Even if I had it, I wouldn't give those pricks my money. Can it go back in time and feed you? No, it can't. Don't worry about it. You're my boy, my lion, any idiot can see that. And he hugged him close again.

Jamal wished it wasn't so easy for people to be introduced to him as blood, and for him to love them so desperately, but he did. He had spent too many years wanting a father to do anything less than accept him, whatever his flaws.

Cevdat misinterpreted his silence. I don't know what she's told you—

She didn't tell me *anything*, Jamal said forcefully, looking him in the eye. I don't know you.

Okay, okay, Cevdat said, but the turn of his mouth showed his doubt. That's why I'm here, oğlum. For you to know me. For me to know you.

They talked for a little bit. Jamal told him he was in the first year of his bachelor degree, that he worked part-time at a cafe, and was going to be an editor because he loved reading. It all sounded plausible and Cevdat seemed pleased. He didn't say that Moses had been sent to Silverwater prison, that he had been walking home when he saw the flashing lights, the car by the side of the road, his brother bent over the trunk, arms behind his back, head twisted to the side. That he kept his eyes down and kept walking until he was out of sight and could run to Rania's house for help. That he might not make it to the second year of the degree, that he couldn't see the path ahead. The distance between what he wanted to say and what he could say was too great for their talk to be anything other than strained and Cevdat gave up shortly.

I'm sorry if I upset you, he said. I just wanted to see you, and to give you this—he took off a large gold ring, inset with a roaring lion, and pressed it into Jamal's hand. They met only a few times after that, trying to work out how they fit together, and each awkward dinner or lunch seemed only to set them running away again for months. His father was never less than enraptured to see him, to feel him near, but he was always going back to Turkey, unable to stay still, unable to hold on to any of his children.

Jamal got used to hearing variations of, This new opportunity is going to set us up for life, you won't have to worry about anything, you'll see! And then Cevdat would be gone, chasing a high just like Hala. Jamal twisted the golden lion on his finger, praying fervently under his breath. Most of a decade later, he was the one chasing the high, chasing his father, who was waiting for him. The plane's engines roared and everything shook as the land rushed to meet him.

&

I can't believe you're really here, Cevdat said. My boy, my boy. He said the words with an almost theatrical relish, more for the sake of saying them than any other need, luxuriating in the sound. They were sitting on the balcony of the family unit in Mersin, looking out onto the street. Dozens of similar flats clumped together, a uniform brown. On the street level there were shops, barbers and bakeries, hawkers with their carts on the road, shouting out their wares. Beyond them, at the edge of sight, the faint glimmer of the sea beckoned.

He's not a boy, he's a man! Ey? Mehmet joined them, carrying a pan with scrambled eggs and sujuk. With his big belly and even bigger arms, Jamal's uncle looked like a brown boulder. Like his brother, he was shirtless, and he had thick tufts of white chest hair across his muscle and flab. The pan joined the tray of cheeses and olives, the plate of diced tomatoes and cucumbers, the bag of fresh bread, the steaming raqweh with its black blood.

That's right, God forgive me, a man. Cevdat flexed his hand on Jamal's neck, took a drag of his cigarette, genuine shock in his voice. Both of them were yet to catch up with reality, which kept flowing with dizzying speed.

Jamal had arrived in Turkey three days ago, after travelling for three days, and each of those hours had been a thin mesh of dream, slow movement within almost understandable images and moments. He was terrified of heights but felt nothing clothed in clouds. He sat in the pressurised tube of the plane, and that's all it was: a rattling box, an arcade game, an imagining completed by the cheap fabric of the seat, the cramped space, random sticky spots and the remnant stink of other people. He was not in the sky. It was too ridiculous to believe, and so he refused it. He was briefly in Dubai, the Arabic on the signs confirmed that, but otherwise it was just another gleaming set of hallways and escalators, until he was back on the ride, and the box rattled as the game loaded Istanbul, and there everything fell apart. Istanbul gouged into his eyes with its grit, its heat, its minarets, the enormity of the Blue Mosque, the long wide expanse of the Bosporus river, the ancient cobbled stones of ten thousand alleys, the hundred thousand cats and dogs wilding the streets, and the men, everywhere, selling fruit and cold bottles of water for one lira. Bottles he touched and water he drank to have something tangible to hang on to, and because he was thirsty, and because—how could it cost so little, how was it everywhere, who were these men? After a terrifying taxi in the night, he slept in a hostel in the Sultanahmet district, in the shadow of the mosque, and woke to the sound of the azan prowling over the city.

He did not for a second think he was back at his aunt's house, and the absence of that instant search for home registered as a chill. Guys and girls in various stages of undress moved around the six-bed room, and envy ripped through him, watching their ease, their bared skin. The casualness in their motions, feigned or not, was alien. He'd slept in his clothes, and changed in the bathroom, hurriedly shoving cloth over still-damp skin, urgency a shaking porcupine in his stomach, pricking him to move faster, to not be seen, to operate at a speed past questioning. In the second year of his bachelor degree—the year he dropped out—his Chinese tutor had warned him that every child of migrants thinks when they 'return' they'll fit in naturally and feel part of the crowd, not apart from it, but actually you stand out to the homeland just as aggressively as any other tourist. Years later, he discovered this didn't apply to him and it only made things worse.

The two days he spent in Istanbul were profoundly lonely. He walked a few steps behind tourists who were besieged by workers trying to spruik their restaurant menus, and as he approached, the Turks melted away, nodding or looking down, dismissing him instantly as one of them—unless he opened his mouth, unless he asked a question in English, then they would answer in confused Turkish, and he had to do the I'm-not-one-of-you dance, I know I know, I don't know, sorry, until he was whittled into nothing.

To be nothing had its own beauty, at least. The throng of people on the streets hummed constantly, and he lost himself in the bewildering array of colours and alleys, until night descended, by which time he started to believe that maybe there were only three types of shops: beads, rugs, and lamps. Or maybe it was all just one shop with three items. He had returned to the hostel numerous times, just to remind himself it was still there, a touchstone before venturing anywhere else—what a shame, he thought, that this was how memory worked, too, only instead of relief, what he circled back to was pain. As he lapped the place, he learned some of the names of his fellow tourists, like Andrew and Jennifer, a British couple who had been backpacking for a year.

On the second night, he tagged along with them to a club in Tahrir Square. He remembered kissing a Turkish man, his perfumed beard. He remembered the pungent taste of Jennifer's cunt, her hands pressing his head deeper, the cold tiles of the bathroom. How she pushed him away when she got bored, and went back to dancing. She and Andrew weren't there in the morning and he couldn't remember how their night ended. As he made his way to the airport, he thought that it wasn't right that he could brush someone's pubes out of his teeth in the morning and not be able to speak to them, to have a chance to own in the day what had passed in the night.

The flight to Adana airport was blessedly brief and at the end of it, these two men were waiting for him. Cevdat, with his silver head, three-quarter cargo pants and Ralph Lauren polo, had the air of a retired CEO. Beside him, Mehmet, in red Puma trackies, looked like his hired muscle. He didn't know either well enough for 'Dad' or 'Uncle' to sit comfortably on them, but this was the story of his life, the slow making of family out of strangers, and so he was at least familiar with the tension of bodies catching up to the burden of their names.

It was an hour's drive to Mersin, alongside a mostly flat plain spotted with shrubs and distant mountains. Jamal stared out the window, exhausted, but still able to appreciate the land, its rugged, almost defiant beauty, the way it wore its scars, its uncompromising shape. Cevdat talked at him the entire time. Istanbul is the greatest city in the world, he boasted, you can get a coffee at 2am and the streets would still be full, you can have a conversation at 2am—that's the mark of a real city! Unlike Australia, that fake country. Tfee. And the people, did he see them all? Fourteen million they say, but it's closer to eighteen, if you count the illegal pricks. (Everyone was a prick to him.) A whole lira for water? You got ripped! It should be half that! Look at this prick, Mem, he can't drive for shit, beep your horn at him. I bet he's another one of these Syrians. This fucking war, you know? But Erdoğan will take care of it, may God bless him, he takes care of everything. Except for Vegemite, there's no Vegemite here, would you believe it? I should have told you to bring me some!

And then they were driving through a city, and walking up stairs to the unit, every step like pushing through a fluid force field, the humidity a constant presence, and finally into this one-bedroom flat. The air con was in the lounge room and it was there that Jamal fell asleep, under the watchful eyes of two brothers he barely knew. He felt he could sleep for another day yet, but his father was sitting next to him on this balcony and saying, You're here now, son. Talk to me, ask me whatever you want.

Jamal stared, appalled. The Smiths were a family of unspoken secrets, of the-walls-are-listening sign language: direct speech was abhorred, a profound thing that had to be earned, and which you were never meant to actually earn, at least not while the adults were alive. They wanted to keep their shames secret, as was proper. The Khans were a completely different animal, if his father was any indication. Jamal had come to meet the man on his own terms, to hold him, to show him he could be held, but he had not expected to succeed, had not known what success would even look like, and now he wanted nothing more than to run. He had to admit Hala might have been right all along. When he told her his plan to stay with his dad in Turkey, she had two reactions. First, she declared that he wasn't going, as if he was asking her permission (since he'd left home, she tried this every now and again, testing to see whether the hook of her old authority had regained any purchase in his blood) and then she'd laughed at him. You're gonna go across the world on two bucks and a prayer? Turn it up, would ya.

This wasn't his first plan—his first plan had been to get a visa and live in Canada for a couple years, and he was so excited, he told everyone about it. He thought living in the Inner West away from his family would be liberating, but even there he struggled to be as free as he wanted, and so he decided he would find another country to be in for a while, the way so many of his peers seemed to be doing. How could he know that his application would be denied, that he would fuck even that up? By which time, his housemate's friend Alex had been dumped, and Jamal had already said he could take his room. The idea of telling the whole world (his 301 friends on Facebook) that he wasn't going anywhere was too much to bear, and it was then that he thought of his father, who had said he could always come to Turkey, he could stay for free if he needed.

He had enough for a return ticket, and a month's rent to spend, but would be relying on his estranged father, a known liar. What could go wrong? Everything. But everything went wrong even when he froze, saying nothing and doing nothing. He was done with that bare minimum kind of living. Let everything go wrong on the back of risk for a change. He shovelled cheese and bread into his mouth, thinking of what to say. Their interactions in the past had always been chaotic, burdened by the pressure to build something in moments that most people created naturally, asleep as much as awake, life and love growing hand in hand. It was an awful thing to have all this love without an equal amount of life to anchor it, an attendant sea of memories to soak it up, give it shape. His father was staring at him expectantly, so he said the first thing that came into his head.

Who is Abdul Khadeir?

Cevdat laughed. Nobody, he said. You think I'd give that prick my real name?

That prick was the hostel receptionist, a thin weasel of a man named Arif, who sat behind his desk and smoked all night, talking shit to his mates. Arif had asked him if his name was Jamal as soon as he got out of the taxi, saying that his father, Abdul Khadeir, had called to check if he had arrived. His English was thick and ended in question marks.

That's not my father's name, Jamal said. And I didn't tell him where I was staying.

Arif's eyebrows lifted. But you are Jamal?

Yes.

He knows secret people, your father?

Jamal shook his head, said he didn't know. He hadn't slept on the plane: despite disbelieving his seat in the sky, he had a hundred other reasons to be anxious, and every inch of him needed sleep. He went to his room, connected to the wi-fi, checked Tango to message his dad he'd arrived, then crashed. He hadn't thought about it since.

How did you know where I was? he asked.

Son, do you see this phone? Cevdat held up a dark metal slab, froth of egg on his lips. I have generals in here, okay, I have politicians in here, if I want to know something, all I have to do is make a call. Don't worry about how I know things.

It's true, oğlum, Mehmet murmured, his voice a smoke-thickened husk. Eat, eat. Can your amca cook or what? He grinned proudly, thumping himself on the chest. Of all of us, I'm the one who cooks the best, isn't it? Isn't it? He didn't wait for Cevdat to nod. Even for grandma, your babbanne, I'm the only one she'll let cook for her.

Jamal nodded, feeling oğlum settle on his shoulders. For some reason, it meant more coming from his uncle, either because he said it without expectation, or because he was the first to have introduced him to the word, and from there to the feeling. The food was delicious, though not as good as babbanne's, whatever his uncle thought. He hadn't spent nearly as much time with the sweet old lady as he wanted; being with her brought on a tide of guilt, like he was betraying his teyta somehow.

Fatma! Cevdat yelled, leaning over the balcony rail. Faaaatma, he said, hand cupped around his lips to help carry his words to her. He dragged out the sound of her name in a long boyish singsong, threading the distance with her vowels, and laughed.

Don't, ya, Mehmet said. I don't want to hear from that crazy bitch.

Cevdat laughed. Mem, I'm just having fun with her. To Jamal, he added, She owns that junk shop across the street, and look, see her taking all the crap out onto the footpath? She does that every day, in and out. His delight was infectious, the way he enjoyed pissing his brother off. Cevdat called out to Fatma in Turkish, and she replied, yelling out over the passing cars.

Both men chuckled, before Cevdat translated, I said I'm sick of watching her pack up her store, and she goes, she's sick of hearing me bitch at her from my balcony. Affection and familiar exasperation laced their voices.

Jamal smiled and looked away, feeling again the edges of a loneliness and despair he would never part from. I need a shower, I feel gross, he said. He was beyond exhausted, and he did need a shower, but he was not going to get one. In the bathroom, there was a tap and a bucket, a stained shit-flap set into the floor, and holes in the tiled walls where a shower was yet to be installed. Jamal laughed hysterically when he saw it, imagining what his mother would say.

I don't get it, he said. You don't shower?

Mehmet flipped the bucket over, next to the tap, then sat on it. He turned the faucet, and water splashed down over his brown feet.

We wash like this, oğlum. We're waiting for the building manager to finish the repairs. He turned the tap off.

And who's the building manager, Mem? Cevdat called from the living room.

Mehmet grinned, his blue eyes sparkling. Me, but I have to take care of the whole building ya, there's a lot of work and everyone's on my back about it.

Get off your fat arse then!

Mehmet responded in Turkish, and Jamal stood there in the unfinished room as the two men vanished.

Scales and Weights

For fuck's sake, shut up already! Jamal shouted into the mottled dark. He was slumped in a seat on the balcony. Below him, the hawker carried his cart down the road, crying out in Turkish. A jet-lagged week of fitful sleep had ground him down, made worse by the incessant time delay of translated conversations, six steps behind every laugh or grimace, to say nothing of the constant standing around, staring vacuously at the various men and women being introduced to him. It was like reliving his childhood, only more painful and strange, because here he had no link to the language, no cousins to run around with in shared ignorance, their speech inflected with enough Arabic to at least tie them to each other. A week of this with his father and his uncle forced him to concede that they were both bums who did nothing but smoke on the balcony and shout at passers-by, or watch TV. He shouldn't judge them, he was in no better position—what could he say for himself except that he had semi-regular contract work, an undergrad drop-out who hadn't lived up to his family's expectations? But they were old, he thought. Weren't things supposed to get better? They weren't meant to be sitting around doing fuck-all, the way he and Ilo and Emir did. He rubbed his puffy eyes and groaned.

A reply floated back up to him: No, *you* shut the fuck up!

Jamal's jaw dropped. He went over to the balcony edge and saw a man below, who looked to be his age, staring up at him. What makes you so great, eh? Orsan is just trying to make a buck. He gestured at the hawker, who was walking on unperturbed, as he probably would until the world ended, or even after.

Jamal turned and rushed back inside, through the crashing snores of the men sprawled like walruses on the couches, and out, down three flights of stairs. He slowed as he came to the door, breathing hard. The air was blue, the night easing into light, and there he stood in black jeans and a worn-out Metallica T-shirt: his name was Kassem, and he was short and thin, with a fine moustache. His initial alarm faded as Jamal babbled on in English, telling him that he was bored sick, he didn't know any Turkish, he couldn't sleep, he hated metal music, and did he want to get a coffee? Kassem smiled, stubbed his cigarette out, and took Jamal by the arm.

Come, he said. Nearby one of the bakeries was open, and the smell of fresh bread enveloped them. Kassem ordered coffee, and a plate of meat and cheese börek—flaky, stuffed pastries that melted in Jamal's mouth. He wasn't up early, he'd just been about to go to bed, on the way home from a disappointing house party, and club crawl. Kassem was studying to be an engineer, but dreamed of poetry. He had nimble hands that darted in the air, punctuating his sentences. Jamal didn't know if Kassem would be interesting in any other circumstance, but in this one, he drank in every word. He hadn't realised just how trapped he felt, knowing he was dependent on his dad and uncle—in Istanbul, it seemed everyone could speak English, he could get around or away on his own. Looking deep into Kassem's honey-flecked brown eyes, he found himself relaxing for the first time since arriving. He told him that he worked as a transcriber on reality TV shows like *MasterChef* and *The Biggest Loser*, that everyone thought he had a plan, but he didn't.

So, why did you come here? Kassem said. Not for your father, clearly.

Is it that obvious?

You're talking to the first stranger you found, instead of him—yeah, it's obvious.

Okay, yeah, I needed to leave.

Australia?

Australia, Jamal agreed. The country was an ugly weight. He was heavier there, every step dragged and drugged with memory. He launched into a rant about racism, putting every inch of his unhappiness on the government, because they deserved it, and because he didn't want to talk about his family, how they had failed him too. Kassem was educated enough to know Australia wasn't all beaches and barbecues, he had distant family there too, but he was still shocked by what Jamal told him. He remembered the Cronulla riots—they had made global news—but didn't know that months later, the Middle Eastern Organised Crime Squad was formed in response. The MEOCS had a literal mandate to target them, and so they did. Jamal remembered coming home after his English HSC exam to find the metal bars had been ripped off the window, the house raided, Hala wandering around the trashed place with a confused look on her face. It was one of many memories that, like cicadas, buried themselves for years until they rose to the surface with a scream. The cops had torn everything to pieces, even his books, searching for drugs and finding nothing. He told Kassem how they got Moses later for carrying with the intent to distribute.

So he was carrying drugs? Kassem said.

Ecstasy, and it was unrelated, Jamal said. I'm not saying we're angels, I'm saying everyone's a devil and there's a decent chance you'll find something no matter who you stop, you know? Especially if they're broke. Or rich. Anyway, that's just one example. Don't even get me started on the offshore prisons where they've locked up hundreds of asylum seekers.

Hundreds? Kassem exclaimed. Is that all? We have three million Syrian refugees here. More, maybe. They're still coming. We took them in.

On the table, their hands were almost touching. Reflexively, Jamal checked over his shoulder, canvassed the area. Up on the third-floor balcony, his father stood, lit by the risen sun, staring back at him. Jamal waved, and the figure retreated. Kassem had moved his hands away by the time he swivelled back. They spoke only a little while longer, the heat stolen from what had been rising between them.

Cevdat was waiting for him by the door when he returned. I woke up and you were gone, there wasn't even a note, he said. Lips mulish. How could you just be gone like that?

Jamal's chest tightened, his heart jerking at the sound of distress in Cevdat's voice. He wanted to repeat the question back at his father, who had never been there for him, but he didn't. It wasn't necessary, the words were always between them.

Cevdat's hand moved in a strange, aborted gesture. I just—we need to get you a sim, son. So you can call, okay? That's all it is, he said. That's all it is.

Okay, Jamal said.

His father looked drawn and tired. White stubble coated his face like frost. So you met Gurkhan's son, he said.

Kassem?

Cevdat nodded slowly. The barber below us, that's his boy.

Okay. Jamal shrugged. So what?

What did you think of him?

He speaks my language, Jamal said, and slipped past into the bedroom, which was dark and hot, a pedestal fan whirring at the foot of the queen bed. His phone reconnected to the internet, and he saw a friend request from Kassem pop up, a small square of radiance. Kassem had his tongue out in the profile photo, a stud shining in the pink, metal sun. Jamal let it burn his retinas for a second. Sleep rushed into him, and he met it smiling.

&

They made sand angels on the burning beach.

Waves entreated Jamal and Kassem to leave the hot grains behind, but they stayed there, half-buried and laughing, because under the sand they could hold hands. The idea was to bake for as long as they could stand it, then run into the water. Under the cry of gulls and the fuss of waves, the yells of children and chatter of friends, they talked. Jamal told him that he'd dropped out of his degree, that he'd been working in the years since and had no plans to go back. It felt so good to tell someone, to finally stop pretending. His family thought he had completed his degree, that he was busy fulfilling his potential, working in television (the nature of the work was lost on them, next to the prestige of the industry). He had never found a way to explain how much he hated his studies, how poorly prepared he was for the work, how poor he was, period, compared to his peers from the Inner West and North Shore. He couldn't explain that he'd never looked down on his family or his own circumstances while he was still with them, having had nothing to compare it to, and that even the flimsy illusion of middle-class living provided by share houses in the city had ruined him.

He told Kassem that after one lecture in Power and Politics, he found a camera left behind by one of the tutors, and that the last photo on it was of the entire Humanities staff, shirtless, the women in bras and undies, the men in ties, forming a human pyramid. Replicating Abu Ghraib, the torture of Iraqis at the hands of Americans, which had resurfaced in the news. Smiling like the soldiers. Here, he knew, was power. He showed Adam, the only other boy from Liverpool who went to his uni, and Adam showed his new film student mates, who decided they had to do their own version to show the teachers that they were just as cool as them and not like, boring, or whatever. He would never forget the queasy expression on Adam's face, his nervous laughter, the way he couldn't look Jamal in the eye. He took his place at the base of the pyramid, and Jamal held a leash attached to his pale body, looking directly at the camera and trying to smile, because he didn't want to be 'boring or whatever', didn't want to lose his new queer friends when he had only just met them. His shame grew and grew with each passing week until he quit the subject, and then the degree.

Kassem looked sad. They say the West is fucked up, you know, and I guess I believed it, but … He shook his head, blew out a breath. That you hated yourself, I get. We are all taught this. It just comes out in different ways. Did anyone else drop out? Was anyone hurt?

No, Jamal said quietly. It would have been too improbable, too silly to say he had hurt himself. What kind of sense did that make? And yet, it was true. In his mind, he stood apart from his white friends, they had not suffered as he suffered, but that day, he and they were the same, pantomiming his people's oppression. And there, there was the wound. That he could no longer say he had a people. His heart was beating so hard, and he was drenched in sweat. He wanted to burst out of the sandy oven and run into the sea already.

I'm not allowed to have a pet, Kassem said, because Baba has allergies. But with all the neighbourhood cats, I never really needed one, I used to feed them whenever I could. One cat, he was this tiny orange thing, but a real tiger, and he wouldn't let anyone pat him except me. I don't know why but I think just for that alone I loved him.

And you're telling me this because?

Because I don't want to think about that depressing shit you just dumped on this beach, Kassem said, spitting out a laugh. Because cats are great! Because fuck you.

Did you kill the cat?

Astugfirullah, Kassem said. What is wrong with you?

You did, didn't you? I can tell—you can't just leave me hanging here feeling like a bag of shit, you gotta give a bad story for a bad story, that's how it works.

Kassem was laughing in earnest now. Who told you that? Then, more seriously, You said it yourself—none of us are angels. So what does punishing yourself achieve? He paused. Do you believe in God?

Mostly, Jamal said.

You think if you punish yourself that He won't?

I don't know, he lied. I was twelve when my aunties told me that being gay was haram. I couldn't understand it. Or even the idea of hell. How could the Most Compassionate, the Most Merciful have less compassion and less mercy than me? How he could He hurt me for being as I was made to be? Or anyone!

I brought you into this world and I can take you out, Kassem murmured.

Exactly, Jamal said. They all talk like that, like they own you.

So you stopped believing?

No. I cried myself to sleep a lot, Jamal laughed.

Kassem grinned. Me too. I was the angstiest kid alive. I'd walk around these alleys yelling and arguing with God every week—until I realised that arguing meant I knew He was listening, that this was all in my head and my heart.

Jamal didn't know what to say to that. He stared at this grinning golden boy, his delicate shoulders, the sheen on his skin, his damp chest hairs, and tried to compare it to the tired, angry guy he'd seen days ago. He wanted very much to kiss the dip in his neck.

What are you looking at? Kassem said, squinting at him.

Nothing, Jamal said. But I know why the cat chose you.

Kassem groaned loudly, then exploded out of the sand, running at the rushing waves. Jamal laughed and ran after him, the shock of the cold so intense it flooded his whole body, the relief its own kind of ecstasy. He dived into the blue, tackling Kassem, and they splashed around. Sometimes wrestling, sometimes floating away, ducking under the waves. Kassem came up close to him after one dive, spitting out water. He looked like a drowned rat with his hair all flat, fringe stuck to his forehead.

When did you know? he said.

I'm still not sure that I do, Jamal said. I mean—he floundered for a second—it's like this, you know, the waves. It never stays, if that makes sense.

Not really, Kassem admitted. We're in it.

Like everyone, Jamal said, nodding at the others around him, kicking his feet to stay afloat. I don't feel like any of the words actually fit me.

I knew when I was six, Kassem said. I kissed my friend Hussein on the cheek and his mother slapped me. He laughed. I'm glad, in retrospect. I never had to make a choice, everyone just knew from then on.

And no one says anything? Jamal said, eyes wide.

Kassem shrugged. Not to my face, he said, and went under.

&

Gold blur, blue sky, haze of houses.

Look out the window, son, see that? Cevdat shouted. That's Ceyhan, that's where we come from! They'd been driving for an hour. Wind buffeted them through the open windows. Mehmet was in the front seat beside his brother, his arm up, holding on to the handle above his head. Cevdat stared out, his thick head of hair ruffled, sunglasses glinting, joy stamped on his face. He was incandescent out on this road, steering wheel in hand, in control, moving, free. There was no comparing him to the man mired in the unit that Jamal had seen these past few days, or even the man he met for the first time in Leichhardt. That confident man was gone. There was something raw and resigned about him here in Turkey, but on the road, he regained a measure of his old fire. As with many of the boys from the area, driving seemed to exert an almost supernatural pull on him. Anything was possible behind the wheel. He pointed out houses he used to own, said he gave them all to his ex-wives. What would have been said bitterly on the balcony, he offered here easily and with a shrug.

You can't hold on to these things, son, he said. When we go to the grave we take only our skin, remember that.

Jamal's teyta appeared in the back seat beside him, smiling; she put her warm hand on his forehead, the smell of citrus blossomed, and then she was gone. Her death lived in him, ragged and awful, made all the more so by her occasional visits—her smile told him the pain he felt was entirely his own. Somehow, he'd deluded himself into thinking he was free of the past, as if it was tied to the land that made it, and here across the sea it could not hurt him. He had the feeling his grandparents had made the same mistake. This land, too, held part of him and his story. A dozen griefs pumped out and through his heart. He closed his eyes, and his uncle began to speak, his voice deep and rocky like the hills.

See those ruins, oğlum? Yilankale, it's called. Snake Castle. They say a lizard person lived on that hill once, and who knows, maybe he still does, it's cursed, we don't go there. Anyway, there was a boy who fell into a well of honey. He dug beneath the honey, and found a cave full of snakes. It was a kind of garden, you know. And then she came to him, their queen, this snake woman, very beautiful, top half woman, bottom snake—

—Like every woman, Cevdat interrupted.

York, ya, shut up, I'm telling the story. Anyway, they fell in love. He lived with her for many years, but he missed the sun and the sea, and so one day he left. She told him not to give away her secret, and to be careful not to bathe with others—he was part of them now too, isn't it? The water would show this, make his skin scaly. Then the king got sick and his advisers told him he needed to eat the snake woman's flesh to survive. Sahmaran, she was called, and the legends said she could cure anything, even age. They told him that those who knew her location would be revealed by water.

Wait a minute, Mem, how could they know that, you just said—?

Did I make this story? No, I didn't. The story was existing already like all the stories, I'm just telling it now.

Seeing that Cevdat was going to continue arguing, Jamal said, Dad, please, and he subsided. Jamal rarely used either word, he knew the danger in them, but he wanted to hear the rest of the story.

Where was I? I bloody forgot, Mehmet said.

Water, Jamal said.

Ah. So the king gave an order—they could do that in those days, just say a thing and everyone had to do it, can you believe it? He ordered everyone to go to the hamam! Everyone had to bathe in public. No secrets that way. And so, the boy, you remember him, who ate the honey, who found the cave, who loved her, he tried to escape, but the guards threw him into the water, and just like she said, his skin became scales. They tortured him until he gave away her location. They brought Sahmaran to the king, and she told them that if they wanted her powers they should eat her tail, it was fat with oil, and if they wanted to die, to eat her head. They cut her into pieces and the king and his guards ate her tail, but her lover, he only wanted to die, the stupid man, so he ate her head.

Mehmet shook his head, dragging at his cigarette.

What happened to him? Jamal said.

Nothing, he said. She lied, the clever bitch. All her power went into him, and the king and the guards died. He's still alive, they say, and that's where he lives, the bastard. Who would eat a woman's head, ya? Jump off a cliff, you idiot.

Jamal burst out laughing and they did too and the wind took whatever was in the car and threw it out into the country. For the next two hours, he thought of little else except the story of doomed and hidden love, how knowledge itself had changed the nameless boy's body and how that change could be made visible. There was a question in there that gnawed within, but the words for it eluded him.

At noon, they arrived in Gaziantep, a large and sprawling city, and buildings began to block the eyeline in every direction, leaving little room for anything else. Heavy and nauseous from the long drive, Jamal faded in and out, only coming to when they parked outside a small travel agency in a near abandoned and graffitied lot. A dozen Turks spilled out, most of them children, along with two men in suits who hugged Cevdat and Mehmet, back-slapping and babbling happily. These were the cousins he'd been brought to meet, and like all the other relatives, they marvelled over Jamal's face, saying, Mashallah, mashallah. He is you, they said to Cevdat, even though Jamal had a thick brown beard, a sullen and woolly disposition. Cevdat grinned, and Jamal kept his expression neutral. There could be no more satisfying a thing to say to a father, and nothing more painful to say to a son.

They took him to the centre of the city where Gaziantep Castle crouched atop a hill, an ancient fortress turned into a museum. The dirt hill, the stone edifice, seemed almost a flagrant slap in the face from history itself. It made every modern thing in the vicinity look fragile and cheap. Jamal wanted to go inside but Cevdat said the museum was for tourists who couldn't see that history was everywhere, that it walked hand in hand with them. He was led instead to the nearby bazaar, the cobbled laneways of artisans and metal workers, which rang with the sound of hammers. Cevdat pointed this out with great excitement.

Your dedde, okay, my dad, he was a metal worker. See these pots and pans? He made them too, he could make anything. Dedde was only twelve when his father died from a heart attack, just an apprentice. He had to sneak into the workshops of the other masters and listen to what they taught their apprentices, because he was now the man of the house. He got into Australia because of what he learned, he bought that unit in Mersin. He had nothing, and he changed every one of our lives. Do you know what I'm trying to tell you? When you can make things with your hands, son, the world is clay.

His jido had made bread with his hands, and his dedde had made metal; all the women made food that kept the family alive, and he, like his father, made nothing. No wonder they were both so hopeless. Cevdat asked after Hala's parents, and Jamal told him that his teyta had passed away last year, that dementia stole her language so she couldn't speak, and ate her memories so she didn't know who she was, but that his grandfather was still alive.

Cevdat shuddered. I don't fear death, son, but that's one thing I pray God keeps from happening to me. I know three languages and I need them all.

Cevdat bought him prayer beads, soft handmade leather shoes, loose linen pants, and Mehmet bought him a fez for a laugh, the two splurging, as if they could bridge the absent years between them with each purchase. By the end of it, Jamal felt light-headed. They tried to get him to eat an Adana kebab—this is what I brought you here for, come on, we're famous for it!—but Jamal's stomach cramped, and he refused. He felt sick, and in sickening, found it hard to think or retain conversation. Had he drank any of the water from the taps? Was he not meant to? He was not meant to. Their concern faded into relieved laughter. You're going to have a bad time, they said, but it will pass. It was normal not to have drinkable water in the taps. He dimly remembered a time in his childhood when the presence of parasites in Sydney's water supply meant for weeks they had to boil water before drinking it, or else have the fizzy kind he hated, but that had been close to two decades ago and never occurred again.

He emptied his guts repeatedly over the next few hours, and as dark fell, they drove back to Mersin. Jamal lay in the back seat, burning up. He concentrated on his nausea with intense focus, because it was all he could manage, making his attention an action, hoping the weight of it could hold his unsettled stomach still. As they went past Yilankale again, the old ruins of a snake man's home, the question inside Jamal unfurled. The man had left Sahmaran, and in leaving, opened the door to catastrophe.

Can you really love someone if you're able to leave them?

He did not know he spoke the question aloud, or that neither man answered.

&

Tell me of your life, son.

They were on the road again, just the two of them. Mehmet chose to stay in Mersin and Jamal wished he could have, too. He wanted to see Kassem again, to be near him. They chatted on Messenger all the time, and it was there that Kassem started sharing more of himself. His mother died giving birth to him. He thought this was why he was gay, because she gave her life for him and no other woman could live up to that. His father never remarried and the community judged him for it, and then again when they knew his son was gay, like it was some kind of tragedy, a wound he needed to doctor. Kassem didn't believe in wounds or healing in such matters, he said the language of the body did not suit the soul. Our bodies heal because they are temporary, made to break. Our spirits are eternal, they don't tear or heal—they change. The question should never be, how do I heal from this, it should be: what am I changing into? People say Baba needs to heal, but they haven't accepted how he has changed, he said. It was this kind of late-night eloquence that made Jamal fall in love with him. Meanwhile, Ilo and Emir were telling him in all caps to make a move already, like it was such an easy thing to do.

Cevdat had woken him early this morning, insisting they go on this trip, that there was something he needed to see. Knowing what he did now, Jamal had a sinking suspicion it was just to get him away from Kassem, that being seen with a gay man was worrying.

What do you want me to say?

Cevdat sighed. You don't talk much, you know that.

The highway was as open and empty as the sky. Tell me what you're thinking, what your dreams are, where you want to be in life, are you seeing any girls?

Not really, Jamal said, answering the last, and the frustration on his father's face deepened into a frown.

Why not? A handsome young man like you should be getting out there.

What do I have to offer anyone? Jamal said. I work as a transcriber. I barely want this life, let alone to share it with anyone else. There's not enough.

Okay, so you don't like your job, but this means you have to be alone and miserable? There are plenty of girls here who would marry you just to go to Australia. Your babbanne already has some picked out.

See, look, it's better not to talk.

Cevdat laughed, incredulous. What, this is good! I want to know you!

No, you want to shape me. To argue me into doing what you want. This is why I don't talk to any of you.

Any of who?

Jamal waved his hand, annoyed. Mum, you, Moses—the whole aileh. It's exhausting.

This is a depression talking, oğlum, it's not you, it's not real. If you don't want to talk to anyone … he trailed off, flabbergasted. That's not what Jamal had said, but *any of you* had translated to everyone, because his father thought family was everything.

Not even your brother? Cevdat shook his head. I would be nothing without my brother, you've seen how we are, I love him more than life.

Of course we speak sometimes, Jamal said, almost growling with annoyance. Just not … not about anything important, and that's how we like it.

Jamal had stayed with Hala while Moses was doing weekends in Silverwater, then left when he successfully appealed for home detention, complete with ankle monitor. Their house had been prison enough for him. He had written a character reference for his brother's appeal, and as far as he was concerned, that made them even.

They pulled into a gas station, and Cevdat turned the car off. Even with the air con, Jamal was sweating. Without it, he was sure he would melt.

Listen, I've had this depression thing, Cevdat said. I know how it is. My son is here and what can I do for him? Nothing, I have nothing. It keeps me awake at night. That's why I'm trying so hard, with these deals, I'm trying to make something happen for us.

Jamal shook his head tiredly. No one asked you to do that.

Look—what's that above your eye?

Jamal shied away from his dad's outstretched hand. He touched his forehead and skin flaked off, a flurry of dead snow. I dunno, eczema maybe?

Euurgh, that's fucking gross, Cevdat said, laughing nervously.

You think your other kids, your other son—what is he, twelve or thirteen now?—you think he cares if you don't have a job right now, or money? Jamal said. All your kids want is for you to be there, I've told you that before.

Maybe, Cevdat said. But it's my job to want more for them, for us.

For him, he meant. Cevdat got out of the car and filled the tank. He grabbed water and snacks when he went to the counter, which Jamal took gratefully. Back on the highway, he turned the radio on and a woman's voice sprang into the silence.

Ah, now this, my boy, this is a love song. Cevdat crooned along with Adele and Jamal relaxed. It was another half an hour before they arrived at their destination, a small private lagoon surrounded by cliffs.

Look! Look, my god. Cevdat beamed at him encouragingly, and Jamal had to admit it was as beautiful a place as any he'd seen. A deep blue with bolts of green dazzled far into the distance. They walked down a slope of flagstones towards a floating boardwalk that jutted out over the water. Recliners and umbrellas were set up across the boards, and a few were occupied while kids splashed about below. Cevdat paid for their entrance, his body shifting as he got out his wallet, his mouth turning down.

I haven't been here for years, he muttered. Back then there wasn't all this shit. Now you have to pay for everything, even the sea. Then, louder, You're going to love this, you'll see.

He wasted no time in taking his shirt off and diving in. Jamal followed him, eager to get out of the heat, and the wet burst with a clap, then rushed back in to hold him. He spluttered and splashed awkwardly, bobbing at the surface, his eyes stinging, his skin and lips smarting with salt. For a minute they both forgot the rest of the world, as it narrowed to kicking in this buoyant weight, to what held a father and his son in the same body. Jamal dived under the surface, loving the shifting coolness, the odd colder and warmer threads, the way it made everything outside itself bearable. He wished that for himself. He returned to the air, and stayed there, blinking bleary. It soon got harder to breathe, his arms and legs started to ache, and he wondered if it had always been this hard to maintain a pleasure, or if he was simply unused to the effort. Thinking of the great unbreathable depth under him, he flopped over to the metal ladder that led up to the boardwalk, and grabbed one of the rusted, algae-encrusted rungs. His father was further out, close to the rocks that mostly separated the lagoon from its ocean mother.

When he saw Jamal next to the ladder, he made his way back, untroubled and glowing in the glimmering all around.

How do you feel? he said. It's good, isn't it. Jamal nodded, but his skin felt painfully tight, and he wanted a break.

That spot is red now, Cevdat said, and reached out to Jamal's forehead. He let him this time, clinging to the ladder, as his father's finger pressed into his temple and rubbed hard until his skin sloughed off.

Cevdat looked repulsed, then strangely delighted. Fucking hell! Look at this, there's so much. He laughed like a kid, rubbing his boy's skin. You needed this, oğlum. Satisfaction poured off him. Here was something he could do with his hands. Jamal's head tilted back under the pressure and he stared into the sun as he was scoured.

Release

I wasn't sure you were coming back. Kassem blew out a wave of smoke. He'd been out already, and dark rings circled his eyes. He reminded Jamal a great deal of Emir then, sulky and angry. I wouldn't have if I were you.

Jamal shivered in the night. Leaned his head against the brick of the apartment building. He radiated heat, like his skin had drunk the sun and didn't want to release it. When he got back, Mehmet had taken him aside and said Kassem had come round asking for him.

What did you say to him?

Nothing, oğlum. I just said your dad took you, isn't it?

Jamal didn't have a sim card yet—it felt too permanent a move—and was reliant still on wi-fi to talk to anyone. He hadn't got any of Kassem's many messages, who now thought Jamal had run from their friendship, because being seen with a known gay man was too much for him.

What would you do if you were me? Jamal said to him now.

Firstly, I would not go to a country that cannot understand me—

Jamal scoffed. You think I'm understood there?

Kassem ignored that. Second, I would do an awesome amount of drugs.

You do that already.

Third, I would—he paused. Swallowed. For a second, he seemed so desperately unhappy that Jamal wanted to reach out to him, fold him into a hug. He watched the second pass, saw the sadness turn inward and ugly.

You have so much, Kassem said, his hands shaking. More than you know. You can leave! You can leave, don't you get it?

Jamal wasn't sure that would be so easy. He'd been fairly certain his dad's threats were idle, that his boasts were three parts bullshit one part exaggeration, but now he had reason to doubt. On the third occasion he met his father, Jamal had been working in Rosebery, not far from Eastlakes, where his babbanne lived. Cevdat had been back in Australia again, pursuing one of his schemes, and he texted to find out where Jamal was, then offered to drive him home to Stanmore. Jamal agreed as long as his housemate and co-worker Dan could get a lift too. They piled into the SUV, and Cevdat started to tell him about a man he knew in Auburn, who was blind, but knew the Quran off by heart, even though he'd never read it. Everyone knew that the angels whispered to the blind man, they told him things, he knew the answers to every question, and this was why they kicked him out of school when he was only a boy.

I can tell you don't believe me, oğlum, but look, just ask Sam—he's the smartest man I know, a Leb, would you believe it, he's got three degrees—ask him and he will tell you the same thing. Sam is the kind of man I can call no matter what. It's important to have good friends, friends that can protect you. He flicked a dismissive glance at Jamal's housemate in the back seat, a pasty Jewish guy with curly hair who looked more likely to faint if he saw a weight than be able to lift it.

You want a friend who says *tell me where to dig* when you say you need to get rid of a body—actually, that reminds me. One time, this was in the early nineties, I had to kidnap somebody, and who did I call? I called Sam. He got in his van just like that and he came over. That's the kind of friend you want. See, back then I was known in the community. I fixed things, you know, this and that. So one day, I got a call from the Turkish ambassador, saying her daughter had run away and she needed someone to get her, and to do it quickly and quietly, because it was a big embarrassment to her. He was successful in this mission, he told them, pulling up to her boyfriend's house and putting a gun in his mouth. They bundled the girl into Sam's van and took her to her mother, who sent her back to Turkey.

Jamal had rolled his eyes then, thinking the whole thing bogus, a middle-aged man's tiresome fantasy, but just yesterday he'd seen a framed photo in which Cevdat was shaking hands with the former Turkish president in his office. If he had met the president, then it wasn't so improbable that he knew an ambassador, or even a general. It made Jamal uneasy to think there could be any truth to the many stories he'd heard, and immediately he recast the man from bullshit artist to dangerous bullshit artist. It meant that he really was at his father's mercy here and perhaps always had been.

Let's say I can leave, Jamal said to Kassem. Are you saying you can't?

Of course not. Who will take care of Baba when he's sick, when he can't work anymore? He's alone. Just yesterday I was getting groceries and Fatma, that old slut, leaned over and said, *There is such a thing as too much pride! He's still young.* They don't give a damn about him, they just want to give him a reason to get rid of me. Kassem stubbed his cigarette out aggressively.

Jamal remembered standing over his teyta's grave and repeatedly being told to stop crying, that sorrow called to the deceased's spirit, it made them restless. He remembered the funeral for Jihad's stillborn son, how his uncles had gathered around the weeping father of the dead, his eyes shattered wells, and told him the same thing, that there was pride in his grief. This isn't love, they said. You're hurting him, haram. Nothing could stop his tears and there was nothing that should have, as far as Jamal was concerned. They had twenty-four hours to put the bodies in the ground and they were not meant to grieve? Maybe the purpose of those claims was simply to make the body buck in rebellion, to grieve harder, to spill every tear in one exhausted explosion, because that was always the outcome, a downpour unlike any other, a long song—not to call the spirit back, but to let them know they were loved and always would be.

I know what you mean, Jamal said. But he's a grown man, he has friends. Do you really think he only accepts you because of what, leverage? Maybe he doesn't want another wife because he's trying to protect you.

Kassem paced, his body tensed so tight veins stood out on his forearms, and he trembled, his breathing shallow and fast. You don't know shit, he said. You think your life is the hardest, but you don't know shit. So you can't speak the language, so fucking what, fuck you!

Jamal wanted to say, Why would you make less of that, why would you make less of yourself? He thought of the old saying, *nobody knows what they have until it's gone*, and how stupid it was—everyone knows, and that knowledge is no protection against loss, or arrogance. People lied about what they knew all the time, to gain advantage, or to diminish others. He thought these things later, because in the moment he was already walking away, and what he spat back over his shoulder was this: Everyone's got a sad fucking story, bro. Get over yourself.

He marched down the street, striding unthinking towards the sea. As he got closer, he slowed, and it was only then he heard his name being called and turned in time to see Kassem collide with him. Wait, damn you, you don't know where you're going. You can't, you don't know, he said—and then they were embracing. Kassem turned it quickly into a friendly arm over the shoulder and led them onward, towards the avenue by the beach, and a promontory that had an upright fighter jet sticking out from it. The tide rushed in, spray reaching up to salt the air. In the shadow of the jet, under that ugly finger pointing at the sky, Jamal kissed Kassem. At first with hesitant flutters, then with increasing urgency and depth, their lips melding and parting as they took turns inviting each other in. Jamal pressed Kassem back, sucking on his neck; Kassem pushed him off before he could leave a mark, and they kissed, again and again.

I should take you to Ataturk Park, Kassem said. Grinding their zippers and belts against each other, aiming for bulge on bulge, hardness to hardness.

Jamal ran a finger over his lips, his moustache. What's there?

Men like us, he said. Though it was late, there were still people out and cars streamed by on the road behind them.

I don't need anyone else, Jamal said.

Kassem frowned, biting the inside of his lip. Jamal knew this 'where will we go to fuck' dance all too well. The most asked question in Western Sydney was probably, Can you host? And if they weren't Anglo, most likely the answer was going to be no. Most of the ethnics in the area lived with their families. Few had the cash or the stomach for a motel, so they hit up the park, or made do in the car. It seemed the same was true even in Turkey. Kassem's father knew about him, but that didn't mean he would let strange men into his home, that didn't mean he could flaunt himself.

Jamal sighed. We don't have to—

Come, Kassem said. I know a place. He took Jamal back to the street with the bakery, the barber, their fathers. Orange eyes honeycombed the dark in the buildings all around them. Kassem unlocked his father's shop, and Jamal followed him inside, the bell above dashing out notes of welcome. There was a heavy curtain drawn across the glass shopfront, and the place smelled like leather, wax and, faintly, detergent from the recently mopped tiles. Kassem vanished into the back, re-emerging with a candle. He lit it, placing it in front of the mirror furthest from the door. He made a show of dusting off the seat, then took a step back, facing Jamal, and pulled off his shirt, He had a hairy tree on his chest, a thin veneer of muscle, and dark nipples. His shoes followed, then his jeans. His dick was hard in his blue and white underwear, peeking out of the top band. Jamal walked over, bending quick to lick the shiny head and tongue the slit; Kassem bucked, shuddering at the sudden sensitive wetness.

Jamal kissed his way up his chest, sucked at his nipples, and then Kassem was tearing his clothes off, and they were both naked, cocks touching, arms around each other.

Kassem pushed Jamal into the seat, tipped it back. Wait, he whispered.

He moved away, grabbing a lotion from among the many bottles on the bench, poured some out. He braced himself there, arse out, and began fingering himself. Outside the fragile light provided by the candle, Jamal had to strain to see more than the pale cheeks, but he could hear the gentle moans, and he'd never been harder in his life. He wanted to shove his face in that moon, but he didn't know what Kassem was applying, if it was edible or not, and he was afraid, too, of breaking the spell that held them. Kassem moved towards him, skin shining, and slid his body up over Jamal's. The chair creaked alarmingly, then settled, as Kassem straddled Jamal. He reached back to line up his cock, and lowered himself with a grunt. Jamal stayed perfectly still as he entered Kassem slowly, all the air hissing out of him. Kassem gripped Jamal's chest as he rocked his hips for a minute, clenching and unclenching. He whimpered. Rested his head against Jamal's neck, gasping, gritting his teeth. Then he drew himself up, and down, and they began to fuck.

This was neither's first time. When Jamal had moved into the share house in Stanmore, he'd even had the privilege of sex in bed, with guys for the most part, as well as the occasional girl, but he had never experienced a moment like this, unrushed despite the peril, a moment when every part of him felt alive, felt wanted, felt loved. He watched in the mirror as Kassem took on his thick dick, as his muscles rippled in response, a cascade of delight. The force surging within Jamal felt almost destructive; he wanted to take over, for his rhythm to be the one they rode to, but Kassem, for all that he was stuffed with dick, stayed in control. What release could be achieved would arrive at his measure, and Jamal gave into that, to being the vessel of another's pleasure. He came inside Kassem, and Kassem came on his chest, biting off a moan as he slumped down. They stayed together for a minute or ten, softening. Jamal pulled at his matted body hair, licking the excess off his fingers, his pecs a bright mess. He wanted more, but Kassem withdrew from him; shaken, afraid.

You should go, he said. I have to clean.

Crawling in the Sky

I want it all, God help me, I want it all, Cevdat said. Why won't this prick call?

They were on the balcony. Jamal had learned not to pay too much attention to which prick's call was coming. The latest scheme had something to do with a lithium deposit in land he had leased, or with finding investors—no, that had been the last one, and the one before that had to do with astroturf. Currently it had something to do with a movie project. He kept trying to pique Jamal's interest, saying things like, You never know, son, maybe I could get you on board as well? You could talk to your people. And Jamal would tell him again that he was only a transcriber, that he wrote down the mangled words of reality TV contestants for hours on end, every *um* and *but* and *you know*, and no one in the production company he worked for would care about anything he had to say, especially about a random Turkish project. He and the other transcribers didn't even have an office, just a couple of desks in a storage closet. It was tedious work, but it paid well enough to make this trip possible, and so he thought of it with gratitude.

Your father is a poet, did you know? Mehmet said, slinging his arm around his nephew. Jamal was starting to suspect that every Middle Eastern man thought he was a poet.

Oh, you should hear him, his uncle continued. I always said he was too smart for his own good. He should have stayed working in insurance, that's when he had all the money, isn't it? Buying this and that, spoiling those rotten girls, your sisters, you know.

As usual, he was shirtless, and sweating from cleaning. The TV was set to YouTube, playing pop songs in the background. Both he and Cevdat were obsessed with cleanliness in a way that disturbed Jamal, who had only ever seen that in his aunties, and on the rare occasion, even his mother. It set his teeth on edge, their frenzy, the way they seemed more animal than person, an uncontrolled and foaming mass. Everything had to be clean, polished into a glare, in case someone came over, in case someone dared to see them unprepared.

Mehmet dragged on his cigarette. But he's always thinking thinking thinking—he knows three languages, ya! Turkish, Arabic and English. Even reading and writing, mashallah.

Arabic, too?

Mehmet nodded. He studied the Quran in Kuwait, your dad, they don't let just anyone do that. He could be a sheikh if he wanted.

Mehmet seemed to be trying to redirect the conversation to Cevdat's accomplishments, and Jamal wasn't sure if it was because his own disappointment was so transparent, or if it was something his uncle felt just as keenly.

If this comes through, Mem, Cevdat said, I'm getting us each an apartment on the Bosporus. Four hundred square metres. You wait and see.

York ya, Mehmet said. That's too much.

What, why? If you dream small, you'll live small.

You gotta crawl before you walk, you know.

I can do that already—fuck walking, I'll fly. Agitated, he went inside.

Mehmet shook his head after him. They had this argument often. You gotta understand, oğlum, he used to have money. He used to know important people. Once you've had whatever you want, it's hard to go back, isn't it?

Jamal sucked in a breath, pained. He knew then why Kassem had withdrawn from him the other night, and that there was nothing he could do to make it easier. How much longer would it be before he found it impossible to go back? He was already contemplating various ways of staying. Cevdat would be thrilled if he did. He was always trying to get Jamal to become a Turkish citizen officially, and Jamal was always saying no. He had no intention of doing mandatory military service. It would be good for you, son, Cevdat said. And because you have a degree, you would start as an officer!

What he meant was that it would be good for him, it would give him a purpose he currently lacked, to have a son in the military, to have someone who needed him completely, to have a reason not to go back to Australia and face the other children he had abandoned. Jamal still hadn't told him he was a drop-out. He couldn't stay just to fix this man's life when he couldn't even fix his own.

You know oğlum, you can tell your amca anything, Mehmet said softly. I will always love you. Jamal couldn't bear his uncle's blue eyes, the compassion and warmth there. He went inside, joining Cevdat on the smaller, more private balcony adjoining the kitchen.

It looked out over the alley at the back of the building and there was only room for the both of them on it.

I have to go home, Dad.

You are home, Cevdat said. You're not going anywhere. He held up his phone, wagging it with a sly look. One call and I could have you snatched at the airport, believe me.

Jamal believed him, but he didn't say anything, and it was his father who looked away first.

When will you go?

At the end of the week, Jamal said. If you let me. He nudged the old man in the side. After a minute of awkward silence, he told him that the new season of *MasterChef* was crewing up and that's why he'd decided to leave, he needed the money. The lie was spontaneous, but he knew it would work. The pursuit of money was something all of his relatives understood. If he said he was working or studying, they usually left him alone. He did not say that Kassem hadn't been answering any of his messages, that he felt unbearably alone, that he was desperate for a shower, or hell, even a bath—anything that wasn't a bucket and a tap. Cevdat asked him if he knew how to cook, having worked on a show like that, and Jamal rolled his eyes. He said there was a difference between hearing and listening, and that it all just passed through him, barely leaving a trace.

Is it true what Amca said about you being a poet? Jamal said.

Eh, Cevdat said. Everyone's a poet, so what. You know who wrote amazing poems? Your mother. My god. She set my blood on fire, that one. How is she?

Jamal tensed. He didn't like when either of his parents spoke about each other, it was almost always an attempt to rewrite themselves through him and he hated the way that made him an instrument. Neither had ever asked what he thought of the other.

She's okay, he said. She and Moses both lived with Jido in his new housing commission in Villawood, a place Hala sneeringly said was full of drug dealers and junkies, even though she'd been both in her life. She might deal and she might use, but neither defined her. Jamal wished he had that power: to resist definition, to be only what he wanted to be, when and as he pleased. But then, maybe that was only a fantasy. Though she frequently threatened to poison Jido's tea, she hadn't yet; she was his daughter no matter how much she despised him. She cooked for him and cleaned for him, but otherwise stayed in the garage that she'd turned into a bedroom for herself, leaving the men alone in the house. It wasn't lost on Jamal that both his mother and father had ended up back in their parents' house.

I remember when I first met her, Cevdat said, musing. It was at a club called Concrete in Auburn. Your mother was the most beautiful woman in the room by a mile.

And, you know, that wasn't the first time I'd seen her either. I drove my mate home to his place in Redfern one day, and as he got out, she pulled up in a blue Toyota. I'll never forget it because the numberplate was just SEX, and she stepped out holding the hands of two little kids, a boy and a girl, and my god, I thought, who is this incredible woman? Straight away, I said, God please—he looked up to the sky and held his hands out in supplication—please give this woman to me. I was married, son, I knew it was a sin, but I prayed for her anyway. Just like that. You see, Jamal? Allah knows what's in our hearts and he will answer if you ask.

Jamal's teeth were pressed so tight together he was sure they would snap, and his blood roared, as his father continued telling the story of his mundane miracle—that he'd seen her again a week later in a club, that they'd hooked up, and it was a lesson, wasn't it, that you should be careful what you wish for. The revelation cycled through him with startling intensity, and he didn't know whether to laugh or cry at the sheer absurd simplicity of it. Simplicity or arrogance, madness or genius, what do you call it when a man prays *to* God for a sin and claims its deliverance as answer?

They left for the airport before dawn, exiting the fog-wrapped city in silence. Jamal loved fog, the way shapes were hinted at beneath its ethereal waves; he lived like this, pulled along by other forces, dampened and confused. Sometimes the fog would break, and light poured through, but it always returned.

He didn't see Kassem again, though they resumed chatting online when he said he was leaving. They talked through the night, saying nothing serious, mostly sending links to YouTube videos they could laugh at, or make inane comments about. Jamal had no intention of sleeping, he was too anxious about missing his flight. Somehow, it felt like he would only have this one chance to leave, and if he missed it, he would be stuck here forever, sweating, shirtless on the balcony with two other men, all of them swollen and hairy and gleaming.

Around 2am, he wrote: Do you like my hair? Maybe I should visit your dad's shop for a touch-up? He let the implication hang.

I like your hair, Kassem wrote back. So fluffy. Maybe trim the sides? He'll tweeze your nose hairs too, and wax your eyebrows.

The sting of rejection was lost to outrage. What's wrong with my eyebrows?!

Nothing. They're perfect.

I'd let you do it, you know.

You want me to cut your hair?

I want you.

Jamal did not wait for a response, he closed the laptop, feeling exposed. Sometimes he wondered if his fixation on anticipation was as painful as—or even worse than—rejection might be if he allowed it to occur. His father was in the lounge with him, watching TV, while Mehmet slept in the bedroom. They took turns in that hot room, while the other two slept on the cold couches.

Chatting to your girlfriend, eh? Cevdat said, hopefully.

No, Jamal said. My friends back home.

You get this from me, you know. This insomnia shit.

Great, thanks.

Cevdat laughed at his sarcasm and Jamal basked in that, the first time he'd moved the man to such melody. His father looked at him fondly, just for a second, and Jamal tucked that look—a warm light in his brown eyes, the crinkling lines in his skin, the slight lifting of his lips—deep into his spirit, where the image became a feeling, sublime.

Cevdat got out his phone then. You wanted to hear my poetry before. Listen.

And he played a recording of a poem in Turkish, his voice echoing with reverb, a music track added in the background, the whole production of it unabashedly romantic.

What does it mean? Jamal said.

It's a love poem, Cevdat said. But more than that. I don't know how to say it in English. He went back to watching TV, and Jamal dozed until morning.

At Adana airport, despite his protests that he was fine, Cevdat and Mehmet accompanied Jamal past security, speaking in rapid-fire Turkish with the guards who laughed. The waiting area was small and mostly empty, with just the one cafe. People trickled in behind them, and as they did, Cevdat gasped, grabbing his brother's bicep.

Look, Mem, he hissed. Oh my god, it's them. Jamal looked at the line, and saw an old man with a white goatee, and a couple of younger men and women.

Oğlum, this is the cast of the show we were watching the other night! Can you believe it, Mem? Cevdat's eyes were wide and shining. You will be on the same flight as stars! My son, this is your destiny, to be among them, I know it.

Jamal hadn't registered any of the TV shows that had been on, long practised in ignoring the foreign soaps his elders watched, and so it was strange to see his father react to these ordinary-looking people as if they had hidden halos. Cevdat was transformed by awe at this meeting of reality and far-flung dream. Kept saying wow, wow, wow, under his breath, hand on his mouth. Mehmet tried to convince him to meet his idols. They're just people, he said, but Cevdat refused. He didn't want to bother anyone, yet he couldn't look away from these forgettable faces. He was inspired, and it was easy to see why. Jamal had grown up with gamblers, he knew the dazzle of this lightning bolt, which turned chance into omen and omen into destiny.

Cevdat turned to him and said, I've been thinking about that poem, you know. How to say it. It's not quite right, but it's something like: All we are is memory and myth, and memory fades.

III

A Matter of Control

The Right Space

The unexpected thing about suicide was the way it coiled inside you, very much alive, and fought to remain there. It did this by eating your voice because it needed silence to survive, it needed to stay hidden.

Jamal sat at his desk and wrote the words that others said, headphones glued to his head. He hadn't looked anyone in the eye in a week, unless you counted the recorded interviews of contestants in this season of *The Biggest Loser*, and even then, he wasn't really looking at them nor they him, so it didn't matter. If he was spoken to, he answered in grunts or monosyllables. Texts were his lifeline, the messages and emails he sent to the script coordinator and post-production manager explaining that he was going through something but couldn't talk about it, he wasn't in the right space. He didn't know what that space was, or how to get there, but he had heard it spoken of in these offices, he'd picked up the soft leash of this language by listening to thousands of hours of desperate people talking to a producer behind a camera as if the producer was their therapist or the country or God. He couldn't talk about it, couldn't look anyone in the eye, because if he did, he was sure they would see his death there, that shameful snake, and he couldn't bear the possibility that they might take it away from him.

Are you seeing this shit? Dan touched his shoulder, and Jamal glanced over at his desktop, where he was scrolling through an article about Trump's Muslim ban loaded with images of chaotic airport protests and close-ups of the agonised expressions of brown people who were now cut off from their family abroad. It's so fucked up, I'm sorry, man. He said it like it was happening to Jamal, right then and there. Jamal nodded to signal that yes he'd seen it, before turning back to the physical trainer making a fortune off the way people hated their bodies. It wasn't that he didn't care, it was just that his rage had long ago guttered out into a numbness. Every month, every year, there was something like this, and Jamal didn't know how to care about everyone and everything all the time. Dan wanted to commiserate, to be seen commiserating; he wanted to say, I'm Jewish, I get it (as he had before and would again), but Jamal didn't have room to include him, not when they were so far from feeling the same thing, not when he was so focused on figuring out how to die. Unlike Jamal, Dan had wealthy parents. He had no HECS debt, and a mansion he could return to whenever he tired of his pretend independence.

Jamal let himself fade into the rapid hammering of the keyboard, the stop-start pause-rewind of speech; there was something soothing in the monotony of it, the great slabs of text, how for once he could direct the pace. He liked knowing what went into this reality. Behind every episode of television, every fifteen-second slice of on-camera interview, there were hours and hours that went unseen, left on the cutting floor—or, more accurately, logged in dozens of binders, thick with pages Jamal had written and printed for a post-producer to read. Everyone thought these shows were fake, scripted, but the truth was stranger. Each episode was massaged into being. *Don't say this if it isn't true, but would you agree that ...* the field producer would prompt, or, when they heard something they wanted in an organic sentence, *That was great, can you say that again, just the end part? Can you say that without all the awkward pauses?* They poked and prodded until narratives peeked out of the shit, and everyone went home convinced they had been themselves, honest, real.

It was easy to see why this genre was so addictive: the structure of meaning was apparent, the way to massage a life into an arc, to mould a nobody into a somebody by virtue of trials overcome or, even more simply, time spent together. The major downside to the work was how it left him unable to read, to escape into his one comfort drug. At the end of all this writing, the last thing he wanted to do at home was stare at more text. Nor did he have the energy to imagine a different kind of life. Jamal typed until his fingers and wrists and neck and ears and back ached.

I don't know how you do it, Moses said to him once, when he explained the work. And Jamal had replied, I don't know how you dig up roads all day either. They had both trained themselves to be in these positions in some way, Moses wanting to be strong, a man located entirely in his body, his physical usefulness, while Jamal was nothing if not an expert at listening and making of his mind an emptiness.

Ilo checked in with him to see if he was still good to go this weekend, and he sent back a thumbs-up emoji. He left work early and Dan stayed behind, to Jamal's profound relief. Sometimes they did this to get a break from each other in the anonymous crush of public transit. He brought up the photo on Instagram that he'd been fixating on this past week, Kassem smiling with another guy, shirtless at the beach. Was this when the snake had wrapped itself around his throat, or was it a month ago, when he had arrived at Sydney airport, dazed, covered in the film of filth that accrues over an eighteen-hour flight, his world shaken by the ease with which he kept upending his life? Somewhere between there and here, between the sea and the stars, he'd sent his father an email using the plane's internet, telling him the truth. He couldn't leave so abruptly, so like his father, without explaining. He didn't want to become the man.

As the long quarantine line inched forward, he received Cevdat's response:

I had a notion of this, son. I told your amca, I said Mem, I'm afraid Jamal may be gay or bisexual, ask him if you don't believe me. Son my dear son, I was afraid that I was going to hear this from you, I swear I had a feeling. I'm not angry at you but at myself for not being there when you needed me. As long as you're not a homosexual and only longing for the same sex, that means you can overcome this. We men have the potential to act in all sexual activities, son, the main thing in life is that you control your desires and don't cross the boundaries.

That is before even putting the creator in the picture, Heaven and Hell, the Day of Reckoning, and so on. Son I love you, we really need to talk. Your babbanne will never accept this, so this she must never hear about. There's a lot that can be said, I can't stop myself from writing, son this is an act of lust we all can have feelings, it's a matter of control—please talk or write to me, I love you, you're my son.

But no longer his lion, or his king.

Someone nudged his shoulder, and Jamal looked up from his phone to see a customs officer gesturing at him to leave the line. He stepped out, wheeling his suitcase to the secondary security area, where a Somali hijabi was being questioned by an olive-skinned officer while her children watched on. Jamal's officer was a compact Black man named Tyrone, who spoke with an American accent. Tyrone handled Jamal's clothes methodically, then had him open his laptop and phone. He stood there as the man slid through his selfies, his camera roll, in case he had been stupid enough to take an incriminating photo with Al-Qaeda, and there it was, a moment he had forgotten, kissing Kassem on the cheek—his eyes closed, face turned into bliss, while Kassem stared straight into the camera, grinning. Daring. He had been so daring, hadn't he? He had been brave, done the unthinkable like his heroes, travelled alone to the other side of the world. Yes, he had been running from the shambles of his life into the arms of yet another man who didn't know how to love him, but it had still been audacious, still more than anyone expected of him. Despite that, he was back where he started, his memories subject to suspicion.

That's my boyfriend, he blurted, and the lie startled him but not the officer. Tyrone just raised an eyebrow and asked if his boyfriend had ever trained with terrorists.

That lie was tied to the email tied to the sour taste in his mouth. Jamal still hadn't replied to his father, and maybe that was when the silence took root, to save him from choking on all that he wanted to say. He looked out the dirty window at the dark denim of oncoming night, the fairy floss made of streetlights as the train passed. He looked at Kassem's happiness again, at the caption 'besties', which might mean only that but definitely didn't, and felt so ashamed that he was anything but happy for him. The photo beneath it was of his father, Gurkhan, a portly man with a sad smile. He remembered Kassem spitting out, *You have so much*, and felt the first flush of anger stir. He did what he was paid to do then, regurgitated those words; hit send. When he got home to the derelict duplex he rented with Dan, he went straight to his room, took off his pants, and opened Grindr. The first week back, he had to sleep on the couch while Alex got his things together, but after that his privacy was reclaimed.

He stroked himself slowly as he scrolled. Jamal's nipples were hard and he came quickly, thinking of Kassem, thinking of Bilal. Desire—or some other need—still pulsed through his body, restless, unrelieved. He went into the bathroom naked, wanting to get a pic before his dick shrank. He took the photo with practised ease, then another, this time with his body angled to hide the swell of his belly, highlighting the curve of his arse. Tops rarely took an interest; he was too tall, too thick, bearded, manly. It was most often bottoms who went after him, wanting to be dominated. His last message was from an old white man offering to worship his feet, and to pay for the privilege. Jamal had asked how much, and the man tried to hedge, saying, 'bits and pieces', 'a bill here and there', like he didn't already have a broke dad to worry about. He blocked him.

After checking a dozen ignored 'hey' messages, he sent his bare cheeks to the top six. It didn't really matter who was behind the profiles, he only interacted with headless torsos or blank squares—they were mostly brown or black men, or occasionally older whites and religious types who still lived under shame's foot. Thank God. They would want to ruin, or be ruined, in secret, and only he would get to see them open, the widening of their eyes, the rising of sweat-slicked hairy chests as they gave in to what ruled them. No one replied. Nude in the dark with only the dim light of his phone touching the black, he walked over to his window that looked over the street. Knee-high grass waved in the yard. He wondered if it would soften his fall, and decided he should tell Abdul, the landlord, to bring his sheep round to reveal the hard earth again. Abdul didn't waste money on lawnmowers.

Jamal opened the window and leaned out into the cold. The world spun. He wished he could hear the manic song of bats again, but there was nothing. Nothing except eyes in the grass arrowing up at him. He blinked. Yakob, Dan's black three-legged rescue cat, who was not allowed outside, was staring up at him, head cocked, as if to say, Well, what are we going to do about this?

Shit, Jamal said. He threw on some pants and hurried down to let the cat in.

You know you're not supposed to be out there, he said sternly, and stupidly, because it was a cat. Yakob was supremely unconcerned. He plomped onto the dusty wooden floor, exposing his belly for pats. Jamal obliged, and the cat began to rumble like an ancient engine. When he straightened up and headed over to the couch, Yakob scrambled to follow, all three limbs flailing, absent any grace. Jamal's lap soon filled with fur and the cat rumbled again as he scratched behind one notched ear. Feral green eyes slowly squeezed shut, almost reluctantly—a slow close, always snapping back open at the last—as if trying to resist, trying to trust, before shutting finally and ecstatically. At the rattle of keys in the door, Yakob pelted off him, claws digging in painfully for the launch, and Jamal yelled, I see how it is, you little slut.

It's nice to see you too, Dan said, laughing. As he knelt to play with the cat, he asked carefully, You okay, bud?

Instead of answering, Jamal mimed pulling the pin off a grenade and lobbing it. Dan's eyes widened, and he flung himself back from the explosion. The tightness in Jamal's chest loosened enough for him to laugh. He approached the limp body. Dan was an aspiring actor, a theatre nerd with anxiety, and sometimes instead of speaking, they filled pauses with pantomimed violence, kitschy kills that were strangely addictive. Dan lunged forward suddenly with a sword, stabbing at Jamal's gut, side and neck with accompanying sound effects. Jamal groaned and recoiled, miming blood pouring explosively out of him, and they laughed. As he headed to their munted couches, Jamal looped his arms over Dan's head and garrotted him. Dan flailed, choking out his last breath with a splutter, before sliding to the floor in a heap.

Nice one, Jamal said. He helped him up and they flopped onto the couch. He didn't need to explain that he wasn't okay, Dan was more than happy to fill the silence, talking about how crazy the world was (and it was crazy, right, it wasn't always like this, there had once been order of a kind?) before putting on the TV. Jamal sat with him for a time, thinking about how this was the right space, this hour filled with someone else's story on the air, their pain and dynamics the perfect channel for his feelings to pour through without the cost of speaking them. He retreated to his room later, exhausted, but knowing sleep would be a long time coming. He checked his phone, opening a small portal into the always crazy world, alongside a billion other tired, scared people. He fell asleep wondering if one day he would hold Dan as he died and how different it might feel if it were real.

Punishment

Moses found the body. It was unusual for Jido not to be up in the morning before him, already seated in his armchair with the news on, so Moses had looked in the bedroom. Winter cold stilled the air, and the old man was unmoving. Jamal huddled outside the morgue attached to Lakemba mosque, along with a host of his relatives, as Moses told them the story, how his own breath had puffed into the room, how Hala's dog Samson had barked and barked but refused to enter it. How when he was a boy, he'd lived with Jido, and it seemed fitting that he had returned to him in the end, that he'd been there in the hour of his death.

Around them, Arab men stood, most in trackies or jeans, one or two in suits. Jamal didn't know most of them, beyond a name or bloodline here and there, and he wasn't alone in that; they stood in half-circles, cliques that only a few moved between. Aside from Jamal, the crescent around Moses included Jihad and Ali. Jihad looked like a Picnic bar, brown and bulging out of his singlet, while Ali had grown a long craggy beard, his upper lip shaved in the Sunni way. Both were married and had children.

Jamal scratched his itchy stubble; he'd shaved before flying, in the vain hope it would make travelling easier, and decided to keep the shadow because it made him feel more dashing than destitute.

At least you didn't find out by Facebook, Jamal said under his breath. Jihad's status update this morning had read: My jido passed away, Allah yerhamou. *God forgive him.* Sad face emoji. The comments a stream of shock and Inna lillahi wa inna illahi rajuns. *From God we come and to God we return.*

What? Moses looked at him directly and Jamal shifted slightly to the side.

Nothing. I said at least you got to spend more time with him, this past year.

Not really, Moses said. I barely saw him, he'd be asleep by the time I got home.

He dug up roads from six to six, uncovering gas and water pipes that needed fixing, as part of their cousin Emad's crew. He had come a long way since serving time in Silverwater and finishing his sentence at home, the latter being worse, he'd said, because he was the only one trapped, surrounded by freedoms everyone else had. The others still reckoned him a kid, and they always would while he was unmarried. Ali had already given Moses a lecture about this in the thirty minutes they'd been there. You've had three KKs already, stop fucking around, bro, he said.

Nah, come on, it was Fatihas only, Moses said, injured.

Kateb kitab, Fatiha, same shit—it's a commitment, Ali growled.

Moses bowed his head at the correction, but he was smiling, the light gleaming on the copper threads in his trimmed beard. He was too pretty for his own good, and women still flocked to him. They didn't say anything about marriage to Jamal.

I heard you were in Turkey, cuz, Ali said, stretching his arms behind his head. Unlike their parents, who had been dragged to the other side of the world, Jamal's generation rarely left the area, let alone the country. None of them had been further than Queensland. They got married and moved into houses as close to their mothers as possible, making clusters of convenience and closeness, not unlike how they were standing now. Jamal sometimes wondered if a map of Lebanon's villages before the war would match where families had ended up in Sydney, if they had unconsciously replicated a way of being that no longer existed.

Yeah, to see my dad, Jamal said. He loved how one sentence could recast a confused, spontaneous and awkward trip into the deliberate execution of a plan. Was it a lie? He couldn't be sure. His intentions were rarely clear, even to him, and this was one of many reasons he spent so long turning over his past, looking for evidence of a plan, of something worth salvaging.

Aw yeah, how was he? Ali said.

Jamal shrugged. He's a flop, he said, and they cracked up. Wallah, he doesn't do anything, doesn't have a job, full lost case.

Yeah, well, you'd know, Moses said, and they laughed again. There was no hostility in it, they all knew he was the odd one, and so long as the oddness went unnamed, it was acceptable.

They're all like that, Moses added. I met mine, too. Biggest mistake. He's fried.

No way, he's out? Jamal said. He dimly recalled Abraham, the man who had driven their mother to jump, the man Jido would not let her divorce even after that. It was their teyta who forced him to relent, threatening to leave him if he didn't give Hala permission.

Nah he's back Inside, Moses said. He prefers it.

Jihad chuckled. Why not, it's a family tradition. Even Jido did time, Allah yerhamou.

What? Jamal said. This was new to him.

Yeah, what do you mean? Moses said. I think my dad got him into the game.

Jido was the OG, Jihad said. He did ten years, cuz.

Shut the fuck up, Ali said. Show some respect, you gronks.

They quieted, and in the quiet, Jamal struggled to regather the torn threads of his family story. He pictured his mother, a little girl taken from Lebanon to Australia, forced to grow up in the shadow of prison, and suddenly her fractured fury made more sense to him.

Should we go in? Jamal said, and Ali said not yet. Their uncles were inside the morgue, washing their father's body. Kholo Ahmad had flown in from Melbourne, and when Jamal first saw him—a bald man with a salt-and-pepper beard—he'd frozen, thinking he was Mahmoud, the first man who had failed to father him. No one was crying, and the absence of that visible and vocal grieving was strange. He only had two other funerals to go by, his grandmother's and Jihad's baby, on opposite ends of life's experience, yet they had been equally dense with sorrow, enough for every witness to sink into, to become stone. This day was clear and cold and weightless.

Kholo Khadeer came out of the morgue, his cheeks drooping, waxen. His eyes were red, and Jamal heard him saying again to Jihad, *This isn't love*, how hoarse his voice had been, because seeing his nephew broken so profoundly monstered his own heart. Jamal turned away from his uncle. He hadn't spoken to him in years, and he had no intention of doing so now.

The men prayed on the ground floor of the mosque, with the women in another room. In front of them was a metal casket, wrapped in a green tapestry threaded with golden Arabic that Jamal couldn't read. Afterwards, they followed the body to Rookwood cemetery, a sprawling expanse of grassy graves, right down to the back where the green turned to brown. This was the new Muslim section, pushing up against the gate. Rookwood was the largest cemetery in the Southern Hemisphere and it was running out of space for their dead. Next to a row of rumpled red clay, the plunging metal jaw of an excavator rested. In one of the earlier settled rows, his grandmother's grave had been undone into green and red clumps. The metal casket was opened, and three sons, Kholo Ahmad, Kholo Buktikh and Kholo Khadeer, carried their cloth-wrapped father out to place above his wife. As Kholo Ahmad descended into the grave first, Jamal remembered how his grandfather had changed when Teyta died, how he'd dwindled, and wept often. He had visited Aunty Rania's house every day in those last months, trying to play the doting husband next to his witless wife, but she would grab on to her walker, shaking, dragging her rotting leg, trying to get away from him. Her mind might have gone, but her muscles and blood had their own unerasable memory.

Jamal was last in a long line of boys and men to grab a clod of dirt and throw a fistful down on the deceased. He wondered if any of these men would be here for his body come the day he returned to earth. As he walked back and the women came forward, led by his aunties, Jamal noticed his mother wasn't among them. He asked

Moses where she was, and he shrugged.

Who knows, bro. She's a disaster. He said he was going to stay with Kholto Nazeero now, that he didn't know and didn't care what Hala was going to do as long as it didn't include him, and then he took off to go back to work.

Everyone's going to my mum's, cuz, do you need a lift? Jihad said. I just need to visit my son first.

Jamal nodded and followed him. Lana was waiting for them by their car, a Maso woman with her hair tied back in a bun and a heart-shaped face, her belly swollen with child. Jihad had been disqualified from driving years ago, so it was Lana who drove them up to the old Muslim section. The two walked down to where Mahmoud was buried, with baby Ali on top of him, marked by a small square of white stones roughly the size of a man's foot. Jamal stayed in the car. He had prayed above that grave once and he would again, but now was not the time. When they came back, Lana was crying, and Jihad enraged. She sat in the driver's seat, weeping into her woollen sleeve, unable to start the car.

Stop fucking crying! Jihad screamed, punching the dashboard in a rapid rain. How many times have I told your family, you can't put these fucking things on a grave? He shook a teddy bear cradling a love heart at her. His eyes were wet and crazed.

My mum doesn't understand, Lana wailed, bending over the steering wheel in a flood. They had always been like this, on the edge of hysteria, or driven within it. As teenagers, they called each other every day and screamed abuse, who are you with, you're fucking around I know you are, fucken slut, fucken shit cunt, I'm gonna kill you, I'm gonna kill myself: drunk on their own desire, unable whatsoever to be apart. It was the most sickening thing Jamal had ever witnessed, and it had made him pale with jealousy. He thought they'd calmed with marriage and age, but maybe not. It wasn't their volume now which bothered him, but confusion, and the clotted ache of wanting to comfort them but knowing he couldn't.

Shu sorred? he said. I don't get it.

Jihad heaved a breath, hitched on a sob of his own. Anything with a form can be possessed, cuz. Angels won't visit a place with something like this, all right—because of her jahsheh of a mum, angels haven't been visiting my son, he said, crushing the bear in his hands, spit flecking his lips. Jamal bowed his head, turning his palms up, and prayed. He didn't know what else to do. They were the last to leave the cemetery.

&

Rania's house leaked smoke laced with the smell of grilled meats. Cars were piled up outside, and tables had been put into the yard, stacked with aluminium trays of food. As light waxed the patriarch's wake, his daughter fed the village. He hugged Fatima, who had grown into a woman, competent and purposeful, and she accepted it with the same brisk ease she accepted hugs from the children clinging to her legs.

You okay? he said, and she snorted. Oh yeah, I'm perfect, my husband was meant to be back with the drinks ten minutes ago and is probably lost, these little demons won't leave me alone, there's gonna be a massive mess that I'll have to clean before going home and doing it all over again, and meanwhile, Jido was a fucking monster and I don't want to be here. Aside from that, I'm just fucking peachy. Humdulilah.

They laughed, but his skin prickled with unease at the vehemence that clipped the word *monster.* As the youngest, Fatima should not have been fielding all this alone, but Sara didn't talk to her siblings anymore, not since her criminal of a husband ripped them off and blood was almost spilled on the steps of the house. Jamal was only getting in Fatima's way, so he stayed out on the driveway, apart from his aunties and uncles, their nonstop stream of ahwa and ash. He was not ready to be back here. One of the many reasons he hated being back in the area was the deluge of memory and judgement it provoked. Gravel crunched as Jihad came to a stop next to him.

Why aren't you coming inside? he said, sparking up.

Jamal eyed the cigarette wearily. Just once he'd like to leave a family visit without breathing like a man who'd been trapped in a burning house.

I don't wanna speak to anyone, he said, gollying on the grass. How'd you manage this anyway? He indicated with his chin the sleek black SUV parked on the kerb, and Jihad's eyes lit up.

She's sexy, uh? Compo, cuz. Didn't my mum tell ya? AC unit clipped me at the warehouse last year. Fell from the top shelf. His chin jutted out with pride. I could have died, but it just fucked up my spine, subhanallah.

Subhanallah. *God is perfect.*

Oof, Jamal said. How bad is it?

He shrugged. Ask my wife, bro. I need a whole pharmacy just to get to sleep, and I still scream. Jihad glanced up and down the street, the muscles in his neck and shoulders suddenly bunched up, as if an enemy might be near.

You know what, fuck it, jump in. He unlocked the doors and slid into the driver's seat. Jamal followed, hostage to a kind of animal obedience. As the engine revved, the flyscreen crashed open and Lana came tearing out.

What are you doing, you dickhead, what the fuck—she screamed, and Jihad stuck his head out the window and screamed back, Skittie wuleh, get back inside, don't you fucken disrespect me like that, and then the radio was blasting *Yeezus* and he reversed into the street. Jihad relaxed as they cruised up the road, all the creases in his face smoothed over, erasing years; he looked at ease behind the wheel, like Cevdat did, like Ali and even Fatima did, in a way Jamal never would.

I didn't know she still got like that, Jamal said, shouting over the music.

Yeah, cuz, what do you mean, she keeps me on my toes, Jihad said, cracking a fierce smile. His jagged black eyebrows always made him look angry, but when he smiled, you could see the world in his brown eyes.

His phone rang, beaming Lana's stern white wog face into the car's display panel. He answered it quickly. Listen, bub, I'm just going to the shops to get a V and smokes, all right, only around the corner, all right. We just came this way and we didn't see any coppers. All right? You want anything? Yullah, okay yullah, love you, bye.

Every time he said *all right* he leaned into it, hunching closer to the phone, like he could force her to feel his sincerity, like his life depended on this moment. Each inch of road they crossed was steeped in their history, it beaded the gravel, dewed the air. There was Ryan's house, Jamal's boyhood best friend, a Koori kid who moved away when Jamal was eight. He rarely saw Ryan after that, except at footy matches. Last Jamal heard about them was Ryan's mother on TV, crying in front of flashing cameras, saying her boy had been jumped, his head cracked open, and for what? The first lockdowns came soon after that. The news called it an epidemic of violence, of coward punches. Aunty Rania said alcohol was to blame, O God knows how the khaffeir loved their poison. There was Mesake's house, his best friend after Ryan, a Tongan boy with a flat nose and a smile that made Jamal's heart accelerate; last he heard, Mesake had crashed a car into a tree, drunk driving on parole and breaking his leg in the process.

Have you seen my mum lately? Jamal said, turning down the music. He knew Jihad and Hala did shit together sometimes, either to sell product or to get high deep into the ugly hours.

Jihad's shoulder twitched. Nah, bro. You know I love your mum, wallah she's got the best heart, better than anyone's, but straight out she's not right in the head. He looked at Jamal from the corner of his eye, then away again. They were on Wonga Road, houses on one side, fields plonked with cows on the other; there were the radio towers, too, that reared up into the sky, and past the fields, a cement lot of warehouses used for God knows what. They sped past, turning onto Hill Road and coming to Lurnea shops, where two small strip malls faced each other. On his right, the old tennis courts had been demolished, a new holistic health centre was being developed, and on the left, the half-built skeleton of a new apartment block leered at the shops.

Did you know she's been helping Kholo Khadeer with his yard for the past few months? Jamal said. As he'd stood on the edge of the driveway, he'd been listening to his aunties and uncles talk, snatching gossip off the wind.

She asked him if she could stay in his garage for a couple days, because Centrelink are kicking her out now Jido's dead. And that fucking kalb said no. Anger pulsed in his body: his teeth ached with it. Why the fuck does no one in this family help her?

Jihad pulled into the shops on the right, where Said's Tobacconist had faithfully served their family for many years, next door to a supermarket and a Lebanese bakery that made half-decent manoush, so the whole place smelled like a mixture of cigarettes, oil and piss. The TAB he'd known was gone.

Look, bro, where the fuck have you even been? Jihad jerked the car to a stop, turning his red-shot eyes onto Jamal. You wanna talk about this now? First of all, yeah, watch your fucken tone or I'll kasr rohsok, and secondly, I've been there for her when you haven't, all because you like sucking dick and couldn't shut up about it, so don't think you can say shit to me, you little gronk.

Jamal stared, shocked. Any lingering doubt about what his cousin knew of him vanished. Why are you geeing up like I came at you? I'm talking about Kholo Khadeer, Ahmad and them.

Like that doesn't include my mum, eh? Jihad sneered. Then he abruptly deflated. We're not kids anymore, bro, he said. Wake up to yourself. He slammed the car door as he got out, sandals slapping as he walked into the supermarket. Jamal struggled to get his breath back as a great fist closed around his lungs. The worst part was that he couldn't dismiss Jihad's words. He still thought of his uncles and aunties as the adults, the ones who were meant to take care of each other and everyone, despite the fact that they never had. How much longer could he justify staying away, holding himself apart?

He accepted that his fear of confrontation made him passive, but had failed to consider even that as a choice with consequences. Some part of him still clung to invisibility, as if invisibility didn't carry a cost. Like the night when Kholo Khadeer visited Rania, not long after Moses went to stay with him, and the adults were all talking while Jamal was in the corner, reading a book. The rhythm of their conversation had changed, becoming sharper, slowly dragging Jamal's attention back to reality, where he heard his uncle say over Rania's protests—

What do you mean just let it go, my sister's a whore!

Yeee, his wife said, and Aunty Rania, her face blank with shock, tsked.

Hatha subbi hon, she said. *The boy is here.*

Khadeer glanced over then, noticing Jamal trying hard to seem engrossed in his book, but it was too late. A red flush crawled up his uncle's fat neck.

I don't care, I don't care, he said. She was my sister first.

Jamal wondered now if his uncle would still make that argument, still claim that hierarchy of care. He doubted it. The older he got the more he realised that the one skill every person learned to perfect was rationalising whatever was most convenient for them in that moment.

He turned his attention to the five Lebs in trackies outside the bakery, scratching their balls, smoking. Watching them, their easy camaraderie, calmed him. When he came back out, Jihad went over to them, shaking their hands with loud dramatic slaps, and in seconds his scratchy chuckling laugh sprayed out over the carpark. Maybe he knew them, but there was every chance he didn't. Nothing stopped Jamal from joining them except the thought that they might know what he was, and that rejection and abuse would follow. Nothing stopped him except himself. That's what Jihad meant: you blame us, but you did this to yourself. It was only partly true, but even a partial truth can wound, and Jamal heard the pain in his words. They had slept in the same room, shoulder to shoulder, in Rania's house of smoke. His aunty, his mother; cousins closer than brothers. Until Jamal was taken away and, after that, left them all behind. Now, aside from the odd Facebook or WhatsApp message, Jamal didn't visit, nor was he visited.

He lurched out of the car, closing the door behind him, sidling around to stand in front of the black bonnet. All the Lebs turned and stared. In an instant, every demon in his blood bayed. You're nothing, ya little faggot, little weirdo, *Aussie*, son of a Turk, khaffeir, Jew! He twisted, ready to go back, and that's when he saw the patrol car creep into view, and turn slowly into the strip. Hot liquid lead poured down his throat. Another reason Jamal hated being back: this feeling following him, the acid taste of terror on his tongue. The copper leaning out the window looked like his face was on fire, his ginger head and beard brushed into flame by the sun.

Who let the dogs out, rou, rou! Jihad sang, thrusting his hips out. He laughed at himself, and Jamal joined him uneasily. No one else laughed. These guys weren't feeling it, they weren't looking the cop in the eyes, their heads were down, they were stubbing their cigarettes out. Jamal hadn't noticed it at first, but these men—

and they were men, not boys—looked defeated. Two went back into the bakery and the other three took off across the road.

Always the joker, ey. Where's your missus, Ji? the cop said.

What? Jihad said, the humour leeched out of him.

I see her car, the cop said. But I don't see her. I'd hate to think you were out driving unlicensed again, that'd be the real joke.

Nah Dennis, no way, as if, you know me. Jihad said it casual, but his eyes tightened. He was afraid, and the copper was pleased.

My cuz here is driving. Jihad's hand pointed out, his finger a loaded gun.

The copper looked Jamal over for a long minute. If he asked for his licence, it was all over: Jamal had never had one. It had once been the biggest thorn his family dug into his side—to be able to drive was an enormous benefit, and more than a status symbol, it meant you could be useful, instead of a burden. He thought about how relieved he would be if that became the biggest problem for them again.

Take a picture ya, it'll last longer, Jihad said. Shu, you want his number or something? You're in luck, bro, he's a big fag, this one. Laughing, he walked over to the passenger side of the car and got in. Yullah Jamal, let's go.

As the cop rolled his eyes, then his window up, Jamal got into the driver's seat and buckled himself in. He sat there, heart pounding, watching as they left. Jihad passed the keys over, and Jamal put them into the ignition. He was numb. Jihad was doing in an hour what he hadn't the courage to do in over a decade: setting ablaze a lifetime of avoidance, side-eyes and coded judgement. He turned the key, and the engine roared to life.

You're gonna have to drive us home, cuz, Jihad said. His voice was soft, the harsh edge dropped. Don't worry, I'll guide you, all right.

Bismillah, Jamal said with a shaky breath. If we survive, I'm going to kill you.

Ooouu, he's religious now! Mashallah, it's a miracle, Jihad said. Yullah, sheikh, put it in reverse, nice and easy now.

He had only ever had three driving lessons as a teenager. One with Moses, where they made it halfway down the road before Jamal noticed a spider on the inside of his door, screamed, and flung himself out onto the road, almost crashing Moses's precious white Nissan Skyline into the kerb. The second time with Abu Omar, a family friend with one good eye and the hairiest mole in the world on his chin, who had Jamal drive him around to see his mates in the area, a bunch of other old uncles with nothing to do, and to get his groceries. The third time, on the highway with a stranger, surrounded by cars and trucks hurtling past at terrifying speeds, left him shaking and sweating. After that, he quit.

The SUV felt huge and menacing. It lurched forward under his heavy feet.

Slowly, slowly! Jihad said. I don't wanna die in this fucking carpark, what a bahedleh.

The little green cedar tree swayed on the rear-view mirror as Jihad gave instructions. Jamal didn't know where his cousin got his nerve from, how he could look a cop in the eye at all, let alone make a joke. He drove slow, terror alive in every cell of his body. He'd always been clumsy, and no matter how hard he tried to be more careful, more awake, more focused, there were too many holes inside him and he kept falling into them and out of the present. How could he trust himself with a two-tonne weapon, what if he froze in a moment that required split-second decision-making?

As they drove up Hill Road, slow as a dying turtle, a lowered blue Suzuki ripped around to overtake, beeping furiously, and Jihad stuck his head out the window and roared, Yeah you're a fucken hero, bro! then rubbernecked back inside. What a gronk, thinks he's all that in his little shitbox. Wallahi, you couldn't pay me to drive it.

Jamal's pulse throbbed out a frantic Morse code, thudding hard as a slingshot.

Straight out, cuz, Jihad said. You know I don't get this gay shit, but you're my brother and I love ya. Just make sure you never tell my mum, he added. She'd flip.

Jamal could only nod, because all he was thinking about was his slippery grip on the wheel and how, at any minute, things could spin out of control. After a nerve-racking twenty minutes, he managed to get them back home alive and unarrested. His pits stank and he was dripping wet, but they had made it. Jihad whooped and clapped him on the back, shouting, That's it, cuzza! I knew you had it in ya! capering around like a man newly freed from shackles, shiny green bottle of V in hand. All the cars were gone, except for Aunty Rania's silver Hyundai. Jihad surveyed the emptied yard with satisfaction.

See, they're like locusts, cuz, you just have to wait them out.

Jamal seriously doubted that was the way to deal with locusts, but he was too tired to argue. He sagged onto the driveway with relief, feeling the cement warmed by the sun against his back, the light gone, swarms of insects dancing behind his eyelids.

If You Are Pleased

Jamal asked Aunty Rania if he could stay the night. He was too drained to hike back to Stanmore. His cousins had long been married off and were renting in nearby streets, so there was room. You still have your key, don't you? she said, and he smiled. Her door had always been open to him. The problem with him was the same as it had always been: he wanted more from home than brick and mortar. He wanted to be safe in his own body, which, while connected to time, was impossible. Especially here. One day back and he'd already had a brush with cops. You couldn't live here and not embody a certain recklessness. It was in the air, a vestige of the wars that flung his people here, the product of colonial violence, or both. How many bodies were in the mud beneath this house?

Aunty Rania said it used to be owned by the army, that's why it was brick and not fibro. Or at least it had been before she cement-rendered it, like most other Arabs in Western Sydney, to make the walls smooth and beige and seamless, a strange and ugly conformity. He said as much once to Hala, who considered herself a font of all things fashion and loved to tear into bad taste, but she shook her head.

You can't blame them, she'd said. Half of them think they're gonna be bombed again. Plus, anything's better than this hideous brick.

Inside, the house was tiled with large unbroken slate grey squares. Big black leather recliners filled the lounge and a flat-screen TV dominated the wall. A square table that was too large for the adjacent dining alcove had replaced the simple oak-brown table he remembered, with its arm-thick plastic cover over a lacy white sheet, that old wog sheikh. It looked like an IKEA catalogue had invaded Rania's house. Everything shone with a grating, prefabricated gleam. She was sitting in her armchair, in her fluffy pink pyjamas, her hijab off, hair tied back in a grey-brown bun. She saw him looking around, and pride beamed out of her pores.

It's not like it used to be, huh? Humdulilah.

Jamal echoed her with a sadness she didn't, and maybe couldn't, feel. It was built and beaten into them to be house-proud and to be hospitable, no matter how little there was to share, no matter how tired their hands, how bent their spine, how cracked the floor. How you lived reflected who you were, after all. It was possible she hated the old furniture he thought of fondly, and that whenever people were visiting she'd felt self-conscious. Fatima's payout finally came through, Aunty Rania told him. It only took the better part of two decades. Multiple surgeries and endless court appearances later, Fatima got a hundred grand for her pain, her shortened leg. She bought a car, and clothes, and decked out her mum's home. She paid for the cement-rendering, too, and now she had nothing left.

No, she doesn't have nothing, you stupid boy, Aunty Rania said, thrusting her lit cigarette at him. She has a husband, humdulilah, a very nice boy, and two beautiful kids. What do you have?

None of the above, Jamal said.

That's right, nothing! Oh, God knows I pray for you, she said.

Jamal sighed. Kholto, what's going on with my mum?

You know how she is, Rania said wearily. I warned her to get it in writing from Centrelink that she could stay if he died, but did she? No. Now look.

Despite her words, she seemed somehow satisfied.

Can't she stay here? he said, knowing already the answer was no. They were either the closest sisters or the most bitter enemies, depending on the day of the week.

Rania shook her head. I'm done taking care of everyone. I told you, things aren't like they used to be. I'm getting old, Jamal.

An uncomfortable silence settled on them. He could tell she was waiting for him to leave, to offer a way out, as he would normally do. He always fled discomfort, thinking it originated in him and was his alone. He was starting to think it was not innate, and he might have only been picking up what was projected around him, as his presence was enough to disturb his family, to shake loose what they tried to keep buried.

My dad told me that my mum deliberately got pregnant, he said. Did you warn her about that too?

Rania shifted in her seat. I don't know about that, she said. But I told her to get an abortion, you know. You're lucky she didn't listen, astugfirullah.

Jamal stared in disbelief. Saint Rania, the holier-than-thou sister, had been the one to suggest abortion? And his mother, the rebel, the dark sheep of the family, had been the one to refuse? He did the maths quickly in his head: Hala was nineteen when she had him, to a man who didn't want either of them, and this was after her first failed marriage to a junkie who beat her half to death. He did not understand her choice.

That's when she changed, you know, Rania said. Your dad's wife put a curse on her. You weren't even born yet. One of the neighbours in the unit, Mona, swears she saw some hijabis throwing sand across the doorway of the building. When you walk across the sand, the writing they put on you takes hold. I wouldn't believe it if I hadn't seen it myself, wallah, my sister changed forever after the spirits they put on her. She became uncontrollable, dark.

A couple of months later, your dad dropped you off here, Rania continued. That was Allah's way of punishing me for what I said, see? Humdulilah.

Of course Rania saw her sister's change as the result of a curse from another woman, and not another betrayal by a man, another love turned wound. He could see why Hala had run away from them all, but now the question he'd carried all these years changed to: *what brought you back?* She would have been his age when she returned. Jamal got up unsteadily. Ibn haram, o ya ibn haram. He'd long known he was a son of sin, but he had never thought to ask to whom the sin belonged.

Rania looked up at him, sorrow etched on her face. Your mum did her best, you know, wallah she did.

He didn't know which woman she was talking about.

I'm going to sleep, he said. As he passed her armchair, he kissed her cheek.

Goodnight, immi.

He let himself into Ali's old bedroom. It was here he'd last seen his grandmother and held her stiff body and kissed her cold forehead on the morning of her death. His old room was at the other end of the hallway, but Rania used it now for storage and to do her sewing. She had a side hustle sewing prayer clothes for Islamic schools, even though she complained that she was too old and tired to be working still, ya Allah, the doctors said her knees and hips and ankles were paper thin, she'd worn them down to nothing, she had to rest, to take it easy. If only she knew what those words meant.

Jamal crashed onto the bed, closing the door with a flick of his foot. In the room was a back-up freezer, an old white block that used to be in the kitchen before being replaced by a silver monochrome monster that had too many buttons and kept threatening to tell him the weather. On top of the old freezer was a small TV, which he switched on. He heard Rania turn hers on too, playing a Turkish soap—dubbed over in Arabic—at full blare because she was nearly deaf and refused to wear hearing aids.

If I put 'em in I can hear the neighbours! she complained.

Rather than compete, Jamal put his on mute, let the captions play. He tugged aside the white curtains and peered out into the inky blue. Distant radio towers scaled the night, a series of red eyes glinting up to the tip; those eyes had haunted his sleep once, but he felt nothing now. The familiar fear had become familiar only, a small part of his lonely body.

Kholto Rania was asleep by 9.30, after the last prayer and last cigarette. She was a creature of habit, her ways set in stone, a stone Jamal knew better than any. He let himself out in silence, careful to turn off the porch spotlight that blared out warning of anyone approaching or leaving. He flipped his hoodie up to cover his head, the cold burn of his fade, and headed towards Bilal's house. Jihad had said he would be there tonight to play 400, the old card game their uncles frequently brawled over, giving it a marker of manhood, of seriousness and intelligence that they'd craved for themselves and had taken up as soon as they could. It helped that they had started years before any of them got phones of their own, let alone a home computer, and it helped even more that it was a good way to take each other's money. In the beginning, though, it was all about hearts, the trump suit, and a circle of boys crowned in smoke, slapping cards down like bombs.

Bilal's house was on a winding back road that led to Lurnea High or Casula Public, depending on which way you turned at the end. He had gone to the latter, but not the former, despite the fact it was closest to them. It struck him as odd now that he'd attended Liverpool Boys, catching a bus to that gated place of long halls and muted brick and stone. Fibro demountable rooms had been added as the diasporas spooled in from the wounds of the world. Principal Egghead once told them proudly that the student body spoke seventy-nine languages, as though he had planned it that way, as though he wanted a medal for it. It was a pride no one else felt. Even the teachers were poor. Mr G didn't have a car, Mr Loukakis lived in the PE staffroom when his wife kicked him out, and the boys burned down the front office not once, not twice, but three times, as if to force them to renovate it. Thinking back on the boys as thwarted interior decorators had Jamal cackling as he went up Bilal's driveway.

It wasn't actually Bilal's, but Jamal so rarely saw his parents there that it was hard to separate the building from Bilal himself, how he occupied it. His dad had another house in Lebanon and worked in both countries, and his mum had a busy schedule of other lonely women to pester every day. Like Rania, she would visit the other women her age for tea, which took about two hours and involved cup readings, dream interpretations, and gossip. A loud shout of light spilled from the garage pad, and Bilal and Jihad were sitting on the couch inside. Fresh air violated the room, swirling an off-putting cocktail of Lynx body spray and the fake citrus scent common to cleaning products. Next to Jihad sat Osman, Bilal's neighbour, who was slightly older, a bony man with shifty eyes, crouched over a blue crate like a crab.

What are you laughing at, you psycho? Osman said, squinting at Jamal as he came out of the dark.

Nothing. Just thinking about Livo Boys, Jamal said.

He's a spinner this one, Jihad said to Osman. This majnun would walk from his house up near Hoxton Park Road all the way to my house, at two or three in the morning. Is that normal?

Wasn't my fault, Jamal said defensively. I couldn't sleep.

Osman ignored that. What about Livo Boys? he said. He'd been in Ali's year and he carried with him the same sense of threat, a readiness to do harm you could feel from a mile away.

Nah nothing, Jamal said. It's just weird how Lurnea High is around the corner, but we all went to Livo.

Not me, Jihad said, I went to Casula High.

You guys don't know shit, Osman said, scratching his pimply goatee. Ali and I *did* go to Lurnea at the start. We were the only Lebs in the school, and it was packed with full Nazis who bashed us every day, so our mums sent us to Livo instead.

There, Jamal knew, that dynamic reversed. It was the Lebs who dealt out beltings. No wonder he and Ali scared the shit out of everyone. They had taken every flogging the white boys had given them, and regurgitated it on others. There were few white people in the area now and the remnants were either tenacious racists, desperately povo or both, like the Hunters. It was mostly Arabs, Pasifikas, Aboriginals, and Asians, with the occasional old-school Greek or Italian who couldn't afford to move out when the others came in.

Osman shook his head. You wouldn't believe how fast it changed, bro, he said. Only six years, but everything was different. Yullah, let's play already.

The game 400 was based on one suit: hearts over everything. Within each suit, ace was highest, and two the lowest. The deck was split evenly among four, and based on your hand, you made a prediction on how many tricks you thought you could win. The objective was to match your prediction. They played in teams. Osman and Jamal against Bilal and Jihad, which made for a tense hour because Oz took it seriously and Jamal was rusty, but they won almost as often as they lost, all of them yelling and taking great satisfaction in volume, in calling each other gronks and shit cunts and lost cases, geeing each other up, swapping this gentle hostility that could at any moment arm itself, spill out of the bounds of their spit, and become something alive that demanded they fight for real. Or else laugh with their whole bodies and truly come close to holiness. If memory served him, they were godly far more than they split each other's lips.

Jamal chanced a look at Bilal's lips. They had never kissed, and the thought had not occurred until now that he might even want that. Everything about Bilal was thick, hairy, solid. He hadn't said anything when Jamal showed up, but his eyes were often on him. After about an hour, Osman got a phone call and he stared down his beak of a nose at them, and said, One sec, boys.

He trotted out into the dark, opening his bumbag as he went. Headlights flared and a car pulled up in front of the house. When he came back, Jamal saw he had a dozen little bags of pot and pills in his bumbag, alongside a roll of cash.

Shu, you want some? he said, seeing the look.

Nah, Jamal said. I'm good. He had spent more than a thousand and one nights in his mother's lounge room as she got high, nights where all he ate was her smoke and they sank into the glimmer of blue-white images; it held no mystery for him and no appeal.

You sure, bro? Genuine concern carried through Osman's voice, the same kind of generous giving that suffused Aunty Rania's voice when she asked if Jamal was still hungry, or wanted another helping. I'll give it to ya, no worries, wallahi.

He had faced this choice a million times and felt the splinter driven deeper every time he refused, every time he passed the blunt, whether in the Inner West or Lurnea, with middle-class whites or broke brothers. Jamal couldn't say why he agreed on this occasion, but he pocketed it, and noticed Bilal twitch as if he might say something, noticed the tightening of his lips as he swallowed it down.

Oof, if Jemz is getting into it, you know shit's serious, Jihad said and laughed. Onya, cuz. Yullah, bust out the bong. He took his own advice and had his mouth over a thick shaft in a second, sucking up the smoke to the sound of bubbles. Jamal waved it away when it was offered to him.

I've been hanging for this all day, Jihad said with a sigh. Nothing like the cemetery to scare the shit out of you.

Osman agreed. The grave scares me more than the hellfire, I swear.

Me too, bro, Jihad said. I need to get my deen right. They say it comes in threes, you know. The whole time I was there, I was thinking, please ya Allah, only take me if you're pleased with me.

Sorry about your jido, boys, Bilal said softly. Allah yerhamou.

Osman blew rings out. I thought youse were cousins?

We are, I think, Jamal said, confused.

No, Jihad said. He's *my* cousin. On my dad's side. You're like second or third or some shit. Like Zakky and Osama, remember them?

Jamal burst out laughing, he couldn't help it, because of course he'd been wrong about this, too. It seemed he couldn't stop making family up. The others laughed with him, because they were high, teasing him that he couldn't handle their residue, but it didn't bother him. Jihad and Osman left soon after. Jamal stayed, and Bilal let him. Bilal revealed his dad was coming back, and that he had a bride in mind for him. Jamal could hear in Bilal's heavy voice the first sign of serious worry. He was used to his independence, and his dad's return meant an end to that. Jamal got up and pulled the garage door lever; it rattled down behind him like a snake. He knelt on the hard concrete and said, Take me only if you are pleased with me—and before he was halfway through, Bilal grabbed him by the neck and dragged him over to the couch. Jamal undid his jeans, pulling his pants down. Bilal tongued his arse, then bent him over the armrest and fucked him hard, his long dick lancing pain and pleasure deep into Jamal's gut. He struggled to hold on to the peeling cushions, moaning like a bitch.

God, he said, drooling onto his hands. Come in me, please.

Later, as they lay naked on the couch, Jamal asked Bilal if he ever thought about coming out.

To what? he said. Nah, I'm good right here, bro. He sounded comfortable and confident. Jamal's ear was pressed to his chest, and he could hear the solid slow thump of his heart. He kissed his brown nipple, idly twirling a finger through his chest hairs. *I'm good right here.* That was the key, he thought. Jamal was not good, not okay, not here, not in a share house, not overseas, not anywhere. There was a snake in his eyes and it was trying to kill him. He had come out to his father as a practice run, powered away from him by literal jet engines, and it had still not been enough. He had to pierce every silence in his life, every unsaid bubble, if he was going to live.

Jamal walked home feeling full and vast, satisfied that he had pleased a man. He knew the song of these streets better than anyone; he'd busted his head and heart and arse all over them, and he was still here. Maybe home wasn't meant to be safe, maybe it was meant to be where you could break, where you could pick up the pieces and regather yourself. When Moses went to prison, there were so many nights when the band of steel around Jamal's chest would not give, keeping sleep at bay, and so he haunted the roads between the two sisters who called him son, driven by an urgency he couldn't name. Jihad didn't understand that Jamal was the scariest thing on the streets in those hours, that he was hoping to get jumped. Hoping to be taken in some animal way, to have a reason to be his own animal self. Kholto would find him curled up on the couch in the morning, when she got up for the dawn prayer, and usher him sleepily to her bed before getting on with her day.

He opened the door with the spare key he had never lost, and walked inside, the way lit by the hallway light Kholto left on because she got up at least once a night to go to the toilet. He felt a deep love for that bare fluorescence, the comfort it provided her—the way it told him, too, that everything was okay.

Haunts

The adhan sank into Jamal's skull and erupted from his eyelids. It was not yet dawn, the day still in its fuzzy undergarments, and he let out an annoyed groan. Sleep yanked at him, but he had to wait out the prayer. The sounds washed over and through his exhausted body. When he got up later, Rania made him scrambled eggs with labneh, fresh Lebanese bread, and a side plate of diced tomatoes and cucumbers. She did it with practised ease, in just a few minutes. He rarely ate breakfast, and most nights he had takeaway, or toast with tuna; this was heaven by comparison. His uncle Mehmet might know how to cook, but Jamal didn't know any other men in his family who could.

I don't know how you do it, Kholto, he said and she looked at him like he was the biggest fool on earth. It's just eggs! But he knew she was pleased. She didn't cook much anymore, she said. Everyone was out of the house and taken care of, thank God. Now shut your mouth, you stupid boy. He remembered all the times he'd seen her in the kitchen with Fatima or Sara at her shoulders, the long unbroken line from Teyta through all her daughters, and how the men were kept apart from that, how every time he asked to learn she'd laughed at him. Rania didn't cook much anymore, except when she wanted her wayward boys to come home, and like well-kept dogs, they came to heel. It was a power all her own, and she was not going to give it up.

When Jamal finished eating, she said that she needed help with her latest Centrelink issue. The rent hadn't been paid, and she needed someone to go into the office to pay the bill. Normally Ali took care of it, but he was busy, and she had other errands to run. Jamal nodded as she spoke. He should have known. Nothing came free in this family. He texted Ilo and Emir, who both still lived with their parents, knowing they did the rent run for them too. They could have had it deducted automatically from their welfare but one thing their migrant families had in common was a profound and nebulous suspicion, particularly when it came to anyone touching their money. They wanted it up-front, and in cash as soon as possible. Ask them what could go wrong and they would shrug. Anything, everything. The money might not make it. Who knows who would see the form filled in with their details? The act of writing by itself made them vulnerable. What if the banks shut down? Or the currency crashed? Or the government failed? It could happen, they knew. It had before. If you asked Jamal, it was stubbornness, pure and simple. They didn't want to admit they didn't know how the new system worked, or else they were afraid if they did anything to bring attention to themselves, if they looked the gift horse in the mouth, they would have their benefits revoked.

After a quick shower, Jamal shuffled out into the brittle light wearing the same jeans and one of Ali's old blue Nautica shirts, heading to the bus stop outside the Hunters' house. It looked the same as ever but Jihad told him they'd been raided last week, and the cops had found an arsenal of guns and drugs; Mick and the boys were done. As he settled in to wait (the app said ten minutes, which meant at least thirty), he saw that the silver bench and its overarching shelter were still graffitied with all the shit tags they'd come up with over a decade ago. Even the cement was marred with their fingerprints, and stray claims. Jaydo loves Lizzie. Mo Waz Ere. Bus Stop Boyz. 1999. Aiden, the prettiest white boy for miles, had done a real number on the girls. He got Lizzie pregnant first, then Tanya, Mesake's sister, before winding up in prison. Both girls still lived in these houses, opposite each other, one white and one brown, raising half-siblings to a tatted-up gronk with a Nickelodeon smile. He couldn't blame them. If he had a womb, and Aiden was willing, there would no doubt be a third child running around, and another body shattered by the experience of obtaining its fantasy. He had been that, a real dream. Clear skin, blue eyes, a jawline to die for, light auburn hair flicked back. Charisma for days. Moses was his twin in that aspect, though dark-haired where he was fair, and they'd been best mates until they started cutting each other's grass.

The bus trundled to a stop in front of Jamal, and he got on, tapped his Opal card. The driver jerked the lever, closing the doors with a hiss. It was narrow and rank and blissfully empty inside. Jamal sat on a gum-blotted, cig-burned seat towards the back, trying not to feel like he was stuck in a sealed disease tube. It never worked. He put his earphones in, focusing on a distant glare of green outside the window, and slipped out of the world.

The bus shuddered and lurched to a stop near Anthony's house. Anthony, with his shit porn; Anthony, his first kiss, the boy who had pegged a loose bit of road at his head, creating the star-shaped scar on the right side of his nose. A burst of blood, a hot wave of red over his mouth. He wondered if he still lived here.

Jamal took one earphone out, startled by the familiar figure of a large, blocky man getting on. Is that you, Zakky? he said.

Zak came closer. Who? he said, without thinking, his voice a low grunt. Then his blue eyes widened. Is that you, cuzzy?

Who? Jamal said, in imitation, nearly killing him—Zak's eyes crossed in confusion. Zak was a big düb. (You know düb?) He lumbered in all things, and to see him think—and you could see it on his face—was painful. He knew it, though, which made him smarter than most people. He had no pretensions to an intellect that society would value, his intelligence lay in knowing himself, in his hands, his muscle and bone, his obvious and profound joys. Whatever he felt, you would know immediately, and this put him in a class all his own.

Yeah, yeah, it's me. Jamal laughed and stood up halfway to shake Zak's hand. As their hands slapped together, Zak let out a disbelieving yell, Faaaar out, it's been ages. He crashed into the seat in front of Jamal, head shaved except for his long fringe, slicked back over and down to his neck. He didn't have much to say, his family was well, alhumdulilah. His younger brother Osama, who was Jamal's age and had shown up to school on maybe three occasions, was back Inside.

Stealing cars. Selling drugs. Tutuhanak. You know how it is.

There was one awkward pause when he asked, with surprising gentleness, Is that Celine Dion you're blasting, bro?

Jamal had tuned out the music, but realised he was right. He was listening to the second verse of Celine Dion's 'It's All Coming Back to Me Now'.

Uh, yeah, he said.

Zak looked at him, and there were a thousand possibilities in that moment, each of them ending in rupture, or refusal. He took none of them.

Aw yeah, he said, I love that bitch. He started humming along, grabbing the dangling earphone, and thrusting his hips dramatically like Mr Bean. Jamal laughed and laughed, a hyena thing that pinballed around the bus. Suddenly he loved Zak all over again and he wasn't just a guy Jamal once knew, barely a distant cousin: all his memories cracked open, and there Zak was, goofballing around Kmart, dumb as rocks, his head glittering with stubble, his jaw as long as Jamal's arm; and there he was on the footy field calling for the ball, bulldozing through the defence; and there he was, swearing to Jihad, Cuz, I've got your back, no matter what, wallahi. He was loyal as a shadow, and never vicious with his strength, always ready with a smile. Maybe Jihad was right and there was a difference because he was only a second cousin, but it didn't feel that way.

Jamal got off the bus outside Westfield's. It had started off as a concrete monstrosity, and only got worse over time. Scaffolding for the new Western Sydney University campus building squatted skeletal over what had once been a meagre selection of shops and an okay hair salon. Livo would finally have a uni 'campus', if this thing was ever finished. Ilo stood out front, smoking, his long black hair a fluent wave tucked across his neck to spill down over his heart. He looked like a tall, beautiful woman in cheap jeans and a black tee. Jamal nodded and Ilo waved at him, his eyes lighting up, cheeks bunching.

Jamal went straight into his arms, and Ilo made a wordless noise of solace. I'm so sorry, babe, he said. You've been going through it lately, goddamn. He kissed Jamal's forehead, and Jamal had to swallow the sudden lump in his throat.

God, don't make me cry here, he said. I'm okay, I'm okay, really. Strangely, that was almost true. The reality of the grave, the dirt in his hands, had punctured his illusions. He'd thought that he longed for oblivion, an end to the constant work and hurt, but behind that was a sharp hunger for proof of grief from everyone—proof that he had been alive and loved. It would be stupid, except that in Islam, the dead were conscious and waiting, so in theory it was possible to gain this knowledge. To gain it and be unable to do anything with it. Jihad was right: he had been selfish for too long, much as it pained him to admit.

Where's E? he said, and Ilo rolled his eyes, pointing to the plaza. Jamal looked and felt the absence in his chest shudder all over again. Emir slouched towards them through a sparse crowd, a short guy in denim with a buzz cut and the heavy eyes of a chronically depressed former emo kid. He walked right past the spot Zak had been killed years ago, stabbed to death by a Viet gang. That's what they said on the news, anyway, and Jamal knew enough to doubt whatever came out of polished TV lips. Zak had gone to Westfield's to fight with a couple boys. A bit of the biff with some lads. He thought his mates would meet him there, make a real go of it. Except they didn't show. He was alone, and the other boys weren't. That's what it came down to in the end. Loyalty. Every week Jamal thought of him running out of this Westfield's, chased down like a dog, and the knives that ended his life.

Hey Vlad, Jamal called out. Go slower, why don't you?

As he crossed the road, anger ignited in Emi's brown eyes and Jamal smiled. It was about the only thing you could make him feel and know for sure he was feeling instead of faking. Or at least, that had once been the case. Emi's beanie read QUEER in gold letters, and he carried himself with a confidence Jamal hadn't seen before.

Finally, as Emi got closer, Jamal said, What's good?

Not you, Saddam, he said. You know, I think I preferred it when you were gone.

Tough shit, dickhead, Jamal said. I'm here.

It came out harsher than he had intended, it always did around Emi, who frowned. Before he could say anything, Jamal brushed past him.

Let's go. I can't stand this place.

They cut across the courthouse and library, then down through the carpark to get to the station. It would be easier to go to the local Centrelink, or to pay at a post office, but there was an Eastern European takeaway shop in Fairfield that did a hectic burek, and besides, this way they killed time, which was all they really wanted. They had killed whole years, shuttling from one shit place to another, inventing reasons to be next to each other for another minute, another hour—anything to get out of Liverpool, anything not to go home.

As they went to the station, Jamal told them that according to his uncle, Saddam Hussein wasn't dead, and neither was Tupac for that matter, although he was getting on in his age. It was all bullshit. Saddam had been an ally of the US, and an enemy of bin Laden (who also wasn't dead, if he'd ever been real), it didn't make any sense. Plus, he was rich, which meant anything was possible. It's all theatre, Buktikh had said, his mean little eyes alive with glee. He loved saying that. He'd never seen a play in his life, what would he know about theatre?

Neither have we, Ilo said, flicking his cigarette into the gutter. Except for that one school excursion.

True, Jamal said. That had been *The Lieutenant of Inishmore*, at Belvoir St. Jamal remembered laughing until he cried, but not much else. It had something to do with a dead cat and sad gangsters.

At the station, a cordon of cops stood around the ticket barriers with a couple of German shepherds, acting staunch: a beachhead of white against a sea of brown and black people, all looking like they couldn't believe this was called freedom. Where were the cops when Zakky had needed them? They only showed up to put brown boys down, or cart their bodies away. He wanted to spit, but swallowed it. He kept his eyes low. As he walked, he glanced into the wet pupils of a dog and saw himself, a dark figure, reflected. The bitch looked away first, and they all sped down to the platform.

The platform was packed. A couple of hijabi glamours gave Jamal the once-over, their skin buffed to gleaming perfection, lips glossy, every article of clothing a top brand name. One wasn't interested, but the other, wearing a pale blue hijab, had a mock invitation in her green eyes, the 'And what? Say something, I dare you' kind of look. Jamal said nothing, glancing away, trusting his periphery to check out her arse. He'd almost forgotten that the girls in the area matched the boys for cockiness and then some.

By the time the train stopped in front of them with a sad exhale, he'd overheard the girls take, then complain about, two separate phone calls from their mothers, who they reassured in Arabic that yes, they were on the way to their classes, Layla/Randa was there with them, the train was about to arrive, they would come straight home of course, and they would stop by the store on the way back.

I swear to God she does that deliberately, the one called Randa said in a thick drawl, It's always gotta be ten calls instead of one 'cause she's bored. Layla agreed, while still flicking looks Jamal's way, and wondered if their mothers egged each other on, if they might even be calling from the same room. One day they'd look behind them in a lecture theatre and see their mothers staring back at them over the lip of a chair, and they would just die. Or worse, their mothers would figure out how many lectures they skipped to hang with their girlfriends and check out boys.

As they were about to step into the next carriage over, Layla yelled out, Ay, give us your number! then she and Randa bolted inside, laughing like kookaburras. Emi and Ilo laughed with them, their giggles higher pitched.

Sluts, Jamal said, with a mixture of wonder and envy. What would it be like to have such courage, or to have a mother who cared enough to call?

You're right, you know, Ilo said thoughtfully. We should be friends with them instead.

Jamal laughed as they got on the train. He knew it wasn't all easy with overbearing mothers. Emir's mother was on his back every day. He complained about it all the time, how much she needed him, while

Jamal felt ill with need to be loved even to a tenth of that degree. Ilo put one of his shoes up on the plush blue seat, the sole flapping open. He pulled a tube of superglue out of his bag, started sealing it up.

There's the ghetto, Jamal said. And then there's *the ghetto.*

Oh god, shut your mouth, Ilo said, laughing.

Ooh, Little Miss Newtown, too good for some glue? Emi said. She thinks she's better than us now.

Please, Jamal said. I've always been better. And it's Stanmore, not Newtown.

He's not wrong, Emi added after a moment. When you're literally carrying glue around, it's time to call it. It's over, sis.

I know, I know, Ilo said. It does the trick, though. He asked if they needed any, and they both checked their shoes. Emi's boots were fine, and while Jamal had a small hole in his right shoe, it wasn't in desperate need of repair. He caught Emi's broken half-smile, and knew they were both thinking the same thing: that Ilo needed to put himself first for a change. He still worked at the McDonald's in Orange Grove, he was a shift manager now, but his money went to his parents to help pay the bills, or to give to their church, and he rarely had anything left over for himself. Enough for some drinks, some smokes, the rare movie.

Anyway, Ilo said, tell us about Turkey, bitch. You miss it?

Not really, Jamal lied. It already feels like a dream.

Damn, the D was that good?

Ha-ha. No, it's like I can barely remember it. Everything's in a fog.

Emir nodded. Yeah, it's like, what I remember most of Bosnia is chickens.

And your cousin's dick, Jamal added.

Emi glared. He literally just did that to you, he said.

Yeah, get your own shitty jokes! Ilo said, and Jamal said, Never! but it was lost in their giggles.

Do you think you'll ever go to Samoa?

Ilo shook his head. Why, so everyone can ask me for money I don't have? No, if I can ever afford it, I'm going to Korea. Ilo was obsessed with K-pop and K-drama, as well as Japanese anime, manga and yaoi. He loved imagining himself as a stereotypical Asian woman—gowned in silk, painted, petite, with all manner of cultural restrictions repressing her desire until she must burst free, or else a warrior who could run across treetops, fierce and fabulous and deadly.

Such a rice queen, it's really probbo, Emi said.

Yeah, you've been all crouching tiger hidden homo for too long, Jamal said, and they laughed until their stomachs hurt. God, he'd missed this; he missed them even as he sat with them. There was still an invisible wall between them, sliver thin, but it was there, because he had left the area, left them. He wanted to say, I'm not better off. The houses might be worth millions but they look like shit, rotting terraces paid for by gangs of students, most of them rich and playing poor so they would have something later in life to refer to as their 'character-building' years. Jamal remembered seeing one of Dan's friends at a house party sneer at his peers that the Inner West has been gentrified, like it was a disturbing evil he'd just encountered and not something his parents had done. I remember when you could get stabbed in Newtown and Redfern of a night, he said. That's when it used to be real. He longed for the grit and drama of that, and looked down on the poncery of his cafe-going, partying friends, even as he joined them. It was a kind of stupid Jamal had never encountered before, and didn't know how to talk about. He was pretty sure Fa'ailo and Emir didn't have to deal with people like that, or feel the almost supernatural aloneness that comes from having no loved ones, no community nearby. At least you have each other, your families, you can be seen if you want, he thought. In Stanmore, no one knew the colour of his eyes, and no one wanted to. He wanted to say these things, but he didn't, because the need to measure suffering against suffering was petty, and born from an insecurity he was determined to leave in the past.

Arrows & Sluts

It's like you're tense your whole life, right, until you finally let go, and that moment, that's your arrow year—you fly furious through everything. Jamal flushed, as he read the article on his phone, and found in the words a resonance that matched the music of his soul. And by fly, I mean fuck, he added.

Oh, the slut year, Emir said. Now I know what you're on about.

Shit, Ilo whispered. You mean we only get a year? Nobody told me!

Like you would have listened anyway, Jamal said, and they laughed. I'm just saying, I dunno, maybe this is mine.

He wanted it to be, anyway. The article writer, a trans Afghan, talked about how being denied desire in your formative years bent you back like a bow, making the eventual release dramatic, if you were lucky enough to get it before the bow broke.

Babe, you had sex with two guys, calm down, Emir said.

Jamal grit his teeth. Can you not be a dick for three seconds? Let me have this.

They both looked away. It had been weird between them since

Jamal returned from Turkey—longer, if he was honest with himself, which he tried not to be, as a rule. Maybe honesty could be more than a hatchet, but he had never seen it used as anything else, and he was so tired of being hurt.

Look on the bright side, Ilo said into the silence. My hair looks great tonight.

Jamal and Emi eyed him askance. You haters! Ilo said, and they both laughed. Whatever. Someone remind me why we're friends again?

Some kind of trauma bonding, Jamal said.

Lack of alternatives, Emir said.

This fucking place, Jamal said, as the train doors opened at Warwick Farm. The moon danced above, or seemed to, as a cold breeze pushed white-blue dresses of cloud over its pale bareness. He hadn't been back here since Teyta died, and that grief, layered over his skin, hair and teeth, a permanent addition to his senses, hummed as he got closer. Once, while standing over the grave of his younger brother in Liverpool's small cemetery, Ilo had told him that a country couldn't hold you until you buried your relatives in it. Jamal's grandparents were both part of the bones of this land now, but he felt no more held by it than before.

It's amazing we never knew we were queer in high school, Jamal said. Like, how dumb could we be?

Wow, Ilo said, dragging out the vowel to cover the street and back. You had to go there. He giggled, and the sound danced in them.

We never had girlfriends, or talked about getting them, and we had sleepovers all the time, just us three, Emir said, counting off his ring-laden fingers. We were mean as fuck and our fave shows were *Will & Grace, Charmed* and *Buffy*. Yeah wow.

I even convinced you one time I had to write gay erotica in order to become a member of a porn site, Jamal said. A story for every category!

That *was* weird. But then, so was the internet, Emir said. And like, I knew, but I didn't, if that makes sense?

They'd all been in on the scam of reading erotica and pretending it was study. It was easy to get away with as the sons of barely literate immigrants who saw reading itself as an incredible act, a tremendous ability that promised social mobility and definitely did not include porn. They only realised later that they'd been reading the same sites, each one rife with the same tropes: the boy/dad next door, the straight best friend you got drunk or were in love with, the straight married man, the college roommate you jerked off with, the promiscuous consensual couple, most of them steeped in shame and violence dressed up as sex. He wished now they had never read a word, never been drenched in the rape and coercion so often presented as normal in them. Get a man hard in his sleep and he will let you do anything, they promised. Waking up to a blow job was the best, who could say no to that? Forget consent. Forget about the risk of asking. For boys unsure how to be men, what could be more irresistible than the song that begins and ends with: *You don't have to be vulnerable.*

Anyway, Emi continued. You were such a masc Leb, it's not like I was going to call you on it.

Jamal's vision fractured. Did they see him as he saw Bilal? Big and blokey? In his family, he'd been the slightest one, the most effeminate. Looking at Ilo now, he realised he was taller than him, and just as wide. Compared to them both, Emi was a twink, or cub at most. Jamal blinked rapidly to dry his eyes, running through the Fatiha in his mind. It always calmed him down, the lilt of his mother's language, the promise of protection. He wasn't sure what upset him more, that his friends had seen him as a man when he was a teenager, or that he still struggled to see himself as one now. Inside, he was always the boy, small and frozen, standing in front of a door his mother would shatter. Some part of him must have known, some part of him had been trying to tell them, and they had seen only the rude Leb, already a man, baiting them.

They were walking by the strip mall opposite the flats his grandparents used to live in. The bottle shop was the only place open. The bakery stood dark, as did the small supermarket with its rotted, rusty Mixed Business sign. The old Viet man who ran it was thin and wrinkled, with black hair and blacker eyes. He reminded Jamal of his jido, except that he despised Jamal and his cousins—he'd turn out their pockets whenever they tried to leave the store, purely because they were Lebs, and stole from him all the time. Up ahead was Durrant Oval, where the school athletic carnival had been held, and in which they never participated, instead sitting on the benches talking shit, secretly fantasising about tall Serb jocks like Nenad, who had eyes clear as light, a voice like a dying mule, and the biggest dick in their year. He liked to measure it through his pants in class with a ruler while the teachers had their backs turned, and the boys around him would stare or pretend not to stare, in a mixture of envy, lust, and disgust. Ironically, going to a homophobic boys school was the gayest experience possible: all the boys did was talk about their dicks, what they wanted to do with them, how they liked to get off. He missed it, despite everything.

Ilo claimed to have hooked up in the toilets at the oval, and on the banks of the creek too, with its overhanging weeping willows. He fucked all around Warwick Farm, in parks, behind El Toro motel or in carparks, not because he loved the outdoors—but because he couldn't take anyone home. He'd never slept with any man in a bed, and he was closer to thirty than not. His family knew, but didn't want to and pretended not to, as they all had during high school, and this way he got to stay home, stay loved, if you could call it that, and they got to keep him close, and his rent closer. For his family he painted the grass, the concrete, the creeks and strip malls and alleys with his need. What had Jamal done, except run at the first opportunity?

Wait, Ilo said. What did you guys do with the porn I loaned you? There had been a phase of burned-CD sharing when everyone with an older brother or a computer passed along what they masturbated to as a kind of weird flex to show how hardcore they were, how not-gay. Ilo and Jamal didn't have computers back then, but they did have older brothers who hoarded nudity, from scraps of magazines to battered videos.

I'd just focus on the guy, Emi said with a shrug. Between them stretched the unspoken: their capacity for self-delusion, for disappearance, was endless.

Ilo's house was ahead, a three-bedroom fibro like most in the area, sitting on a large slice of land. Large enough for a netted trampoline, a Hills hoist, a shed, a gnarled tree, mounds of firewood and a long vegetable garden. Inside, the lounge had dark wooden floors, a couch, an armchair. Ilo's father sat in the chair, a tall wide man with short brown hair and a gut that dipped over his jeans. Hi boys, he said, keeping his eye on the TV, and they chorused their hellos, teenagers again. Four silver key-shaped frames gleamed on the wall, faded photos of Ilo's family within. Jamal had slept on the fold-out couch a hundred times, looking up at them, unsure of their significance, imagining they held the dead or that they opened the gates of heaven. When he'd finally asked, it turned out they were customary 21st birthday presents, a key only to the house, and life within it as an adult. Ilo's mum was still at work, and Jamal missed her warm smile, the shine of her dark gold caps.

They tramped through the kitchen, straight into the backyard. There had been no talk about sleeping over, yet they all knew it was happening. They relied so much on the muscle memory of friendship. After gathering some wood, Ilo got the fire going. The flames crackled and spat, darting like snakes. Jamal stayed as still as stone. Emi had his Echo out, music playing, the orange light of the fire licking his black nail polish, the beads and bangles on his wrists. Ilo's older sister Tasi came out with garlic bread wrapped in foil, wearing a singlet and work-out tights that squeezed her thick thighs. She buried the silver bundle beneath the burning wood, told them to call her when it was done. Their talk turned back to high school. Once the floodgates of nostalgia were opened, they couldn't be closed, no matter who was swept away. Darko had two kids. Amandeep was a cop, tfeh. Elias was a PE teacher. Shigenori had gone back to Japan, no one had heard from him in years. Steven had murdered his ex-girlfriend and was in prison. A half-dozen were gay but still in the closet. On and on. People they weren't friends with, and did not care for, but who they nonetheless carried as a body carried scars. Emir, as usual, mostly listened with ill-concealed contempt, except when someone he hated was mentioned, particularly the Serbs, who had uniformly bullied him.

Ilo stirred the fire, and a flurry of gold sparks spat into the dark. The smell of garlic wafted around them. Jamal's stomach gurgled, and his blood thickened with memory. Ilo dislodged the buried garlic, calling his sister's name. Tasi came out with Booty—a big fluffy border collie with black fur all over, except for the chest and paws and snout, which were white—bounding at her heels. Booty obeyed no one except Tasi, who lavished attention on her, feeding her fresh roast chickens from Woolies; the dog ate better than all of them. Tasi asked if they'd had dinner, and Ilo said with false cheer, Eating is cheating!

Bitch, you know we're gonna eat, Jamal said, and he laughed.

Well, there's plenty of food, Tasi said, retreating inside. Ilo, don't forget to send me your application. He grimaced at her back. She was the assistant manager at a courier company, and there was a job opening. He was dragging his heels. He'd been at Maccas since high school.

What, you wanna be a Lifer, after all? Jamal said. Their friends at school used to make fun of Lifers, people who stayed in the retail and hospitality jobs they only deigned to take to make pocket money, or because their parents had demanded it of them. The three of them had taken it up for a while, but it never sat right, like they were just feeling out if using the same words could give them the same opportunity, the same arrogance of knowing you were above certain kinds of work, above stasis of any kind, or could keep them from living with, or around the corner from, their families.

Ilo's eyes narrowed and he sat up straight. Fuck you, bitch. He smiled because he had to, and Jamal wanted to bite back the words. He didn't know how to kick this habit of treating every sentence as a chance to score a hit.

You need to go for this, Jamal said. You deserve better.

I know, I know, Ilo said. But …

You scared? Emir said, sotto voce.

What softness Emir and Jamal had they shared with Ilo, if not each other.

No! Ilo said. Then, Maybe? I dunno. What if I don't get it and I really am stuck?

Jamal snorted. As if. Tasi will get it for you. You just have to apply so she can pretend it was legit.

What if I *can't* do it? What if I'm just not good enough?

Ilo could travel from the highs of *ooh bitch I look great* to the deepest pit of self-loathing faster than anyone Jamal knew. It was a kind of queer superpower, the continual suppression of abundance, and he had it bad. Emir told him he'd be fine. He worked in hospitality with his mum at the Park Hyatt in Circular Quay, he knew all about customer service. Jamal let the music wash over their words. He'd never had a job like that. For work experience in school, he went to the local Coles, hoping it would lead to a paying job. Two weeks of stacking shelves for free led to nothing. It was only luck that he had met Dan at uni before he dropped out. Dan's parents worked in media, and it was through him that Jamal had picked up his precious mindless transcribing. It was the opposite of what he knew, which was based in forgetting, in repressing or ignoring, and slowly but surely, the rigour of that attention was bleeding into him. The demand to remember was getting stronger, it was tearing into time, and he couldn't stop it.

Jamal tilted his head up, focusing on the tiny undead light of the stars. In their remembered fire another fire: Ilo's 19th birthday, right here, tables of food, fewer rellos, no longer high-schoolers, a sense of breaking pervading everything. Things with Emir had changed, but they were friends still, albeit ones liable to break into argument at any moment. Emir had come out to his parents after the incident, and despite not being religious, they sent him to a counsellor known to the community, to explain why he was committing sin, and how to stop. Conversion therapy nearly destroyed him but, as he said, at least they hadn't kicked him out.

Jamal had told Ilo what happened, but neither of them was able to come out to each other even then. In the aftermath of abuse, their own truths took on a dangerous light. Until this night, this spirit pouring down Jamal's throat as he drank for the first time. He wore a muscle shirt to proudly display the small amount of tone and definition he'd gained, and a beard to distract from the bags under his sleepless eyes. He kept catching looks from one of the Maccas girls, a Eurasian or Filo maybe, she had sharp cheekbones and a short red dress he wanted to take off with his teeth. Next to her was an Asian guy with thick lips who kept trying to get in Jamal's way, out of lust or rage, he wasn't sure, he was having too much fun, halfway to drunk, and it went on like that until midnight when Ilo, with the suddenness of dream, started to cry.

They moved him away from the fire, his family, to the mulberry tree in the back of the yard. No one noticed amid the loud festivities. No one will ever love me, Ilo said, knuckling his eyes, sucking in his lips, trying to hold back, to not let it develop into the kind of sobbing from which there was no return. His face was smooth and round and dark, he was gentle and funny and could sing the moon down—they all loved him, obviously, but not the way he wanted. It was not enough.

The hairs on Jamal's arms stood up, and into the silence of the little circle under the tree, he said, If I was gay—I mean, actually—he stopped. Sweat popped up and beaded his forehead, neck and armpits. You know what, I'm bi, so I can say this, anybody would be lucky to have you, he said.

Ilo looked up with sudden hope, his breathing ragged. I think … I am too, yeah, I dunno. I love you guys.

A weight left them then, rising into the smoky sky, and they hugged. Jamal put his head on Ilo's shoulder, and Emi put his head on Jamal's, but only to hiss under his breath, I knew it!

Later, giddy with revelations, music and fire pulsing in their blood, Emi and Jamal kissed. It was bruising and desperate, their teeth clashing, Emi's hands roving, and Jamal pulling away even before Tasi coughed pointedly and said, Guys, wrap it up. She and her mother, a sturdy woman with kind eyes, were clearing tables and cleaning up. Ilo's mum always greeted the boys with a kiss whenever they came over. This is your home, you are my sons too, she'd say, but she wasn't looking at them this night, and Jamal sobered up, or at least gained a painful sense of clarity, like swimming through perfect water. His legs wobbled, Emi half on top of him, hands wriggling cold under the back of Jamal's jeans to feel his arse. He was gone, lost to his hunger, not for Jamal's body so much as a balancing of the scales, as if to touch him now, awake, would undo his last touch.

Panicked, Jamal shot away, stumbling onto the grass, then back up, tilting with the world into the house. Ilo had his mattress on the floor next to the couch, and Jamal dived over it, scuttling across the couch to press his back against the wall. Emir walked in, bowed like a servant to his lord, and threw up in the hall.

It's okay, it's okay darted out of mouths, and shapes shifted through the murk.

Jamal faded away, a confusion of unmet need. Ilo lay Emir down on the mattress, wiping the vomit off his mouth. Jamal heard his mother's low voice, the swelling of another language, her door closing. Ilo joined him on the couch, and they lay awake together. I'm gay, he said under his breath, and Jamal said, I know.

His hand was on Jamal's thigh. Can I? he whispered, and Jamal said yes. Ilo sucked Jamal's cock under the blanket. Permission and shame fanned through Jamal's body in strange eddies as he was emptied. Ilo slept after that and Jamal lay awake, wondering why he'd said yes, whether it was because Ilo had been the first and only person to ask, because it was too hard to say I don't love you like that, or because it was his birthday. Silver keys glimmered above.

Jamal dreamt he stood before three glass doors. In his hands, a key. Behind one door, the hot girl from earlier, naked, twirling. Behind the other, the Asian guy, sweat dripping down his pecs, his thick thighs. He was bare and erect where she had a bush. The third door's glass was clouded. He looked closer at the key in his hand, engraved with two words: *not yours.* He held a metal bat, not a key, and he swung hard, smashing the doors into ninety-nine jagged pieces.

Jamal rose again into his body, the dark house, Ilo's snores trampling the air. Emir had crept over to the bottom of the couch, and now lay part way across both their legs. He rested his head against the wall, and looked at Jamal. Moving slowly, so slowly, he began peeling off Jamal's socks. He kneaded Jamal's feet. When his hands touched Jamal's skin, electric shivers marched across his chest. As he looked at his friend under his foot, something vicious uncurled within. This was right, he decided. Emir kissed his toes, licking and sucking each one individually, before bobbing on as much of his foot as he could, eyes closed, trying to say with his mouth what he couldn't bring himself to utter, a lather of devotion and perhaps apology. Jamal knew then that Emi was in love with him, and that he didn't return the feeling. Pleasure throbbed through his veins. He was hard, so hard he could break, and he knew he would use Emir anyway.

Jamal put his hands out over the little sunset: he didn't want it to end, to dim, for them to go inside. Out here, under the gauzy lights, anything was possible. He put his head on Emir's shoulder, and Emi put his cheek against Jamal's hair. He was telling a story about his last late shift, delivering room service to a pot-bellied old white man, a Hugh Hefner wannabe in a bathrobe, with a dozen naked ladies and lines of coke racked up.

When you think about it, he said, it's sad I've seen more pussy than you, hey.

Jamal moved off him. No, what's sad is that you have to be some white guy's slave every night, and not even get any dick at the end of it.

True, Emir said. I was just like, ew! And ran out of there.

Ilo's chuckle turned into a roar of laughter, and they all joined in. Of the three, Emir was the most uncomfortable whenever the topic of race came up. It was only in the past few years that he'd started to talk about whiteness as a phenomenon distinct from himself, after he went back to Bosnia for six months; he had a culture of his own, one separate to the Anglo mainstream, which seemed for the most part ambivalent about his features. He was both included and not, which was why he wore the Queer beanie so proudly—it was an unambiguous disadvantage, an easily understood hatred. He was figuring these things out tentatively, mostly by sharing memes on social media, feeling out this new language for a frustration he'd always had.

I wish you wouldn't do that, Jamal said, staring at him directly.

Do what? he said.

Wave it away. When I bring up white shit.

Emir reared up, furious. And I wish you would stop calling me John Malkovich or Werner Herzog or any other non-Bosnian name, but we don't all get what we want.

Okay, Marin Čilić, settle down.

Fuck, I hate you, he said. He made little claw motions with his hands, then subsided with a helpless giggle. Whatever.

I'm only joking, Jamal said, baffled.

No, you love throwing it in my face, it's weird. Emi was deflecting, but as usual, he knew what to say to irk Jamal enough that it didn't matter.

You're right, Jamal said. I treat you like a brother, and that's clearly a mistake. Right, Moana?

Ilo was shaking his head before Jamal finished. This is all you two—actually I think my mum's back from work, bye. He took off to the kitchen, calling for her.

Coward! Emi and Jamal shouted at the same time. Then, softer, Ugh.

Jamal went to the back of the yard and grabbed more wood. He took his time, feeling each step in the damp grass, the rough texture of the bark, flicking off errant bugs. By the fire, Emir was still, a bent shadow. He'd never lost his sadness, the hostility that Jamal had on some level recognised when he first transferred to Liverpool Boys. He dumped the wood and sat down with an exaggerated oomph beside his friend.

How's your mum doing anyway? Jamal said.

Not great, Emi said. His mother's early-onset arthritis left her bedridden most days, and she had once again kicked his dad out. His father was a brickie, a tough wiry man with a lively laugh and a thick moustache. Emi still resented him for the condition that he could only live at home so long as his younger brother didn't turn out gay as well. As if it were a disease you could pass on. And with no thought whatsoever to turning a brother's eye upon his sibling with suspicious fear threaded through his love.

What about yours? he said.

No one knows, Jamal said. And I'm too scared to call her.

Yeah, no shit, she's terrifying, Emi said.

The first time Hala met Emi, she had visibly recoiled. Get a haircut, she said, You look like a girl. His hesitant smile had withered and he shot Jamal a murderous look as she breezed past, indifferent. He knew all about her reign of terror and neglect, the beatings, the chain she put on Jamal's bedroom door to lock him in. He knew Jamal's sad furious years as well as Jamal knew his, and to let go of each other, of this tangled and wounded tenderness, would be to surrender having been known at all. It was too much to ask, in the absence of any other security. This was the problem with building a wall around the people you love: you had to weather everything together, even after you changed.

I told my dad I'm bi, Jamal said. And I think he hates me now. Or at least he won't stop going on about how it's like being a pedo.

Oh baby, no, Emi said and hugged him hard. Fuck that and fuck him!

Jamal cried into his neck. If there were any words in his sobbing, no one but he knew what they were: Is it wrong that I'm sick of arguing for how I want to live? Am I evil, really? I swear I don't know anymore.

Ilo returned, hauling a laundry basket with him, muttering that he should have stayed put. Jamal was wiping his eyes, regaining his breath. Ilo hung up clothes while the buttery light from the kitchen window spread out, thinning over the fire, giving Jamal time to recover. He fluttered over to press close to the house, to look in and say, Hi Mama, drinking in his Samoan mother's smile like a moth addicted to love. Her glaucoma was bothering her, but she was fine otherwise, Praise God. She asked if they were hungry but Jamal told her they'd ordered halal snack packs and not to worry.

Emi ran inside saying he had to shit, leaving Jamal alone with Ilo and the golden crackling pit.

You two good? Ilo said. I saw you having a moment.

Yeah, I guess.

Ilo sighed. Ever since that night, I've felt like that *thing* has been, like, the fourth member of our group, you know? I'm glad you talked about it finally. I'm here for you, okay, no matter what.

Jamal's eyes locked on to the glazed bathroom window, only a few metres away, which was open an inch. The toilet backed up against it, and he squinted to see if he could make out the back of Emir's head, but it was no use. He wished that he had the courage Ilo imagined, but there was a reason he so often brought up their high school years, a reason he summoned those ghosts rather than tread new ground, and it was because none of them were willing to look the truth in the eye, and because it affirmed that however hard things were now, it had been worse once. He didn't correct Ilo, and the food arrived soon after, two large pizza boxes full of hot chips, with sliced kebab meat slathered in hot chilli and garlic sauce, melted cheese layered throughout. They stuffed their snouts in it, mouths greasy with oil, eating until their stomachs groaned in protest, and then some. Jamal flopped back onto the grass and rubbed his belly. He was so full he felt sick, on the verge of pain, a sensation he knew better than any other. Emi and Ilo joined him as the flames flickered down, and the whitened wood refused to become ash.

Why'd you come back? Emi said after a while. I didn't mean it, earlier, about preferring you gone, but even before your holiday, you weren't around as much, you know? It feels different now.

Jamal blinked and the moon swam into the stars. His hands clenched around the grass. There were questions within the question, a hurt he didn't quite understand.

I never thought of it as leaving, he said. Not from you two, 'cause you're always with me, you know? But I guess I've never said that before.

You don't have to, Ilo said quickly, rushing as always to soothe. We get you.

No, it's okay. Jamal put his head on Ilo's shoulder, and they cuddled. Some things need to be said. I needed to leave to prove I had the choice, if that makes sense? It's the difference between being stuck and being still because you want to be.

There was quiet for a second, and then Emi said, Ooh, she thinks she's Shakespeare now, and Ilo laughed and Jamal turned to fart in his direction and the hour dissolved. Soon, they would head inside the black and hushed house. The couch would be set up for Jamal, and Emi would go with Ilo to his room, both saying goodnight softly. Jamal would almost call for them to stay. Every time it came to that moment, he almost called for them to stay, for all of them to sleep in the same room again, to drift into dream talking shit, comfortable with their animal noises, skin in close proximity. It should have been possible, they were grown after all, everything was different, and everything was not. So Jamal would say nothing, staring up at the four silver keys, Ilo's face now alongside his siblings, a joint owner of all that transpired there.

That was one thing missing from the article, he thought. What to do when your arrows were mistimed, when you ripped through each other and didn't know how to say sorry, or how to heal.

Can we stay out here? Jamal said, tearing up the vision.

Ilo propped himself up on his elbow, quirked an eyebrow. What, like fucking animals?

Yes, like fucking animals.

He rolled his eyes, then shrugged. Okay fine, but I'm getting blankets and pillows, it's cold as shit out here.

IV

Ibn

Pretenders

The dead man's bed was being delivered today, and the fact that it was his jido who left this life on it didn't make it okay. Jamal had tried refusing a dozen times already, but Hala persisted.

Don't be silly, she said, it's a brand-new queen. Barely touched. I'll get Moses to drop it off.

He stood outside on the ragged grass, waiting. In the sky, a pilot manoeuvred a small plane around like a pen, leaving a trail of letters that spelled out *Vote No*. On WhatsApp, Jamal's relatives, close and distant, sent links urging each other to vote no in the same-sex marriage plebiscite, as if trying to shore up their bigotry. He was used to ignoring their nonsense. The whole country was debating the legal validity of love, churches and mosques and Liberals unleashing all the hatred and fear they'd spent so long cultivating. He was used to the negative will of strange millions, too; what he wasn't used to was fighting back against it, one on one with his distant father, in strained emails. Sometimes he didn't know if he was talking to his Muslim father or the Christian evangelicals in government who linked queerness to paedophilia and bestiality.

The one key difference between them was Cevdat's avowed belief in transness:

When I was in primary school, there was a boy in my class who was like a girl, he acted just like one, you know, he couldn't play soccer or cricket, the way he walked and the way he used his hands when he talked, he looked just like a girl, but he wasn't, he was a girl in a boy's body, his spirit was surely female. Now I would have no hesitation to believe this boy if he fell in love with another man, this person has the right to believe he has those feelings because it's true.

If a male can do everything like a man does and then this person wants to have sex with the same sex, I can only say (and by the way it's not just me, I have friends who are doctors who are saying this) that it's lust and they're just indulging in another way of enjoyment, so to speak. Son, I may not have been with you long, but I know you're not like that! You're a man!

It was almost impressive how he managed to make even a pro-trans stance homophobic, affirming it strictly on the basis that it was wrong for men to desire men or women to desire women and therefore the body itself had to be the lie. Had to be corrected. Jamal's mannerisms were too masculine to be gay, to register a feminine spirit that Cevdat would recognise. Recognition was everything and Jamal had played to what others recognised all his life: he was nothing if not an able student. The first year of living with Hala taught him that. She had moved Jamal and Moses to a duplex on Kurrajong Road, close to the mall and Prestons Public. He still saw his cousins most days, and walked home with them after school, because Rania always had a pot on the stove with something delicious. His new mum rarely cooked. She tried once, making a Lebanese stew that looked like swamp water, and he'd sat in front of it, too revolted to eat, but unable to leave the table. She paced behind him, her frustration a needle digging under his shoulder blades, until the answer arrived in a brilliant flash.

I feel sick, he said. I can't eat it.

You're sick, are you? she said in that light voice he learned later to dread.

Like I'm going to vomit, he said. She grabbed him by the arm and ripped him away from the table. The chair crashed to the ground and he yelled out, legs flailing for purchase. Her collarbone stood out sharp against her skin as she dragged him to the bathroom, forcing his head over the lip of the bathtub, which was the same plain white as the tiled walls and floor. When she switched the light on, the room blazed.

You're going to vomit? Well? Go on! She stood over him, sweating and furious. He tried to retch but it was no good, there was nothing in him, and she knew it. Lek kus ummok, she screamed, and slapped him with such force his head slammed into the wall. *Fuck your mother*. He moaned and ducked his head under his arms as she ranted and raved in Arabic, spit flying from her lips, but she didn't hit him again. The cracked tile in the wall said enough, so she sent him to bed hungry. Moses came and checked on him after she left.

You should have just eaten it like I did, he said over Jamal's muffled sobbing.

I didn't like it!

So what? Just pretend.

Jamal turned his nose up at so much Lebanese food that they called him an Aussie, but it had never been a problem before: Rania let him eat Vegemite or Nutella sandwiches if he wanted. Later that week, there was a school fundraiser and Jamal stopped by the sale tables on the way out. A black handbag caught his eye; the gold chain strap gleamed, and the latch was a pretty black bow. One thing he knew about his mum was that she was beautiful, and she liked beautiful things. She had stacks of magazines full of pretty pictures of purses and things. The lady behind the table asked if he wanted it, maybe a nice gift for mum? When he said yes, but that he didn't have a dollar, she gave it to him for free.

Jamal half-walked and half-skipped home, the handbag on his arm, swinging against his hip. He felt light inside, he felt like he could fly. Cars beeped at him and he beamed. When he got home, Hala saw him wearing the handbag and he knew in an instant she was going to hurt him. He all but saw the djinn take over her eyes. She pounced on him, snatching it off his arm. What's this? she said, shaking the bag above him, and as she shook it, some evil transformed his gift into a used, one-dollar plastic bag. What's this? she shouted, whacking him with it. The latch opened and a wad of tissues fell out, along with a ridged, square blue packet and some lint. It's for you, he said, flinching away, and she told him what a useless dumb shit he was, what did he take her for, a fucking whore? She hurled it into the bin. Ya Allah, spare her the tyranny of idiots.

It was one of many corrections she issued to him. His mother had taught him how to be a man well enough to fool even his father. She'd be proud of that, no doubt. He didn't explain this to Cevdat.

They came from different worlds, there was too much to bridge, too much they both wanted to change. Last night, after much back and forth with Ilo and Emir about how to word it, he sent his final response: *I'm not going to argue anymore, I love who I love.*

As he waited for his brother to arrive, he remembered how Hala became an angel whenever the devil left her and the bruises bloomed on their skin. How she would buy them gifts, take them to the movies, even bought them a PlayStation, which no one else they knew could afford. How the Quran didn't play in their house, how she never prayed. How she was gone most nights and slept through the day, leaving Jamal and Moses alone for the most part. How with her, they suddenly had a wild and hungry freedom, and it was within that freedom that he began to think for himself.

The blare of a car's horn startled him, and he found Moses staring at him from the front of the ute pulling into the driveway.

What are you doing, you full lost case? Moses said, as he got out.

Nothing, I was waiting.

You scare me, you know that? He went to the back of the ute to unstrap the large white mattress, and laughed when Jamal moved to help. You and what muscles, bro? His own bunched into being, veins popping in his biceps, and he heaved the heavy foam off, struggling mightily every step he took towards the house. Jamal rolled his eyes and opened the door for him, saying, Up the stairs you hero, and his brother told him to get fucked, watch this, watch bro. And he launched himself up the narrow stairs without a problem.

A rusted green Ford Fiesta stopped by the kerb, and Jamal was stunned to see his mother step out of it. She was short and dark like old wood, wearing ripped jeans and a furry vest over a white singlet.

Her bumbag had S-L-U-T spelled out in diamantes, and the sun bounced off the diamonds in her earrings and on her rings.

So this is where it's all been happening, she said. God, what a dump.

He kissed her dutifully on the cheek, then impulsively wrapped her in a hug. She stiffened at once, before chuckling and patting him on the back. Okay yes hello hi, we're here.

I didn't know you were coming, he said, and her brilliant black eyes bored into him with reproach. I didn't mean—

She sniffed. God knows I'd cark it if I kept waiting for you to invite me, she said, brushing past him.

He forced a laugh, following her inside. Yeah right, you were so keen on visiting you never called once.

Don't be a creep, Jamal! You think 'cause you grew a beard you're a man now?

How am I—

You are, you're being a creep, I don't like it. She inspected the small living area, the broken mustard-coloured couch and worn oval coffee table, with displeasure. There were books everywhere, in tattered piles that Yakob loved to knock down.

Christ, you couldn't swing a dead cat in here, she said, then screamed when Yakob stumped into view from the kitchen. Oh! Haram, look at him, he's all fucked up, poor little thing. Her voice became gooey and she leaned down to pat the cat. Moses hurled Jamal's old king single mattress down the stairs, where it flopped into a shapeless stained mass. He followed after, and dragged it outside.

You, sir, disgust me, he said on his way out.

He's not yours, is he? Hala said, standing up.

No, he's my housemate's. He's at work.

Which was where Jamal should be, and would be, if not for this intrusion. He had a couple days off 'to deal with' losing his grandfather, as if he had him to begin with, as if the dead didn't stay with you forever.

Good, because vets are a fucking nightmare. Samson has cost me a goddamn fortune, she said, walking into the kitchen. She loved her dog even more than Princess, who had been hit by a car. It had taken her ten years to even think about getting a new pet, and now that she had, she doted on him. Jamal heard her open the fridge and snort at its mostly empty shelves.

You good, bro? Okay great! Moses said from the door, not waiting for an answer.

Jamal was about to chase after him when Hala gasped, and he turned so fast he almost tripped over Yakob, who yowled pathetically. In the kitchen, she stood in front of the open freezer, her face cold, a bottle of icy vodka gripped in her hands.

You keep alcohol in your house, wulah?

He leaned against the doorway, relieved and incredulous. He hadn't had a drink in years, nor would he ever again. It's not mine, but even if it was, so what? You smoke pot every day, are you seriously going to lecture me about alcohol? He could never grasp how any of his family were able to routinely break whatever custom they liked, and still try to lecture or shame each other about the ones they chose to follow.

It's not the same! she snapped.

Why not? he said. What's the difference?

Oh please, hashish is harmless. You'd never hurt a fly on pot.

But get a man drunk and he'll come home one night and rape his daughter, too fucked up to know what bed he's in. She slammed the freezer door shut and shoved the Absolut bottle into his arms as she walked past. He stayed there for a long time, holding the coldness close to his chest.

A Bomb in a Nation

Dad told me everything. Ur an abomination.

Jamal read the message on his lunch break. Though he didn't speak much to his Turkish sister Emine, the words still ripped into his heart, not because he cared what she thought, but because the frozen child inside him was always saying *you're an abomination* on loop. It made him feel safe almost, content—it was proof that he deserved to suffer, to be apart from his family, to not pursue his dreams, to not try, to simply stagger from one temporary job to another. He was standing at the kitchen bar, half-eaten sandwich on his plate, wondering if he should go back to assembling a shitty reality for others while his own continued to unravel. The other transcribers had gone out to lunch and he had declined, withdrawing again into spectral silence. There were ads on the news and pamphlets in mailboxes and bumper stickers galore, all spreading speculation about how allowing two men to marry would destroy society, as if men marrying women was so fantastic, as if those men didn't murder women every single week, as if everyone wasn't some shade of miserable. And there was his sister, in his phone, telling him that homosexuality will be the end of society, like the politicians who said Islam would be the end of society, or Arabs would be the end of society, a babushka doll of endings a millennium long all claiming that he was a bomb in a nation. He wished it were true.

Hey friend, Alice said with grating cheer. Dude. Pal. Pal-erino? No, okay, that was terrible.

A middle-aged white woman with a blonde bob, she held a plate of cookies out to him. As the post-production manager, she was also his boss, so he couldn't ignore her. He took his earphones out and she smiled at him with real sympathy.

Look, I know you're struggling and I wanted to ask if, uh, maybe if you've considered counselling? It's totally okay if you want to, we can manage without you. She said this last part as if it was gracious, instead of the last thing he wanted to be reminded of—that he was disposable, easily replaceable. Her red lips kept wriggling. She was so uncomfortable she was making him nauseous.

Look, I've got one, she continued. And mine's been great helping me get over my zombie phobia. I know right, I get that look a lot, but they freak me out!

People like her assumed you had the same resources they did, that because you happened to be in the same space, you were on the same level. Jamal feinted towards her, biting the air with a growl, teeth snapping shut with a click, and she staggered backwards, terror blanking her eyes—cookies rained in a backward arc as her arms jerked up. Fuck!

Oh shit, I'm sorry, I—He stood there, his pulse racing. I thought you were joking, he finished limply. He bent down to pick up the cookies, and after a second she joined him, half-laughing at herself.

So, how come—

My therapist says it's a fear of homogeneity, Alice said. You know, being the same as everyone. Or something. She took a deep, shaky breath. I think it would be good maybe, for you, I mean, if you took the rest of the day off, hey.

He didn't argue with her. He'd been thinking of leaving anyway. Not just for now, but for good. Maybe he'd go back to uni, get on Centrelink. On the way home, he called his mother. He was still thinking about her visit, still thinking about Jido's bed, which he had not been able to sleep in, and never would. He slept on the couch instead.

She answered on the first ring. Jamal! I'm at Coles. Is everything okay?

Yeah, I'm good.

Oh, cool. How's the bed?

It's great, he said. How's everything with you?

There was a moment of silence. I can't speak right now, there are people around, she said in hushed Arabic. Then in English, I'll call you back.

When she did, she told him—still in a whisper—that she had lost her case, and Centrelink was evicting her. Had done so, in fact, and a sheriff had already been around once with the orders. The house and garage had been emptied, everything in storage—this was why Moses left to stay with Kholto Nazeero. She'd been squatting in the garage the past two nights, sleeping on blankets, and she didn't mind it, except, haram, her poor dogs. She couldn't do this to them anymore.

Can I stay with you? she said. Just for a couple days till I get my shit together. Wallahi, I didn't think it would come to this, these pricks, they've ruined my life.

There wasn't much left to ruin, he thought. He couldn't believe that she thought she had to ask, that she thought there was even a chance he would say no, and now he had yet another reason to hate himself, which he dutifully filed away.

Of course you can, immi, he said.

You're the best, she said. I'm making you my favourite son now.

She needed a few hours to get her things together, and then she'd be over. He had to figure out how to tell Dan that his mum was homeless and needed to stay with them. Shame crashed over him in a wave. He had seen her reaction to how he lived, the shabby millennial manner that for some was a momentary choice, but for him was the most he could manage, the highest rung on the ladder. He liked it well enough, and Jido's housing commission in Villawood was hardly better, which was what hurt so much—that she had looked at his home with disgust, happily pretending her own situation was fine, or maybe even believing it. She'd made a hundred pointed remarks about the condition of his home—the mould in the shower, the dust on the floors, the doors that didn't latch shut properly—and she would be reduced to living in it now, which meant neither of them could deny the other's reality.

Dan was more than gracious when Jamal texted him. It turned out his parents were at their holiday house in the US, which meant their Sydney mansion was empty.

I'll stay there with Yakob, Dan told him. You can sleep in my room.

Jamal felt weak with gratitude. He wouldn't have to worry about what Dan would see. He only had to worry about her, and how to survive living with her for another week. The next two hours he worked himself into a fever, vacuuming and mopping the floors. He washed his sheets for the first time in months, and found in his closet the brown woollen blanket his babbanne had given him, with a design of pale pink roses blooming across it. When the bed was presentable, he grabbed cans of Coke and Tim Tams from the corner store, and brought the mail in, which included his postal vote. His hopes that his mother would notice or care were dashed in an instant.

She arrived as the Earth covered her face in shadow. She dumped a cardboard box on the table, her two frantic dogs milling around, keening for her attention—Samson needed a Delilah, she said, he was too sad by himself—and then took off again. The dogs scrabbled along the floorboards, barking, jumping over each other, shaggy little mutts with white-yellow fur and pleading black eyes. Samson was bigger, but not by much, and apart from size Jamal couldn't distinguish between the two. They ran up the stairs, snuffling, then back down, and as they returned, the putrid stink of shit wafted towards him and he saw that one or both of them had squirted liquid diarrhoea down the stairs, and they were now tracking faecal paw prints all over the floor. He seized Samson around the neck, feeling the violent trembling under his hands, and ground the dog's nose in the shit, just like he remembered his mother doing with Princess, her face an angry bronze mask.

Bad! Bad dog! he shouted, trying to drown out Samson's wretched squeals. He felt furious and hopeless. Delilah ran behind the couch, shitting in fear, and it was into this scene that Hala came back with a box of cherries.

Oh ya Allah, she said. Jamal! Don't be like that. She took his hands off the dog, whose whines were embedded forever in his heart, and Samson bolted away.

Why? he said, breathing hard. Isn't this what you do?

Yonks ago, maybe, she said. But not anymore. They're just scared. Come on, let's get you outside, you wanna go for walkies? She led her animals into the backyard, then came back in to clean the mess. He helped her, working up another sweat.

This is so yuck, she said as they finished wiping the shit off the stairs. I'll have to wash them now, before it dries in their fur. And you, why are you sweating so much, are you fat now?

I'm fine, he said sourly.

No, tell me the truth, she said. Do you look good nude?

He stood there with a shit-drenched rag in his hands, the smell of dog diarrhoea clinging to his beard, and stared at her. Are you being serious?

It's very serious! Her voice climbed high, her chest jutted out. She looked like an old show pony. If you don't look good nude, you'll be alone forever.

Yaraat! he shouted—*if only*—and she laughed a warm throaty laugh. He watched her wash the dogs in the yard, soaping them into frothy clouds, laughing and singing and talking to them. He brought her an extension cord and her hair dryer as she towelled the dogs dry, then brushed them methodically with a metal comb. She had done this for Princess, too. Samson and Delilah were gambolling about, the terror and trauma of only an hour ago gone, tails wagging. Under her hands, they shone, brilliant and beautiful.

&

Allah Leik Ya Sidi! Moses sang, music blasting out the speakers. *Oh my lord and master!* Albak dab fi eedy! *Your heart melted in my hand!* He danced in the passenger seat as their cousin Hazem drove, shaking his head, but smiling. Hazem was Kholto Nazeero's eldest, a squat man just handsome enough to be smarmy about it, but not enough to get away with it. He and his siblings had been brought up in a Bankstown mansion, with every whim catered to, and BMWs for their birthdays, on the back of his father's successful dry-cleaning business. He never looked less than healthy, his skin was glossy, his teeth could sell toothpaste, and he only wore luxury brands. Jamal wasn't surprised that Moses chose to stay with them, but he was surprised by his response to his call, and it kept rattling around his head.

She's a nightmare, Moses said. She barely cooks, barely cleans, and is always asking for money. What's the point of her? He went on to explain that while he had to pay rent at their aunty's, at least she cooked dinner and cleaned his clothes, neither of which he knew how to do himself. He put on a high mocking voice to quote their mother, 'Babes, I just need two hundred, I'll give it back by the end of the week, I swear', 'Babes, I've got a job lined up at Ingham's factory, you know the one in Casula, just front me three hundred, you'll have it next week, don't be a creep.'

That doesn't sound so bad, Jamal had said.

Bro, they demolished that factory ages ago. Wallah, I've tried and I keep trying, but at some point you snap. I'm glad she's with you, but it won't last. Then he told him to hang tight, that he'd swing past and grab him for a joy ride to Granville.

As another car drove past with laughing girls in the front, Jamal squirmed in the back seat. Can you *not* already, please? he shouted.

Moses paused the song, twisting to look back at him. Why? Let 'em look, bro, what's it to you? Trust me, they love it.

Jamal groaned, rolling his eyes.

How are you embarrassed right now, I don't get it—you're literally doing nothing! Look at him, Haz, unjud, look.

I'm driving ya, hehl'ani, Haz said, sipping at his silver vape.

Well, if you looked, you'd see the biggest cat in your life.

Sorry I don't wanna make a dick of myself, Jamal said.

Nur. Wipe your chin, habibi, you're dribbling shit. Do you know what embarrassment is, bro—b'izm Allah, I'm being serious now—do you know what it is?

Jamal stared. Tell me.

It's fear. That's it. Who gives a shit if people look, or what people think.

He turned back around and started blasting the song again. Jamal sat within the sounds and fumed. When his brother had called, he'd jumped at the excuse to get out of the house, but he regretted it already.

I care, Jamal said quietly. He'd never been good enough for his brother. He didn't wear the right clothes, wasn't stylish enough, never got his hair done the way it should be, and Moses was always the first to tell him every single time, to name his every deficiency, yet here he was lecturing him that he shouldn't care about being judged.

I know you do, bro, but khalas already. That's all I'm saying.

You try relaxing with Mum in your house.

Moses laughed. Yeah, you got me there. Turn here, Haz.

They pulled into a concrete lot of warehouses and offices in Granville. A lanky Leb with a wonky head was waiting for them outside in the carpark. He wore a white dishdasha and waved them in slowly, a gesture that reeked of self-importance. Jamal had a bad feeling. The only thing Moses had said was that he and Haz were going to see something hectic, and now he wished he'd asked more questions, the fundamental kind, like: are you going to a meth lab?

Wait till you see this, Haz, you'll freak, Moses said as he stepped out. He's got a million bucks in stock alone. It's a millie, yeah Sammy?

Sam grinned. One point four, cuz. He swiped them into a small warehouse stacked with thousands of boxes, a dizzying variety of vape kits, from slim metallic pens to bulkier flasks. There was little room to move, with only a few narrow avenues between the boxes, appearing more by chance than design. Sam's store was online only, and he worked alone. Towards the back, the boxes dwindled, and they came to a clearing, some tables where Sam did his admin. On one side of the room was a wall of shelves that held dozens of large transparent jugs filled with vibrant liquids. Each one had a handwritten label listing the flavour of smoke it would produce, from the ambiguous 'candy sunrise' and 'lemon lite' to 'banana bread' and 'meat pie'.

Smell it, bro, smell it, Moses said. He grabbed one jug, took the lid off and held it out for him. Jamal sniffed cautiously and the scent of freshly baked banana bread spiked his nostrils so strongly he could almost taste it.

What the fuck?

Food flavours are all chemicals, Sam said. It messes with your head hard, ay. Some days after mixing this shit I don't want to eat again, wallah. Full turns you off. A stack of boxes crashed in the back, and he ran over to Haz, yelling at him to be careful.

Jamal turned to his brother. Where'd you find this Willy Wonka motherfucker?

Moses laughed. Oztag, he said.

Hazem held up a box. All good if we tax some, yeah Sam? he said, and Sam shrugged, so he started rooting around in the stock with vigour.

Moses lobbed a black box at Jamal. Inset was a sparkly purple vape.

Take that to Mardi Gras, why don't you, he said, and Jamal's eyes flicked to his in alarm. Heat flared up his neck and cheeks.

What, bro? Moses said, challenging him. Say something.

He imagined he could feel Sam staring at him, and once again embarrassment kicked in as a reflex. He didn't know whether he would ever get past it, or even if he should—and with that thought came a clear, hard anger.

It wasn't enough for you to run me out of the house, you gotta still be doing this shit now, bro? Do you hate me that much?

Sorry? Moses's jaw dropped in comical disbelief. Run what out of where? He closed the distance between them in an instant, a wall of muscle, his mouth a thin line. Let's get one thing straight—see what I did there? You're not the only one good with words, dicknose—you're the one who left. He bit down on the *me* that wanted to end that sentence, but it was there anyway.

Oh, like I could stay with you threatening every other day to say what you knew?

Is that what I did, ya k'zab?

You might as well have. Anyway, that's not what this is about, I'm talking about this shit. Jamal waved the glittering purple vape.

Moses's eyebrows lifted. What about it? I was joking!

And as Jamal went to say, *No, you were rubbing it in my face*, he spluttered and almost choked. He had said the same thing to Emir, and there was some truth to it: he had been trying to include him, to show they were all the same, despite knowing that Emir wasn't comfortable with his own skin, how he could pass and not pass, that it was a bruise he could press to wring a reaction. He'd done it anyway, because his intentions mattered more than his friend's feelings, because he was pissed at Emir, and on some level, he always would be.

Jamal sighed. Whenever he thought he'd found the line between care and cruelty, it vanished again. Forget I said anything. He put the box down carefully. Besides, I don't smoke.

They left soon after, Hazem laden with free goods and Moses satisfied he'd proven his value. He was proud of Sam's achievements as if they were his own, and it reminded Jamal of his father, the way he mistook proximity to wealth and power as being the same as having it. He didn't think it was a question of oversight, but a reflection of their own generosity; if they had this money, power, fame, there was no doubt in them that they would share it with everyone in their lives. On the way home Moses asked if he'd heard that Bilal was marrying some import from Lebanon, they'd already done the kateb kitab, and the reception was in a fortnight.

Good for him, Jamal said.

Yeah it is, Moses said, missing the sarcasm. I've gotta sort myself out, too. I'm over this shit.

Then why don't you? You could have anyone, couldn't you?

That's the problem, Hazem laughed. The talk turned to fantasy football, and Jamal let himself fade into the stream of traffic. Bilal didn't owe him anything; he had to look to his own happiness, wherever it might be found.

Oy, majnun, we're here, Moses said, and Jamal realised they were parked outside the front of his house, its dark eyes lidded. Is Mum here?

Who knows, Jamal said.

Can you for once talk like a normal human being, like what's going on in that fat head, ya? Moses said, exasperated.

Okay fine, Jamal said. I was thinking that I really hope Mum's not in there, and that I hate how easy it is for her or you, or fucking anyone really, to spin me out, and maybe it's not anyone's fault except mine, yaani I'm just barely holding on but it's always when I'm around youse that I recognise it, and in recognising it, want to fucking neck myself.

The engine murmured idly, the vape clicked as Hazem sucked in, and the sickly sweet smell of grapefruit-flavoured smoke poured out into their sweat and stink.

I take it back, Moses said. Never tell us anything.

Yeah, you need to get laid, cuz, Hazem said. Smoke a jay or something.

Everyone wants to neck themselves, Moses said. You think you're special? Get out of here, la.

Then why don't they? Jamal burst out.

His brother shrugged. Because it's haram. Plus, for devils like you, this is as good as it gets, bro, I wouldn't be in a rush to go anywhere else—and they all howled.

Paradise Is Burning

Silver hooves stamped gently on his eyelids. The horse trampled the air, along with the other animals, and muted light sprayed over the assembled kingdom of breath. He drew on the blunt, his back to the couch, his mother by his side, her hair a black syntax, strange cursive telling its own tale. Samson snoozed on her lap, and Delilah licked her fingers, their fur a white shine, the scent of mutt and soap a thick cloak. Hala chopped up as Jamal finished the last of Osman's joint, taking in the memory of fire. He ignored the hand curled in Hala's hair, the figure on the couch. On the table in front of them was the postal vote for marriage equality. It was important to have the conversation, every bigot and every Tumblr teen seemed to agree. Important to bellow again each hateful word in retribution or reclamation, but to bellow it, in the hope that a body somewhere could use the sound to climb out of silence, or more likely, that a body attuned to hate would resound with it until numb and stupefied. Some silences kept hearts beating. Others strangled them still. How to know what can and cannot be dragged from time's unknowable rivers was the hard part. Queer suicides were rising ever higher, according to the news. National hotlines were overwhelmed. In Warwick Farm, Ilo's father heard this on the radio and the question inside him about his son suddenly broke into irrelevance. He called to Ilo, wrapped him in a hug, said he loved him. Oh my son, I'm sorry, he said, and Jamal rose with the tide of his brother's joy, his abrupt miracle.

The djinn said, This is not for you, ya ibn haram. And its voice was a burning armchair, its voice was a police baton meeting flesh, its voice was Moses screaming. Jamal looked at the figure on the couch then, an androgynous aurora, slight and undulating, one moment shaped like a man, like a mass of unblooming flowers, reversing into seed, the other like a dirty flame, like—he turned away again. No, what lay ahead for him was more of the same cutting comments, the staggered and warped back and forth of people who don't know how to talk to each other without trying to *win*, to force the other to concede. In a state of constant war, there were no winners and no boundaries, everything was on the table all the time. He would be coming out all the time, to nothing and no one, he would be ibn haram forever.

The djinn tinkled, a tangle of bells. O son of harm! Forbidden one, sacred son, inviolate and set aside, you know neither your own tongue nor our Lord, the Most High.

Just ignore the bastard, Hala said, and Jamal nodded. She was in the same old jeans and vest, and there were heavy bags under her eyes. He could see her scalp where her dark hair had thinned on the sides from years of being straightened, years of the acidic hairspray she sprayed on each morning. She passed him the joint and he saw her nails were half-painted, a ragged peeling pink, and he felt the rough bark of her calloused fingers. She didn't have a job she knew how to keep, which was why she had many, a rotating collection of back-scratches and barters that made little sense even to her and her junkie friends, but which most of all kept them moving, crashing from one crisis to another. He took another hit. His blood had been replaced with jelly, a trembling.

Why weren't you at Jido's funeral? he said.

She sniffed. Because I would have spat at every one of those cunts. He couldn't stand them—where were they when he was alive? Did any of them take him in? No, that's right. They all have houses, yeah, with their jobs and that, but I'm the fucking majnouneh who took care of him because no one else wanted a bar of him. They can all get nicked.

Have you been to the grave yet?

I went the next morning. You know—

—On the first day, the dead are scared and lonely, yeah, I remember.

He exhaled smoke through his nostrils, and hoped he didn't look as goofy as he felt. Hoped he was doing it right. He wasn't sure when he was supposed to feel high, if ever. He felt the same as he always did. He sent a text to Bilal telling him to cancel his wedding.

So I did teach you something! Hala said. Go me! I'm the best mum, honest.

What I don't understand, Jamal said slowly—so slowly the pizza arrived while he was saying it, and they ate half of it—is why you did anything for him?

He was my father, don't be stupid. And yeah, he was an alcoholic, he used to do horrible things, um … Prison was the best thing for him, really, it got him off that shit. But he was a haj at the end, don't forget. She sounded dubious, despite her words.

Teyta still hated him even then, he said. And she was a hajjeh.

They'd both gone to Mecca, completing the pilgrimage while they were able, and returned cleared of wrongdoing. What did it mean to make a holy pilgrimage step by step with a man you despised? To walk towards salvation beside the husband you wanted saving from. He shivered.

Hala chuckled. Yeah, she did. She prayed for him to get caught, you know, and for his sentence to be ten years, which is exactly what he got. We never told him, of course, but we used to laugh about that. We would visit him every week, you know, all the way up at Cessnock Correctional.

There's no point holding on to the past, though. Teyta did, and it ate her up inside, haram. Look how she died. But Jido? Never got sick, not once, and went in his sleep. He smoked his whole life and I never saw him cough once. We all pay in different ways, don't worry about that.

She cleared her throat, started rolling another joint. I got that from him, too. I've never had a cold, the flu, nothing. So it wasn't all bad, I guess.

Kholto says this life is a test, Jamal said. And if you suffer now, that's good, because Jannah will be next and it's everlasting. There was no need to specify which aunty, there was only one between them. Rania: her sister, her rival.

She would say that, the miserable cow. That way she never has to do anything, just wait till you die. How fucking boring. Can you imagine?

The djinn laughed, flowing up to join the animals swirling around the ceiling, one minute a snake, the next a bird. It dived into Hala's eyes, and out her mouth, flying up again, burning the dust that might otherwise become illness.

Jamal went into the kitchen, stomach rumbling. The sink was piled with plates, a black and ash-strewn muck, an old dented raqweh on top. He rinsed it, filled it up, and put it on the stove. He was talking to his mother, really talking to her, not as a child to their parent, but as two adults. Whole sentences! Actual stories about their family, like the fact his grandfather had slept with a gun under his pillow because the paranoia of the war never left him, and even that small fragment helped make sense of him, his years of silence in front of the TV. As the brew bubbled, his phone buzzed. Bilal was on his way. Samson and Delilah began to bark, hacking bullets that punched the air, and Hala yelled at them to be quiet. In a cardboard box on the bench, Jamal found a couple of Arabic coffee cups, and grinned.

Your ahwa's ready, Mum, he said.

She didn't answer, so he grabbed the end of the raqweh in one hand, a cup in the other, and took them into the lounge. Hala was leaning over the coffee table, legs outstretched around it. She had the postal vote in one hand, pen in the other.

Jamal shifted onto the tips of his toes, approaching her back as soundlessly as he could. Trying not to breathe, he leaned over, tilting dangerously but he was too far back to see. He took two quick steps, and Delilah darted at his legs. He was so startled by the leaping bitch that he yelled out and swung away, almost falling, the raqweh tipping as he moved. He had a choice then—the djinn showed it to him clear as day—as to where the burning coffee would fall. Onto his mother or Delilah, her body or what she loved more than life. Boiling hot darkness splashed onto Hala's foot. She screamed and the dogs barked and the last thing he saw was the skin melting off her foot and ankle like a rotten sleeve, the way to paradise burning in front of his eyes.

Bilal took them to the late-night discount chemist. Hala had argued against going to the hospital, that it wasn't that bad, come on. The chemist said that they were all in shock, and it was best to wait for an ambulance. Hala was barefoot, her hair a mess. Jamal found it hard to focus. His face stung where the spilled coffee had reached him on the floor and where his mother had slapped him awake. Christ, she said. If anyone should faint, it's me. Get up.

Sterile white light, endless sale signs. Jamal let himself sink to the ground, saying, I'm just gonna sit for a bit. On the cold white tiles, his mother's feet stood stark: one seared a grisly red-yellow, one brown and untouched. He had the sudden urge to kiss her unburned foot, and almost threw up.

Immi, he said. I'm sorry. He leaned his head against Bilal's solid leg. Hala looked down with huge eyes, her expression more troubled than he could remember seeing.

For what? she said. It was an accident.

For being a faggot, he said. Bilal's thigh tensed, and Jamal clung to the frozen muscle, rough denim. He thought about the postal vote, how as Hala had dragged him up, he saw that she'd drawn the outline of a hairy dick between *Yes* and *No*, and had to bury a hysterical giggle.

Oh is that all? she said, sarcastically. Yeah, right. Great.

And for wanting to kill myself, he said. For giving up. I'm not going to, okay? I'm going to fight you.

Okay, she said. She was on the floor beside him.

Mum?

Yes, Mum, she said, like he was a boy again.

I need to know—do you forgive me?

For what? Her voice was infinitely weary.

He had the sense that he might have asked her before, that he might not have ever stopped asking. He tried to remember, and couldn't. That's the problem with revelations—they're not made for memories, that's why they have to be written down. He thought that maybe he wasn't saying what he wanted to, that it wasn't a question at all, it was something about what they were only able to do for each other, what he had already done for her.

I'll settle for everything, he said.

An Accounting

I used to think I was more compassionate than God. Man, the arrogance. I was such a drama queen. Still am, I guess. I see now that what I meant when I said 'Allah' was 'my family'. I was so angry, so bound up in my pain. Kassem would say that it's not a question of hurt or wounds but of changes, and maybe that's true, maybe my spirit had to change so often and so quickly I became a stranger even to myself, closed down, shutting myself off. Maybe that's the only real distinction between a wound and a change: understanding. Baba, I know it's late, but I still want to say sorry.

Jamal glanced up from his phone, his unsent email. Aunty Rania was on a stepladder in front of him, picking at the long vine leaves growing in her yard. His eyes were level with the cracked backs of her open-toed shahayta. The midday sun hit her hijab, the stunted lemon tree, the wood latticework around which the dark green vines twisted, and he had to squint as he listened to her complain about her aching arms, her useless children who weren't there to help her, ya Allah where had she gone wrong, and so on. Her heels were as cracked as the back of her shoes, and he huffed out a small laugh thinking about how often he'd had to dodge the thrown missiles, how he was never fast enough, how easy it had once been for violence to become a game.

What are you looking at, you stupid boy? she said. That he had been silent for a full minute registered at the same time as her words, her pet phrase for him. He was taking too long to answer. Rania's smooth oval face was concerned within her brown hood, lips pursed; she looked like an owl, avid and pensive.

Nothing, he said finally. They had just passed the same-sex marriage law. He was glad on some level for everyone it would help, but it made no difference to his life, nor to anyone in his family.

Rania sniffed and kept snipping at the vines, putting the leaves into the bag tied to her hips. You know how I feel about that stuff. Don't tell anyone. Especially your mum.

Jamal hid a smile at that, the way his relatives all doubted each other, keeping hidden their own grace. Do you want help? he said, knowing that she would say no.

Like you could, she said. This was Teyta's favourite, you know. She taught me.

Jamal's grandmother had stood where his aunty stood and picked the vines in just the same way, letting loose the same complaints. She didn't have a tree of her own nor a yard, so she would come here when the season was right to prepare warra eynab. Jamal used to adore watching her sit on the floor inside, a sheet spread out before her, as she rolled rice into each green palm. Squinting in the bright light, Aunty Rania could almost have been her, which was what she wanted more than anything. Maybe we all secretly want to be our mothers, he thought. It would explain why he was such a fuck-up, at least. A car horn honked on the street, and a door slammed.

That'll be Mum, Jamal said. He never felt comfortable using the word around his aunty. Sometimes Rania still called him son, and sometimes he still thought of Hala as the other woman, the one who had taken him away.

Sis! Hala shouted, coming round to the backyard. I knew you'd be out here. Isn't it fabulous? Hala had built the latticework and planted the vines, she'd put in stone benches, the lemon and apple trees, the shrubs along the fences, each fresh dark circle of soil crowned by white pebbles.

About time! Rania said. It took you that long.

Hala snorted. You're such a dag, honest.

Jamal couldn't help comparing them. Hala was still darker and fiercer, her once famed beauty sawn into hard, sun-roughened angles, while Rania had become softer and quieter, her pains less obvious to the naked eye, but still present. As always now, he wondered which daughter's bed his grandfather had climbed into, drunk one night, whether it was either of his mothers, or his aunty Nazeero, all or none of them. What chance was there that Hala had conjured such a specific example on the fly? How much weight should be given to a sentence? His therapist told him that it was none of his business, and that his desire to account for sins, to name and measure them, was tied to his need to punish himself and to exert control on the uncontrollable. He had told Alice he was finally getting help in the form of a mental health plan and ten subsidised sessions. He didn't think it would be enough; there was no cure for what he had lived through, for having to live this way, but at the very least it meant he could now enter conversations with 'My therapist said', which lent whatever followed a kind of jaded gravitas.

Check it out! Hala said, extending her right foot, which had an uneven darkness across the arch, a deep sunburst. How good is it?

Humdulilah, Rania said, without looking.

They had to take skin off the back of her thigh, and the doctors said she was lucky not to have lost the foot. She spent six weeks in the burns ward with no one allowed to visit her—she had escaped the first day, gone off to get high with a junkie mate, but returned the next day screaming, so they kept a closer eye on her after that. He thought of her lying in the hospital bed like crumpled sandpaper the first time he visited. It was remarkable how much she had healed in the weeks since, but then, she was protected by a higher being, even if that higher being didn't pay rent. Jamal had sold Jido's deathbed and given the cash to her. She was renting a granny flat in Bass Hill now.

Jamal echoed his aunty, Humdulilah. You ready to go?

Yullah, she said. I'll water the plants first, and then we'll be off. I still can't believe your father carked it, Allah yerhamou. He was so young.

Jamal didn't believe it either, and he had watched the man's body enter the earth. The week he burned his mother's foot, Cevdat had a small heart attack in Turkey, and returned to Australia for free treatment. He died in his sleep, in his mother's unit in Eastlakes. There were three things that Jamal would remember forever, wrapped in the unreality of grief: his sister's text saying, *Dad's dead, you broke his heart*; a hundred shoes piled up outside his grandma's door; the dozens of Turks crammed inside, weeping and wailing, a sense of heat and closeness as of wings wrapped around a body. Mehmet took him to the funeral house; no longer a solid boulder, he looked hollow and old, his hair and moustache undyed and white. A harried-looking bearded man stepped out of the door opposite the waiting room, and jerked his head to reel Jamal into his office. He sat behind a desk loaded with paperwork and said something in Turkish, to which Jamal could only shrug.

English, sorry, Jamal said.

The man frowned. You knew the deceased?

I'm his son, Jamal said.

Aha, he said, picking up his pen. Was he married?

I don't know, Jamal said, remembering Cevdat's claim to be seeing multiple women. Anything was possible.

What was his address?

I don't know.

How old was he?

I don't know.

The man looked up, annoyed. You knew the deceased, yes?

I … Jamal shrugged, helpless. I'm his son, he said again, and left the room.

He saw his father's body wheeled out on a gurney, pale as starlight, cotton stuffed into his big nose. Later, in the cemetery, a hundred strange-familiars wept on Jamal, trailing their hands over his face, saying, Mashallah, mashallah, you are him. He realised they weren't seeing him and never had, they were seeing the past, and trying to touch it. He could not have borne any of this, not even a second of it, had Moses not been there with him, sombre in his high-vis vest, his thick mud-splattered workboots, arm around his shoulder, hand over his heart. Hands were capable of so much more than work, they could touch, knead and anchor: his brother's hand was all that held his heart together.

He didn't know why, but he had been unable to grieve properly then, he felt suspended in time, and he didn't cry until four days later when Mehmet followed his brother into the grave, his heart crushing itself on a plane between Turkey and Sydney.

It comes in threes, Jihad had said. His dull suspension snapped, and he wept until his body became a desert. Everyone kept saying things like, *At least he died peacefully*, as if peace were possible, as if every life and every exit wasn't a protracted war to find and hold on to love.

Beneath the mountain of loss, Jamal felt only relief. He knew now that he would not want to live in this world without his brother, either. At least his uncle wasn't doomed to be alone on that balcony in Mersin—it wasn't right to think of that place without both men smoking and grumbling and laughing on it. His reality had broken past comprehension, it was no more and no less than a savage sea flecked with the debris of his memory. Somehow this comforted him. There was no such thing as control, only surrender, he thought as he belted himself into his mother's car. Trash littered the floor, and the back was full of paint buckets, bags of soil, odd tools, and a whipper snipper stuffed diagonally across the space. She had transformed herself into a handyman, a guru of growing greens, her arms hard with muscle and flecked with paint. Like any diamond, there was no give in her, and there never would be: she was everything she needed to be in order to survive.

On the way to Rookwood, Hala told him that his father was the most beautiful man she'd ever seen.

Even after everything with Abraham, I still fell for him. Shows what a dumb bitch I am, she laughed. His brother was fabulous too, though. Poor bastard. He's the one who told me that Cevdat's wife didn't know. I did everything halal. We were married by the sheikh, but it's only okay if his wife agrees to it, you get me? No wonder the cow tried to curse me. He was wrong to do that to us, but anyway, you can't change the past.

He didn't wonder why she suddenly felt the need to tell her side of the story, why she had insisted on this trip to pay her respects. He wasn't the only person doing faulty accounting. He and Emi had begun to talk haltingly about what had passed between them when they were teenagers. I didn't even know if you remembered, Emi had said, weeping. I'm so sorry. And they hugged, but inside Jamal felt cold. He had hoped for some kind of catharsis, but Kassem had been right all along—the boy who needed it was long gone, as much as the boy Emi had been was gone, and there was a long road ahead to figure out who they had become. After settling into his new job, Ilo told his family he needed to move out. He loved them, but it was time.

The last awkward structures of adolescence were falling away, and they were letting them go without letting go of each other, which they had not imagined possible. In the wake of these deaths, Jamal knew he had to learn how to hold a reckoning without retribution, to be present in alignment with the past, instead of at war with it. He was beginning to see the way. His lips quirked as he remembered how often, in telling some story of his life, his friends like Adam or

Dan would look at him with mingled disbelief and wonderment, saying, Your life is like a soap opera—because there were too many characters, too much death, nothing at all like the kind of spare, elegant novels they studied in school. He had forgotten more life than those books and their writers had bothered to imagine.

What are you smiling at? Hala said, as they drove into the green city of the dead.

Nothing, he said. Just thinking about Kholto's favourite saying, 'Life sucks, and then you die'. They both laughed.

At the new Muslim section in the cemetery, there were dozens of freshly dug rows. It was hard to get your bearing in a place where the dead kept growing, but Jamal let memory take over, and he guided his mother to his father. He recited the Fatiha over his dad's grave, and Hala grabbed a bucket of water to pour onto the recently laid grass. She wiped the bird shit off his gleaming black and gold headstone, making the letters 'Khan' shine, then went to attend to her own parents.

Jamal knelt on the soft unsettled grass, feeling the attention of the angels on him, the many spirits of flame and light and elsewhere drifting on the breeze, hanging from the trees. He took off the ring Cevdat had given him, placing it in the grass, the roaring lion given a crown of green. He had never wanted to be a lion or a king, only a son.

Hey, Dad, he said. Would you believe this prick at the funeral house asked me if I knew you? He shook his head, laughing a little. Who else can say they know the sound of your poetry at 2am, eh?

He took his phone out, and began reading aloud the email he'd been writing since his baba left him.

I'm not sure what name I'll be buried under, Khaddaj or Khan or something else, but I want you to know, Baba, that I don't have an ounce of forgiveness in my heart. I understand now just how far away I am from God. It has nothing to do with sex or love, no matter what you think. It has nothing to do with you, either. I may not have had a father growing up, but I had two mothers, two pathways to heaven, and nobody can ask for more than that.

I thought I was more caring than my family, that I was kinder, all the while I judged them—astugfirullah—before I gave them a chance to show me otherwise. I looked into my heart and I did not find forgiveness, it shames me to admit, but I did find Allah there, where Allah has always been, and I know this will please you.

'You asked me once to tell you of my life, you were so hungry to know me, to shape me as only a father shapes a son, and I said no, because it was the only power I had. And because I was scared to admit I don't remember most of it. I know, I know, you'll say that's crazy, but most of it is blotted out. I have only these strange details, and details do not make a life: that's what love and time are for. Still, this is what remains, and I am ready to share it, to shape you as only a son can a father. And more, to shape myself. I have been walking in fog, in silence, for too long. It isn't much, I'm sorry, but it starts with ahwa, which I know would make you smile …

When he finished wiping away the tears, he saw Hala waiting for him. He didn't know how long she had been standing there, or how much time had passed. His eyes were heavy but his body felt at ease and wholly his own. As they walked back to the car, he cleared his throat.

Tell me about your life, Mum, he said. The truth this time.

God, how boring, she said. Where would I even start?

Start with Abraham—where'd you meet?

In Lebanon, she said. Jido took me back when I was thirteen, the war was on, but never mind that, he had to get me a husband. Abe was off his head, even then. When we met he shot up a donkey with heroin, because that was his idea of fun. Of course it died straight away. Every week, I think about that poor donkey.

Acknowledgements

First and foremost I would like to thank Jamal, my distant avatar, for carrying the weight of my unreal life. This is a work of fiction, which is to say a stylised and imaginative construct, but the pain I had him shoulder is very real. Second, thank you to my loved ones, to my friends and family for being the reason I persist in this world. I have been profoundly lucky in my life and my blessings include a Create NSW grant, without which I do not know how I would have managed to get to the finish line. Thank you to Affirm Press, to Martin especially, for being behind me every step of the way. Thank you to Dr Michael Mohammed Ahmad, first for commissioning and editing 'White Flu', which led to this novel, and subsequently for his editing on my first attempt at expanding that work into a manuscript. Thank you to Camha Pham for her excellent editing throughout the final drafts, and to Alison Croggon and Caitlin Maling for initial feedback. Endless thanks are owed to Randa Abdel-Fattah, for her generous support not only of me but of so many younger writers in our budding community, may God bless her forever. Thank you to Alexis Wright, to Christos Tsiolkas,

Sisonke Msimang, Hannah Kent, Hala Alyan and Zeyn Joukhadar—to have writers I admire so much gift me with their time and words is a dream and a debt I can never repay.

To every reader who has helped me become who I am today: thank you.

To my beloved Tolouli, I thank God for you and your love every day.

To my wife, my light, my life, Hannah, words can never convey how much I love you.

To every version of every person I have known, imagined and real: may we all heal together, in language, and in life.

Salaam,

Omar